VISCERAL REACTION

A TORN WORLDS ROMANCE

DONNA AUGUSTINE

Edited by https://editing720.blogspot.com

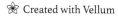 Created with Vellum

S assy

The sound of laughter drifted outside of the rambling mausoleum my sister now called home as she said goodnight to the last of her dinner guests. Ever since she'd married the current alpha werewolf of the district, Penelope had become D.C. royalty. I wasn't sure if she enjoyed it, but she was damned good at the role.

I was always invited to the shindigs but preferred a cigarette in the shadows of the garage. I'd taken up smoking a few weeks ago, along with a list of other bad habits too long to recite. It was sort of ironic that my impending death had led to a fuller life.

Well, *fuller* might not be the best term. More exciting existence? That might not be quite right either. A life of depravity. I wasn't quite there, but it was a good goalpost.

I took another swig from the bottle of bourbon I'd

grabbed from my brother-in-law's stash, letting the burn wash away all thoughts of the faraway future. Another several gulps and I wouldn't care that there wouldn't be a next year for me. I had today, tomorrow, maybe next month, and a long list of things I was going to accomplish before I left this world.

The back door to the house opened. Donovan scanned the lawn and headed over to where I lurked in the shadows.

"That's not going to help matters," he said, pointing to the cigarette hanging from my fingers.

I lifted it and took another drag, looking the other way. We didn't discuss my sickness, and I had no plans on changing that now. He might have had a lapse in memory, but that didn't mean I would.

"Are you going to tell her before we leave?" he asked, not taking the hint.

I'd never met someone as stubborn as myself until my sister found him. It was like she was trying to double down on the pains in the asses in her life.

"No, I'm not." As much as I wanted to ignore the topic, this was something I couldn't afford to leave murky.

"What if you're not here when she gets back?" Donovan stepped closer, a hint of the menace this shifter was capable of right beneath the surface.

I didn't even straighten off the wall as I continued to smoke. He'd take a bullet for my sister, and I'd realized soon enough that he'd take some shrapnel for me too, simply because I was an extension of her. There was no doubt his bite was lethal, but he was all bark at the moment.

"If you tell her, she'll stay. Is that what you want? Because I don't." And he didn't either.

He stood still, staring up at the night sky as if he could wrench some answers out of it if he tried hard enough. "We could delay our leaving. We'd still go, but—"

"Wait for me to die first? Make her sit here and watch me wither away when there's nothing she can do? I'm not doing that to her, and you won't either."

There were very few things I was sure of in life, and the feelings Donovan had for my sister were among them. It helped me sleep at night that she wouldn't be alone after I was gone. He'd have her back until the bitter end. I might be doomed to die before I hit my twenty-fifth birthday, but she'd have him. They had one of those love stories that you couldn't help but envy, that only the luckiest of the luckiest would ever experience.

He took a step away, dropped his head, hands in his pockets as he still tried to search for a solution that would save my sister pain.

"The doctor might still be able to fix you. We don't know if this is it."

It was hard not to laugh. The "cure" that had bought me some time wasn't working anymore. His personal doctor had been poking and prodding at me for over a year, and all it had done was slow the progress. But I was still dying.

"It's time to get her out of here and start a new life. I need to know that she's somewhere happy and safe, away from all this mess." As the wife of an alpha, and one that bore him an alpha son, she was protected to a certain degree from the chaos that was this world.

But if you were human? This wasn't the place to live. Ever since the vampires and werewolves had made a pact and taken over the U.S., humans had become nothing more than slave labor and a food source. She was lucky.

Most humans couldn't get out. She could, and she'd be doing it if I had my way, which I intended.

"Somewhere happy, safe, and expecting you to follow?" His voice was gruff as he glanced over at me.

"Yes, if that's what it takes."

"You should come."

"Did you miss the part about me withering away? Her choices have been about me for far too long. I want her to have a fresh start with no bad memories attached. I'm not going to keep dragging her down, making her worry. She can have a great life with you, and I want her to start living it."

He didn't respond, and the tilt of his head didn't give me any confidence that this would be the end of the discussion.

"You'll keep my secret, right?" He hadn't given me up yet, but that didn't mean it was a guarantee. I hadn't yet been able to wriggle the promise out of him. He'd been keeping my secret for a long time now, and for a man that was usually up front, it had to be a strain.

He dropped his gaze to the ground and kept it there.

"It's better for her this way," I said, knowing that trumped all in his world.

He reached over and slipped the cigarette from my fingers, taking a drag of it. "It's your secret to tell." He crushed it under his heel after he did. "By the way, these things will kill you."

I laughed at his bad joke because we both knew the Sucking Sickness would kill me long before the cigarettes would.

As far as brothers-in-law went, I'd done pretty well with Donovan, even if he was technically the enemy. His unfortunate status as a werewolf I wrote off as an accident of birth.

"By the way, what happened to your wayward guest?" I asked.

Donovan laughed before he said, "Cole arrives when he wants."

"You sure this is the guy that should be taking over the pack?" From the little I'd heard, the guy sounded like a total dick. I guess you needed to be a dick to step in as an alpha to a pack that didn't know you.

"He might be the only one who can."

"What about Huddy?" I asked, knowing it was already a done deal.

"He's got the ability but zero desire. For what's coming, only someone brutal will do anyway."

For what's coming...

No one knew for sure how long the pact with the vampires and werewolves would last, but the tensions with all the races had been running high. Most humans didn't have work or a steady supply of food. The situation between the vampires and the werewolves was rumored to be developing cracks. All the creatures that had crawled out of the woodwork with them had a stake in this messed-up situation. You couldn't walk down the street and not feel the tension in every breathing being, and there were many that had crawled out of the depths after the war and takeover.

"That's why you need to get her out of here," I said to Donovan.

"I will." He gave me a last look, brimming with the things he wished he could do and regrets for the things that were coming.

Just when I thought I'd crack under the heaviness of

the reality he was dishing out, he gave me a nod and retreated back to the house, as he would disappear from this hell.

I took a few more swigs from the bottle, trying to wash away the unpleasant thoughts he'd left. I'd drown them in alcohol along with the rest of the things I didn't like to think about.

Donovan hadn't been gone for more than ten minutes or so when something large leapt over the back wall a few hundred feet away. I jerked back into the shadows, my hand going for the knife tucked into my boot. My reflexes were only a split second slower than they were a few chugs of bourbon ago, but much slower than they were before the night started.

The man strolling across the lawn had too much confidence and brazenness to be an intruder. Looked like the wayward alpha, Donovan's soon-to-be replacement, had finally decided to arrive. He'd been here for a week already but had barely been at the house. I'd yet to meet him, and I ducked farther into the shadows, along the path to the side door, hoping to prolong my winning streak.

"Hey, you." Cole's voice was deep, carrying easily across the sprawling lawn.

I kept walking. He might think he was going to be in charge of the D.C. district, but I wasn't going to be one of his charges, no matter where I lived.

"Stop," he said.

Stop? Not "Excuse me, miss?" or even "Hello." Oh yes, this werewolf reeked of alpha, even more so than my brother-in-law.

"I told you to stop," he said. There was a breeze of

motion, and then he was blocking my way to the door. "Did you not hear me?"

His shoulders filled the side door I'd been about to enter, his body all hard, coiled muscles underneath his t-shirt, just ready to strike. Messy, dark locks, nearly black, contrasted with eyes so grey, as to nearly appear silver, and added a chill to his sun-warmed skin.

Donovan had said he needed someone tough, cold— raw, even—to step into the alpha position. He hadn't been kidding. The man that stood in front of me sucked up all the air around him the way a bomb did right before it leveled a city. The glint in his steel eyes left no doubt he'd walk away from the destruction without a shred of regret as he stepped over the bodies on his way out.

The aroma of bourbon drifted off him. That I could smell it after what I'd put down didn't bode well for his intake—or mine. I definitely needed to drink some more.

He ran his eyes over the length of me, taking in the ripped jeans and snug sweater with a snag on the hem. The rough quality of my clothing didn't seem to deter his appreciation of my form.

"You off work for the night?" he asked, leaning a shoulder on the doorjamb as he gave me a lazy smile.

He thought I was a servant. Or maybe even a whore. He didn't know my sister would've ripped Donovan apart if he touched another woman, but then, she was a human. Most shifters had the lowest opinions of us.

Part of me wanted to punch him in the face. A larger part of me wanted to take him up on the offer he was presenting.

He was dark, dangerous, and disposable. He was everything a dying girl needed to feel alive without remorse when I walked away after the fun was over. In other words, the perfect ending to my evening.

I edged in closer, leaning on the opposite side of the door.

"My evening *might* be free, depending." My words might've been biting, but the smile made it clear I wasn't opposed to his invitation.

His eyes ran the length of me, stopping on my breasts and then my hips before nodding. "If I'd known you were going to be here, I might've come sooner."

He leaned closer, raising a finger to trail over my lower lip before moving his hand down to graze the skin of my neck.

Oh yes, he'd be perfect for the evening. My good nights were running in short supply. Everyone had a finite amount of time, but the urgency in grabbing all the joy out of life you could rose as that clock started ticking down. I was watching the final sands run out and needed to make the most of the time I had left. I was down to counting good nights, and I planned on having as many as possible.

Why not fuck him? What did I have left to hold on to? There would never be a mister right in my life.

There was only one little catch. Did I warn him now or let him find out at a later date? I didn't particularly like surprises.

"Just an FYI, I'm Sassy, Penelope's sister—Donovan's sister-in-law." Even if I did decide to fuck him, it was best to get that out of the way. Didn't need any awkward shocks after the fact when I ran into him at the family dinner or something.

"Does that matter for some reason?" he asked, a smirk appearing because clearly *he* didn't think it mattered.

"Not to me," I said, arching slightly.

"Then we agree." He reached around to the base of my skull, pulling me closer.

He pressed me into the door as his lips grazed mine, then he weaved his fingers into my thick platinum locks. If the way he kissed was any indication, and it usually was, this was going to be a good night.

This man would know exactly what he was doing and wouldn't be shy in doing it. Why shouldn't I spend the night with him?

He pulled back, his mouth hovering near mine. We stood there frozen for a moment as he breathed in my scent, examining my face as if he hadn't quite seen me the first time. If I hadn't been confident in my appeal, I might've pulled back first from the read I was getting off him.

The heat from his eyes cooled and they shuttered, becoming void of emotion. He dropped his fingers from my hair, taking a strand with them in his eagerness to untangle from me.

"Maybe another time," he said, putting a few more steps in between us and giving me a smile like he'd just handed me a wilted bunch of flowers in a beauty pageant I'd taken second place in. "Donovan wouldn't like me messing around with his little sister."

I knew bullshit when I heard it. Not even seconds ago, it hadn't mattered one bit. This man was an alpha to his core. They did as they pleased, always.

"I'm sure I'll see you around."

He turned, walking away, leaving me staring at his back, trying to piece the situation together.

My breath might've smelled of booze, but so did his. He could hardly fault me for that.

Stupid, stupid, Sassy. He was an *alpha*.

"It's because I'm sick."

He froze and then turned back toward me. His eyes flickered for a second with...pity? Remorse? I couldn't tell; it had been too fleeting, only there long enough to add to the insult.

"Some things aren't meant to be." He shrugged and continued on.

My shoulder crashed into the wall as I leaned against it, feeling all of two inches tall. He smelled the Sucking Sickness on me. He didn't want to fuck the sick girl.

I stayed glued to the wall for some time with only my bottle of bourbon to warm me.

2

C *ole*

I dreamt of the sick girl, Donovan's sister-in-law, for the third night in a row. Her big, whiskey-colored eyes staring at me with so much heat, and then even more hurt. No matter how I forced the memory of her out of my daytime thoughts, she snuck back in while I was sleeping.

She'd been utterly captivating, so full of life, and then I smelled death on her. I couldn't get that close to death. I'd had enough of it, and if my plans worked out, I'd be seeing more. But I couldn't watch it happen, couldn't lie with someone walking their way to the grave, not right now.

I rose and hopped in the shower, trying to scrub away the memory. The maid was waiting in my room when I got out.

"Would you like me to get you a towel? I could help

you dry off, if you'd like?" She eyed my dripping frame like I was a rump roast she wanted to sink her little human canines into.

She wasn't a bad little piece, but I found I had an inclination for petite blondes with lots of curves suddenly.

"I'm fine." I didn't bother grabbing a towel or covering up. Werewolves weren't particular bashful beings, and I was even less so than average. If she wanted to get a full look, let her. Considering how frail most human males looked, I could understand—but after a few minutes, my patience grew thin. "Was there something else?"

She straightened, getting the hint that it wasn't going to happen. "Mr. Donovan would like to speak with you," she said, losing the sultry pitch of her earlier tone.

"I'll be there in a few." I tilted my head toward the door. She left, muttering something about how I looked good but couldn't get the job done.

Clearly Sassy hadn't wasted much time salvaging her ego with all who'd listen. I ignored it, much worse having been said about me, and got dressed.

I made my way down to Donovan's office, finding myself scanning the halls for a blonde as I walked. It wasn't because I wanted to see her—I wanted to avoid her, of course.

Donovan was in his office, as expected.

"Shut the door if you don't mind," he said as I came in.

I'd already suspected that this was a business meeting, but that solidified it.

I settled into the seat across from him, eyeing the office that could be mine if I wanted it. I didn't. I might sleep here until I found somewhere else suitable, but that was about it. There was something about this place that made the werewolf inside me want to howl and rip something apart.

"There's something I need from you as the future leader of the D.C. pack."

I stretched out in the chair. He needed me. Did he really think he could lay out a list of terms and conditions now? He better not think that I'd accept commands from him or anyone else. Wasn't in my DNA to take orders.

I raised a brow, waiting to hear his terms before I told him to fuck off. The curiosity was getting the better of me.

"Pen's sister."

Not the girl. Anything but the girl.

I didn't so much as twitch a muscle. Inside I was groaning like I'd been issued a death warrant. I'd already met the sister. Hot as burning coals on the outside but with a ticking time bomb in her chest. I'd had enough of death. I'd wanted her at first sight, but now I wanted to keep as far away from her as possible.

Donovan waited for some sign of encouragement.

He gave up quickly and continued to talk. "She's a little wild and has the propensity to get herself into trouble. But I'd appreciate it if you could watch out for her. I know she's a little reckless, but she's got a good heart. I need someone to keep an eye on her while I'm gone. I'm not saying it's an easy thing, but if something untoward happened, it would kill my wife. And to be honest, the little shit has sort of grown on me."

He flipped the pen in his hand, top over bottom, as he waited for my response. He didn't have to wait long.

"I said I'd step in as alpha. I didn't sign up for a babysitting gig."

He nodded slightly. We weren't so dissimilar, he and I. Or we hadn't been. Seeing him lately made me wonder what had happened to him. That he'd asked such a thing meant he was getting soft. That was a sin that would get you killed faster than drinking poison in this world. It was good he was getting out. I hoped he stayed wherever he landed, or he'd be another carcass in this war.

"I'm not asking you to do it because I think you should. It would be a personal favor to me. My wife doesn't have much family. I need this girl to stay..." He leaned back, clasping his hands in front of him as he tried to find the words that soft-pedaled the reality of the situation. Those words that didn't exist in the human vocabulary.

"I heard she's dying anyway. How long does she really have?" To a human, that might've seemed like a cruel question, but with our kind, especially an alpha who could smell death coming, it was part of the job.

"How'd you hear?" He didn't flinch, but his shoulders tensed.

"I ran into her in the hallway the other night. Could smell death on her." That might've cut out a few pertinent points, but it was the gist of it. "What's wrong with her? I couldn't tell."

His lips pressed together for another second, as if he didn't like to speak about the reality of her situation. Then he sighed, like someone who'd come to accept it anyway.

"Sucking Sickness," he said. "Random vampire attack took out my wife's mother and condemned Sassy to death in one night."

Once in a blue moon, there was something off about a human's blood that killed a vampire instantly. The human would die as well, but it was a long, drawn-out death, with no known cure.

"It's one thing if she dies a peaceful death. I can't have her getting herself killed first," he said.

"She's got the Sucking Sickness. A quick death might be better." There was nothing peaceful about going out that way. There were plenty of stories, and none of them were good. There were never mysterious recoveries. An accident might be a godsend.

"Look, I'd consider it a favor. It would mean a lot to me."

Dammit. That was the last thing I wanted to hear, but I should've expected it from him. Donovan was a stand-up guy. He wouldn't force me to do this petty shit. Which now meant I'd have to, because he wasn't being a dick about it. How could I turn him down when he was asking as a favor? There were some newer men on the scene that might not know better, but I wasn't one of them. When a fellow alpha asked for a favor, you stepped up, or you should be ashamed to show your mug again.

I got to my feet, stalling the inevitable acceptance.

"Well? Will you help me out?"

"Cut the shit. You know I will."

He smiled, coming just shy of laughing at how nicely I was trapped.

"Now that I have your word, there's a few more details that need to be wrapped up."

I leaned back as we eyed each other up. "And what would that be?" I asked.

"Sassy has a tendency toward trouble. She might have minor ties to the rebellion. I need to make sure that she's not only unharmed but sheltered from backlash."

"The human rebellion that's causing all the issues with the vampire and werewolf pact?"

"Yes. That one."

"And I'm going to do all of this because you're staying out of my way?" Donovan was far from an idiot. He knew my motivations for coming here. Would being alpha perhaps make accomplishing my goal a little easier? Yes. Was it going to make or break my success? Definitely not.

"Yes. And because we have ties that go deeper than either of us will ever admit to. Plus, you already gave me your word."

I'd thought Donovan was a stand-up guy. He'd just walked me into a trap. It was my own fault, though. I should've seen this coming a mile away. I would've seen it if I hadn't let our past history cloud my judgment. Now I was stuck taking care of the sick girl who was on a mission to get herself killed.

"How long do you think she has left?"

His gaze dropped to the top of his desk as he picked up a pen and tapped it repeatedly. "I don't know. She's a tough one. She's not going to go quietly, but while she's alive, she doesn't get touched, not by anyone."

I had a hunch that the warning included me. It wasn't needed. The girl had nothing but "pain in the ass" written all over her, and then there was the fact she was dying...

I stood and walked toward the door, wanting to get out of there and go for a long run, but stopped before I left. "And Donovan? You know I'll get you back for this."

"Oh, I know you will."

3

S *assy*

Cole sat across the table, black hair pushed back from his tanned skin. My sister didn't allow cigars to be smoked in her house but no one seemed to have alerted him to this, including her. His legs were outstretched to the side as he flipped over the lighter in his hand absently. His deep-set eyes looked like they could've belonged to the devil himself. He glanced about the room the way only an alpha could, as if he could claim everything in it on a whim.

In this new world of ours, being an alpha and a were-wolf, he probably could. Fairies, dwarves, gnomes, and every other freak show that had slithered out of their dark shadows had pledged allegiance and helped them. Even half of the humans left seemed to be vying for favor. Unless they were like me, and wanted to kill them.

Considering I was my sister's dinner guest and bloodshed wouldn't be appreciated, I forced my gaze from the enemy. If I looked upon him for one more second, I'd tear his skin from his bones. So instead, I fixated on my wine glass, my cuticles, a scuff on my heel, and the hem of the nice dress. I'd begrudgingly donned it after my sister browbeat me into looking civilized.

Donovan spoke, but it barely registered. My sister was speaking now, trying to hold up the conversation for the other half of the dinner participants who were silent.

Even having them here as buffers didn't make this any more bearable. I would've gladly paid to not have to ever see this man again.

Donovan cleared his throat, and then my sister kicked me under the table, dragging my attention back to them.

"Sassy, you know Cole's stepping in for Donovan while we're away, right?" Pen asked, her stubborn streak showing up like a flare in the night.

"Yes. Interesting times." That came out even flatter than I felt about it.

Of course I knew. She'd told me ten times, on top of the five times Donovan mentioned it. What neither of them seemed to comprehend was that I didn't care if he was going to be the new alpha.

Donovan looked at me, and then Cole, before glancing at Penelope. She gave him the slightest shrug with a tiny head bend to the right. It was her *this is as good as it's going to get* look. She nailed that one.

"I asked you both to dinner tonight in hopes that you could get better acquainted before we left." Donovan, stubborn man that he was, refused to throw in the towel.

"I think we're both acquainted well enough," I said, keeping my tone neutral.

Cole's gaze landed on me. It was hard not to feel like the fires of hell were blazing in my direction. Not sure what his problem was. Last time I checked, I'd been the insulted party.

I stared back, hard.

He could torch me with his hellish stare all night. I wasn't scared of hell, the devil, or death. I'd been facing them for years and come to terms with my future, and nothing he had to offer was going to make me shrink into my chair.

His gaze lingered on me for a few seconds, as if he could sense every thought running around in my head.

"I'd have to agree with her on this, at least. We're as acquainted as needed." He looked back to the lighter he was turning over in his fingers, as if that were infinitely more interesting than me. The feeling was mutual.

I countered with a disgusted sigh.

"Could someone enlighten me on what went down between you two that I am unaware of?" Donovan asked.

"Nothing," Cole and I answered in unison. Another thing we could agree upon. The short interaction between us had absolutely no meaning.

Donovan and Pen were glancing back and forth. Donovan shook his head and shrugged.

Finally, maybe they'd give up.

"Sassy, did I show you that painting Donovan had in the attic I dug out?"

"You mean the old one that you had restored and hung three months ago? Yes." I had a few sips of wine left. If this dinner went on for another hour, someone was going to have to pop another bottle just for me or I wouldn't make it. Maybe they should break out the hard stuff. A bottle of wine to myself still might not be enough.

"Let me show it to you again."

She manacled her hand around my wrist and dragged me out of my seat before I could wrap my hand around the last of my wine. She tugged me all the way over to the fireplace across the room.

"What exactly happened with you two that you can barely be civil to each other?" she asked, keeping a hold on me as if she were afraid I'd try to make a break for it.

"Nothing. Some people just don't mesh. We're two of them. It happens." That was the story I was going with, because if I told her the truth—the entire truth about how he wouldn't fuck a sick chick—she'd never leave here. Penelope *had* to leave here. It was her only chance at a happy life, and I'd be damned if I let anything ruin that for her.

"You say that, but this seems awfully strong for someone you barely know. It's like you hate each other."

"I don't hate him. I barely know him." I glanced across the room to where Cole was reclined in his seat as Donovan did all the talking, wondering how much longer I'd have to stay here and tolerate Cole being alive.

"Why? You didn't like the way he said hello or something?" Pen asked, grasping at straws.

"Something like that." I shrugged.

"He's going to be in charge of this area while Donovan is gone. You need to get along. Why do you have to be so damned difficult all the time?" Her cheeks were getting red.

How many times had I heard that? *Why can't you be easier? Why are you so difficult? Be more like Penelope.*

"It'll be fine. I won't even see him." I wished I weren't seeing him now.

She leaned closer, giving me her stern look. "Can you try harder to get along?"

The smell of desperation was almost pungent. She thought that if she could ease the way between Cole and me, things would be fine. It would be like when she and Donovan were here and Cole would look after me or some crazy shit. Who knew what the deal was?

She didn't realize the type of man they were leaving in charge. Cole was no Donovan. Donovan was tough, would hold the pack together and do what he had to. Cole was a cold-hearted killer. I could see it in his eyes. I'd seen enough others to know that dead, flat look. I wasn't sure what his life had been like before now, but something had burned any softness out of him.

"Pen, you don't have to worry. I'll be fine. You know I hate everyone I meet in the beginning, and then they grow on me. It'll be the same with him. You know, I'm prickly for a while, and then I warm up and win them over."

What a whopper that one was. I would never warm up to that man, ever. Luckily, I'd already had a few glasses of wine. I always lied better under the influence. Plus Pen wanted to believe me. A willing participant greased the wheels.

"Do me a favor and play nice with him sooner rather than later? It's not going to hurt to have him in your corner."

My sister's big, pleading eyes were the same shape and color as mine. The only difference was that hers were filled with trust and hope. She'd been on her way to being as cynical as I was. She might never have gotten to my full-blown stage of disgust, but she'd at least been more real-istic about the state of affairs and the monsters who'd taken over our world. Now she was brimming with optimism and trust again. She actually thought that monster would watch out for me if I smiled at him. It was good she was leaving. No one this blind and happy was safe in this world, not even with a man like Donovan by her side.

She smiled at me encouragingly and then grabbed my arm, tugging me across the room again.

Something about the disdain in Cole's eyes seemed to scream that he'd gotten a similar talking-to. I wasn't sure what Donovan had said to him, but from the reclined position and the bored look on Cole's face, I was sure it hadn't worked. Then again, Pen's hadn't either, but I was putting more effort into faking it.

"Why don't we all have a glass of port on the patio? I have the loveliest new bottle that came in that I want you all to try," Pen said as we rejoined the men.

"Sure." Cole got to his feet, looking like he would agree to anything that got more space in between us.

A few minutes later, we all made our way outside, glasses in hand.

The second the fresh air hit us, my sister said, "Oh no, this wasn't the right one. I'll be right back."

"This is great. Perfect," I said, not looking to go through a second round.

"Tastes good to me," Cole added.

At least the two of us agreed on one thing. We wanted this night over with.

"No, no. You have to try the new one. Donovan, come help me?"

"Of course." Donovan turned to us, stalling for a second. "You both better still be here when we get back."

"Fine," I said.

Cole simply shook his head.

As soon as they were both out of earshot, I turned to him. "Could you at least fake some civility so this night can end?"

He turned his head very slowly to me, his eyebrow rising. "Now you want to fake civility, princess? After you told anyone who would listen to your story?"

I stiffened, trying to think back on what I might've said about him and to whom. I got nothing but a blank. If anything, I'd avoided speaking about him at all, but I had gotten pretty drunk the night I met him, finishing off that bottle of bourbon. Had I said something to someone about what happened? It was possible, but I wasn't going to open that can of worms now. This situation was messy enough.

"Just pretend to be a gentleman so we can get through this night." I crossed my arms and turned my head before adding, "And don't call me that."

"Oh, all right, then, since that's the way you want it. From what I hear, everything has to happen the way princess wants it." He leaned on the patio table, crossing his arms as if he was done with this evening.

"You know it all, don't you? Here for a hot five seconds but already king, as if you earned anything, but that's not predictable." I walked closer, not because I wanted to be near him but because I was afraid the staff over by an open door might overhear.

He turned to me, smiling. "About as predictable as a spoiled little girl who wreaks havoc wherever she goes and then calls her big sister and brother to bail her out."

He leaned there, not worrying about dirtying pants that probably cost more than my entire wardrobe.

"If you're such hot shit, why don't you have a pack of your own? Why'd you have to come here and take over someone else's? What happened? No one wants you because you're a lunatic, even among your own kind? That's it, isn't it? You got run off for being unhinged?"

He laughed and took another sip of port. "I bet you know a thing or two about that state of being. Even your own family thinks you can't manage your own affairs."

I lifted my fist to punch him.

He caught it, tugging me closer until I was standing in between his spread legs. "If you touch me, I'm going to assume it's okay to reciprocate. Or is that what you're angling for?" He smirked, as if he really thought I still wanted him.

"The other night was a one-time offer made from over imbibing. That's fully rescinded." I yanked my hand free, putting a few feet in between us.

"I'm sure that lovely disposition of yours has people flocking to you," he said, his voice calm even as I saw the telltale sign of tension in his shoulders.

"If you think I act like an animal, it's because it was the only way to survive you monsters." I took a deep breath, trying to calm my nerves as Pen and Donovan walked through the back door toward us.

"What were you two chatting about while we were gone?" Pen asked as she approached, shooting a nervous glance between the two of us.

I mentally calmed myself, knowing my sister would pick up on any tension.

"Just how charming your sister can be," Cole said, smiling at me. He shot me a look, silently telling me to suck it up if we wanted to get away from each other.

I swallowed, needing to put a little more effort into faking it.

"I might've misjudged Cole a little. First impressions

can be deceiving." Oh, had I misjudged. Cole was much worse than I'd initially assumed. I took the glass of port from my sister and downed half of it in one gulp.

I downed the rest, about to make my exit when Cole straightened and did it for me.

"It was a wonderful evening. Thank you," Cole said to Pen and Donovan. "A pleasure," he said, turning to me.

"Let me walk you out," Donovan said, leaving with Cole.

Cole walked away, and I hoped to never see him again.

4

S *assy*

My phone buzzed again.

There'll be a car at the house for you in an hour. —Pen

It was the fifth message today, as if I'd miss her party tonight. I might've missed a few random parties in the past, but it was because I had a job. I couldn't tell her why because I couldn't tell her about my job. Any party that didn't conflict with work, I was there. Her shindigs were the best place to pick up intel, especially with the new recruits we were getting lately.

Fred, newly appointed strategist in the group, tapped the map of the city before pushing his thick glasses back up his nose. "What about here? We could set the first explosion here. That could work."

I shot a look over Fred's bent form to Mattie, my second-in-command. He might look like an angel, but he was avoiding my stares like he was very guilty. It had been his brilliant idea to appoint Fred as a strategist. I'd stayed silent even with a mountain of doubts, unlike quite a few others in the crew. But standing here listening to Fred's ideas, it made me feel like I was dodging boulders coming down that aforementioned mountain.

"No. We put them there, and the squads that always hang out at this coffee shop"—I tapped the map in case he had no idea what I was referring to—"will be on to us in under two minutes flat. They aren't there for coffee. It's one of their lookout points to watch all the traffic in and out of this area."

Vicki, our best tech and wiring person, gave me owl eyes across the table. Harlow, our chemical and bomb guy, wasn't saying much of anything, which was highly unlike him. He always had opinions and was free with them all. Jess, Ellie, and Pat, part of the ground operations, weren't commenting at all.

"What about if we station people here, here, and here as lookouts for when they're looking out," he said, pointing out different places around the coffee shop.

Don't scream at him. Don't. Scream. Leaders inspired, not berated. I'd heard that somewhere. At least he wasn't a quitter. I'd take an idiot over a quitter any day, just not in a position where he could get us all killed.

I straightened and took a few deep breaths while the rest of the crew watched on, except for Mattie, who wasn't looking at me at all.

Another deep breath. "Those spots have heavy surveillance."

"But there are cameras everywhere," Fred said.

"Yes, but the difference is, the cameras here? They're monitored by a private firm that has live agents watching them at all times, and they have facial recognition. We'll be spotted before we get within twenty feet of our objective."

Harlow shook his head and jumped in. "How often do you pull your head out of your ass? We can't use that spot for a group of humans after curfew, toting machine guns, heading toward one of their favorite places to hang out."

This meeting had to get shut down now, because the lid on Harlow's opinions had officially been blown. Once that happened, they usually kept on coming, and Fred already looked like he was going to go home and roll into a ball.

"Look, we're all tired right now. I'll look over everything tomorrow and figure it out. Right now, I've got to go." I swung my bag onto my back while Mattie followed me.

We stopped outside the door.

Mattie was a crucial part of the resistance, handling the crew on a day-to-day basis the way I'd never have the patience for. But Fred? Had he drunk too much the night of that decision?

I waited until I got to my bike to speak. "You need to find somewhere else to put him. He's going to get one of us killed, maybe several. I get it. His sister died, and you're trying to help him fill the void. But this isn't the place he should be. His input is making my brain bleed. He's too stupid for strategy." He might be too stupid to change a light bulb, but we'd find some place for him. As far as I was concerned, anyone who wanted to fight for the human race belonged with us—as long as they passed the vetting process, that was.

Mattie sighed as he looked back toward the back door of our building. "I'll tell him as soon as I get him alone."

I climbed onto my bike, but Mattie grabbed the handlebars before I could take off.

"Don't take any chances tonight," he said.

Mattie and I typically shared a bottle of bourbon together after a strategy session, but tonight there was work to be done.

"I only get as crazy as I have to."

He shook his head, laughing softly before he headed back inside the old flag factory. It was on the outskirts of town, set off by itself, serving no purpose to anyone but us. It was also a bit of a hike home and not a lot of time to do it in.

I stepped into my sister's house in a black dress that fell below my knees, sleeves that came to my wrists, and a modest boat neckline. In spite of the fact it showed very little flesh, it might be the most seductive dress I owned. The fabric clung to every curve, and there were a lot. I'd been blessed with a tiny waist and ample breasts. The curves of my hips and butt would've made a basketball deflate in envy. I might prefer my beaten jeans and boots on most days, but that didn't mean I couldn't rock a pair of six-inch spikes when the need arose.

My mass of blond hair was doing its wild come-hither thing, and the pink highlight added a certain ditzy flair that was only accentuated when I spun the lock around my finger. As I'd heard more than once in my life,

I looked like I was made to fuck and not much else. It was an impression that was very useful in these moments, when the liquor was flowing and the lips were loose.

My sister came over to the door to greet me, took one look at my attire, and instantly dropped her brows.

"Don't stress me out tonight. You promised you were going to limit contact with *those* people," she said.

Those people. If she had any idea how deep in I was with *those* people, she'd be grabbing me by the hair and dragging me off to Europe with her and Donovan.

"Can't I look nice for the last dinner before you leave?"

"You're saying you look like that for me?" Pen raised an eyebrow.

"Just wanted to look nice, is all." I glanced around, looking for a new subject to broach. "Where's the little killer?"

"With the monster-in-law." Pen talked about Donovan's mother the way people discussed a mold problem in their basement or the neighbor's dog shitting on their lawn.

I nodded. Donovan's mother might hate my sister, but she doted on her grandson, the newest alpha to be born to the pack, like he was her own. Plus, the way that kid bit, it was hard to get babysitters. He had the face of a cherub and the teeth of a saber-tooth tiger.

"Come on, let's go in." She locked her arm around mine as we headed toward the sounds of people mingling. "Cole's already here, too. I'm really glad you smoothed things over before we left."

"Yeah. Great." It was Cole's party to introduce him around before Pen and Donovan left. He should be here, but I'd half assumed he wouldn't be, since he hadn't shown for anything else since he'd arrived. Or maybe I'd hoped he wouldn't.

We were about as "smooth" as the ocean in a hurricane. I hated him, he hated me, and we'd never speak again unless absolutely necessary. That was as smooth as it got for us.

Pen would never know that we'd initially hit it off like fireworks on the Fourth of July, because that would lead to what happened next, and why it happened. Cole didn't fuck sick chicks. That was a tough pill to swallow, and an even harder one to rehash to a sister who didn't know you *were* sick.

We walked into the room. It was supposed to be a small gathering, but that was rarely the case. These shifters were too cliquey by far. No one liked to be left out, and from the looks of it, the entire D.C. pack was here, plus some. I liked a crowded party. More information I could gather.

Without warning, she steered us over to the group in the corner with Cole. He happened to be with Donovan, but I didn't doubt she would've found him eventually anyway, because she wasn't one to let something be.

Donovan greeted me, and so did Huddy, his second-in-command and generally nice guy, as far as shifters went.

"Cole, of course you remember my sister," Pen said.

"Of course." He gave a slight nod, eyeing me up, his expression chilly even as it lingered a hair longer than it should've.

I forced a smile.

"And this is..." My sister smiled as she tried to recall the name of the woman who was currently hanging on to

Cole's arm as if it were the only thing keeping her standing.

"Huh?" the woman asked, wobbling forward, a breast precariously close to falling out of her dress.

I turned my attention to Cole, waiting for him to step in and offer her name. I wasn't the only one. Huddy, Donovan, my sister—everyone had their attention trained on him.

Another second ticked by before Cole lifted a brow and gave a half shrug.

He had no idea what his date's name was? It was as if the universe wanted to remind me yet again of what a jerk he was. If I were her, I'd walk out of here right now, but she looked beyond able to take that many steps on her own.

Instead, she sipped her drink, like some more wine was what she needed.

"Beautiful lady, what was your name again?" Huddy asked, loud enough to make sure he was heard.

"Marlaine," she said, then hiccupped.

A young waitress circled the room with more drinks on her tray. It was the same catering staff they used from time to time. My sister didn't like having a large staff around all the time, and neither did Donovan.

The girl slowed in front of Cole, offering her tray and —from the smile—herself as well. He placed his glass on it and then took a fresh one, returning the smile, oblivious to the fact he already had a date.

Was he really flirting with the waitress in front of his date?

I turned to Pen, not having to say a word, since she could read my expression clearly.

She gave me her owl eyes, the expression that seemed to defy gravity because her eyeballs didn't drop out of her head. I didn't need the warning. I hadn't planned on speaking. And if the guy was so sensitive he couldn't handle a few judgmental stares, he shouldn't commit the crime.

A servant waved from the doorway.

"Dinner is ready if we all want to go to the other room," Pen said.

Donovan moved to her side to walk into the dining room with her. They were one of *those* couples. As happy as I was for my sister, it would be nice for them to chill on the *I'd die without you* looks. We were about to eat, after all, and you could only stomach so much in one sitting.

Cole walked toward the dining room as well, his date barely staying upright as she went. It wasn't clear whether he didn't notice she could use a hand or didn't care.

"I know you hate these dinners," Huddy said, offering me his arm.

Of all the werewolves I'd met since the world turned upside down, Huddy was in my top two.

"Yeah, well, couldn't blow off the new alphas welcoming dinner. Too bad you didn't want the job. Wouldn't have needed to bother with all these introductions," I said as the swarms of people, mostly shifters, made their way in for the dinner.

"Some people aren't cut out for the role," he said.

"I know you. There's steel under that skin."

His lips turned up slightly, but not enough to form a true smile. "Not the kind that will hold up under what's coming or what might need to be done. Now, Cole, on the other hand—he's been through things that would've broken another man. His edges are jagged and the surface is rough, but he'd breeze through a nuclear war if that was what came."

Huddy detached from me as we searched out our names on the place settings. Most people were probably hoping they'd be seated next to someone important, like the new alpha. I was hoping I'd been placed down the other end, plopped right in between two idiots discussing things they shouldn't.

No such luck. I was toward the top of the table, right across the table from Cole and No Name.

I took my seat, ignoring the way Cole's eyes kept shooting over to me. He was probably plotting how he'd off me after Donovan was gone.

Cole's attention kept shifting back to me, but every time I looked, his gaze was somewhere else. I watched everyone else but couldn't seem to pull my attention from him. Mostly because his attention seemed to be on me.

"Did you hear about the attack?" Noah asked. He was a lower-level shifter from a neighboring pack sitting beside Cole.

I'd met him once or twice before. He was pretty close-mouthed unless he was drinking the hard stuff. The glass in front of him looked like exactly what I needed. Maybe tonight would yield a couple of interesting tidbits after all.

"Everyone's heard about the attack. Has there been any rumors on the rebel group behind it?" Cole asked, and for the first time tonight, it felt like his attention was completely off of me.

Any arrogance, act, or charade was dropped and his true colors shone as sharp as a laser sight on a rifle. This wasn't the playboy enjoying a drink with his floozy date. This Cole wasn't just jagged edges—he was lethal. This was the man Donovan was leaving in charge of the pack.

My position on the other side of his law suddenly chilled me more than the ice cooling the champagne in the nearby bucket.

I didn't catch a chill easily. My nerves were wrapped and insulated from being in the trenches for longer than I'd ever admit. Pen thought my nefarious affairs had started in the last couple years. In truth, they'd begun the month after the war. They started as soon as I could figure out a way to fight back. Turned out I was a born fighter. I'd found my way fast and easy.

"No idea," Noah said. "But the vampires are searching high and low. They're calling it the Night of a Thousand Deaths." He picked up his glass, downing the rest of it.

"Did they figure out how many fatalities there were yet? The vampires are saying not many, but that's bull-shit if you ask me," an older shifter a few seats down said.

"I heard from a girl who was messing around with one of them that they got hit bad," Noah answered.

For all the work we'd put in, I hoped so. You'd think one of these idiots could at least have found out a body count.

"But only vampires. No coordinated hits on us. Strange for a rebellion like that. Most of them tend to hit across the board, but not this group," the older shifter said.

He wouldn't think it was so strange if he was the one with uncomfortable connections to the enemy, whom I'd unfortunately grown fond of. For now, or at least until Donovan and my sister left and stayed gone, we were a vampire-only resistance.

My sister struck up a conversation about greenhouses in winter, but that didn't stop Noah.

"It's crazy. Only thing we've managed to hear is that they're led by a person named Ghost," Noah said.

"The guy's got to be some sort of tactical genius," the older shifter added, assuming Ghost was a guy.

Cole's attention was solely on the resistance talk. He wasn't saying much, but he was sure taking it all in.

"Do you have any plans on how you'll handle things while you're in charge?" Donovan asked, finally making his voice heard in the conversation.

It sounded a little like an interview question. Was someone else finally realizing Cole might not be the best shifter for the job? They needed to tell this guy to get packing and make Huddy step up, whether he wanted to or not.

"A few," Cole said.

I sipped my wine and forced myself to chew, as I was all ears on the situation. *Go ahead, stick your foot in it and let Donovan send you packing.*

"Care to share one or two of those ideas?" Donovan put his glass down and gave Cole every ounce of his attention.

"Am I giving you my plan or seeking your approval?" Cole asked, that razor's edge in his tone, the one that could slice a person to pieces if they didn't watch out.

Donovan could handle it. He had some sharp steel of his own.

"Just having a friendly conversation," Donovan said, draining the tension.

And it was Cole for the win. If this kept happening, it was going to get real old, fast.

"Then, in that spirit, I'll tell you this: I'd let that rebellion do whatever it wants, maybe even hand them over some supplies if needed. After they're done doing our dirty work and no longer needed, I'll kill them. They might be focusing on the vampires now, but they'll make the mistake of targeting us sooner or later. Then I'll hunt them down and personally kill them all, because nobody crosses me and walks away."

I didn't miss the way my sister looked at me under her lashes.

Donovan picked up his glass, his jaw twitching.

5

S *assy*

I was getting some air in my usual spot in the backyard, not because I was rattled but because this was what I always did, Cole or no Cole.

Unfortunately, my sister knew exactly where to find me. I'd known this was coming as soon as Cole ran his mouth about killing everyone like a psychopath. They'd chosen poorly, and now I'd have to hear about it.

Pen was looking all over the yard, as if it were her ass about to get slaughtered. "I don't know what your ties to the resistance are, but please, you need to stay as far away from them as possible. We won't be here to shield you when they fall. The top will topple, and they'll give up all the little people to buy themselves some leverage."

A squirrel jumped in a nearby tree, and she jumped

like it had been a grenade. I loved her, but she would've made a horrible resistance fighter.

I, on the other hand, was a very good one and had no intentions of being caught or toppling. If she only knew how insulting the assumption that there would be a toppling was. Unfortunately, I couldn't air my grievances fully, but I didn't have plans on getting caught, at least in whatever time I had left. I might die on a whimper, but I'd be making an awfully loud bang before that happened.

If my timeline was right, I might have four or five months left, and I was going to make a mark for all humankind before then. I wouldn't have lived a life in vain.

"Sassy, promise me," she said, looking as if she would crack if I didn't.

"I promise you, I won't be in a position to get thrown under the bus for some bigwig looking to skate." After all, I couldn't tattle on myself.

She nodded, looking a little less fidgety than she had a minute ago.

"Pen, I promise I'll be okay," I said.

She nodded again. "Okay. But if you do something stupid, I'll come back here and kill you."

"I know." I smiled, knowing I was going to have a gaping void in my life as soon as she left. She didn't realize this, but she might never be back. The writing was on the wall. Tensions were high. Food shortages were everywhere. Whatever civilization left, shifter or vampire in charge, was collapsing. There'd be nothing left to come back to soon. I would've hugged her and cried if I wasn't afraid of keeping her here.

"Pen?" Donovan was on the patio, waving to her.

"I'll talk to you later," she said, knowing I was staying over for their last night here.

She left, and like clockwork, tonight's guest of honor seemed to appear out of nowhere.

He walked across the yard, all in black. Or maybe that was just the color of his soul. I inched back a few feet farther into the shadows, hoping he'd take the hint and walk past me.

He angled his way over like he was already the alpha of D.C., and it made me want to knee him in the balls. I'd never had a shot of him ignoring me. Cole wouldn't miss an opportunity to ruin my night.

He stopped too close, like he had the right. A lot of very dumb women had probably convinced him that he did. I'd almost been one of them.

I didn't move another hair from my spot. I didn't say hello. That would imply I was happy to see him. I pretended he wasn't crowding me as I took a cigarette out of its pack and lit it.

He leaned a hand on the wall a little too close for comfort.

"How's the princess tonight?"

I'd gotten called that more times than I could count. It might've been the blond hair and general look. For some reason, people assumed women who looked like me were put upon a pedestal.

Any semblance of a good life had ended when my mother died and my father became a drunk. I would've argued the point, but then I'd have to talk to him. It was also none of his business.

He leaned in, plucking the cigarette from my lips and then crushing it under his black boot.

"You did not just do that." I turned my full glare on

him now, conscious of exactly how close he was. I hated that he smelled so good. Evil people should smell like rotting corpses to warn others off. Not an exotic, spicy scent and a walk through the trees.

"I'm doing you a favor, since you're clearly too stupid to know better. These things kill humans."

I gave him my haughtiest once-over before I said, "You need to keep walking. Now, if you don't mind..." I waved my hand toward the house before taking another swig from the bottle.

He stepped in and stole that.

"What? Now I'm not allowed to drink either?"

"I think you've had enough, and I need you sober to hear what I'm going to tell you."

"I don't care what you have to say."

He took a swig from my bottle and then at least had the decency to hand it back. It soothed my nerves just shy of wanting to kick him in the groin.

"You'll care about this," he said.

I'd lay money against that one, but I didn't see a reason to continue speaking. It simply encouraged him to stay here and annoy me. I'd let him get whatever it was out of his system and hopefully that would be the end of it.

"Donavan asked me to watch out for you after he's gone."

I shrugged.

Donovan. Now there were two men I wanted to punch. The man might not know what I was doing, but he surely suspected. Was singling me out for attention with the new alpha really the best call, dearest brother?

"Well, I'm officially letting you off the hook. I don't need you to watch out for me. I don't need anyone to check in or walk me home. I'm getting along fine without you." I also didn't need people following me around as I handled my business, which most certainly would not be looked upon favorably.

"It's not a favor for you, so you can't release me from it." He leaned closer, blocking out the light from the house. "I've asked around, and there's lots of rumors swirling. Keep your nose clean and we won't have any issues. You'll never have to see me again."

He stood there, running his gaze over my face and pausing on my lips for a few seconds too long.

"Is that all? Done. Now please, go somewhere else. I was having a very nice evening before you arrived." That was a lie. I'd been having a shitty night and a shittier week, but the last thing I needed to add was more issues with him.

"Don't forget what I said." He hovered for another minute before leaving.

I watched him walk away, knowing I'd never see him again. It should've made me happy. It did. Sort of.

No, it *did*.

6

C *ole*

There were voices below, coming from the driveway. I moved to the window, where Sassy was saying goodbye to her sister and nephew.

"Is that enough?" Sassy asked, looking at the piles of luggage loaded into the back of the SUV.

"It's not all mine." Pen held the baby out to Sassy. "Here, can you hold your nephew for a minute while I make sure I have my sunglasses?"

"He's young. He won't remember me shunning him. It'll be okay," Sassy said as she stepped back, eyeing the baby in her sister's arms.

I laughed. That kid had a cherubic face that would have sold a million jars of baby food, but one nasty bite. I'd learned it myself the first day here. Underneath that innocent exterior was a born killer. He'd be a hell of an alpha one day—if there was a pack left to lead.

"He's your nephew," Pen said, pushing the kid at her.

"And I love him, even if I don't want him within a few feet of me."

The baby laughed, waving his chunky little arms toward her. The perfect little predator, luring her in with his cuteness.

"Oh, all right." Sassy took the little munchkin from her sister. "You bite me and you're going right back."

The baby giggled, like he knew exactly what he was doing.

Pen checked her purse and then stood there, staring at her sister. "You can still come. Just get in the car with us and go. Donovan will smooth things out."

"Nah, it's good for you two to get some alone time and bond as a family." Sassy kissed the baby's cheeks, holding him a little tighter for all her protests.

"You're my family too. Get out of here for a while. Take a break from this mess."

Pen had no idea that they weren't coming back. I hadn't been told either, but the writing was on the wall. Donovan wanted his family out of here, and I didn't blame him.

Sassy knew. Even from here, I could see the sadness in her eyes when her sister wasn't paying attention. She was hiding it well, though.

"I'll come meet up with you as soon as you get bored."

Donovan walked out of the house, and Sassy handed off the little monster to him. She turned and hugged her sister. Her expression, hidden from their view, was nearly heartbreaking, and I didn't think I had a heart left to break.

"You're sure you don't want to come?" Donovan asked.

"I told you both, I'll be fine here for a while."

Donovan and his wife and child pulled away as Sassy watched. She stood there in the driveway, arms wrapped around her midsection as the car disappeared from sight.

I went back to getting dressed, but something kept luring me to the window.

Sassy was still standing there, ten minutes later. It wasn't like she couldn't have gone with them. Donovan would do anything for his wife, including smuggling people out of here. Was Sassy going to stand there and make a spectacle of herself?

"You should've gone with them," I said as I walked outside a few minutes later, not knowing why I was approaching her at all. She'd leave soon, and I'd have this pain in the ass out of my hair for at least a while.

"Why? So you could run this territory into the ground with fewer witnesses?" She gave me a side glance, loaded with pure venom.

Something about her claws had a way of turning me on. There'd been others like her. Many. Most of them lost all their feistiness and fight after a couple of rounds in the bedroom, making me wonder if there'd ever been much steel there to begin with. She'd surely be the same.

"By the way, I thought I didn't have to see you again." She lifted her hand and had the audacity to wave it at me.

I raised a brow even as I wanted to laugh at her antics. She definitely had some amusement value, even out of the bedroom.

"Perhaps you shouldn't have stayed over at my current residence, then."

She turned to say something and then shook her head, as if she were done with me. She walked over to her bike that looked like it was about to rust through. She was going to kill herself with that thing.

"Sassy."

"What?" she asked as she pulled her hair into a ponytail.

"You need to back off whatever you're involved in. Play nice, little human, and we won't have a problem. If you cross the line, it won't go well for you, no matter who you're connected to."

She might have long claws, but hopefully she wasn't a complete idiot. That warning would scare off the hardest in my pack. Although they knew me and she didn't. Still, she was just a little piece of fluff. She'd start watching her step.

I didn't bother taking in her reaction, knowing I'd made my point. I turned to leave, and the fluff stepped in front of me.

"I'm not sure what Donovan was thinking when he left a barbarian like you in charge, or what backwoods you crawled out of, but this place takes a little more finesse, even with you people in charge. Maybe you should go run back to the swamps and thicket, because you're out of your league."

I lifted her under the arms, bringing her to eye level. "Don't push me. You have no idea what kind of monster I can be."

I set her to the side and walked in the house. She might be a problem, but damned if she didn't make the day a little more interesting.

7

C *ole*

One month later

Lonzo walked into the office at the club that was the de facto headquarters of the D.C. pack. He looked like he'd strolled out of a cave. The only difference between the two of us was that I attempted to appear civilized. He didn't bother with the act. That was fine, as polish wasn't necessary for his position. In fact, his rough edges might smooth the way in certain circumstances, and loyalty was the only thing I valued.

"The skirmish last night, the three dead vampires?" He stopped walking and shook his head.

I leaned back, pinching the bridge of my nose.

Watch out for her. I know she's a little reckless, but she's got a good heart. Those were Donovan's words. Had he really been that blind? The only thing in that girl's chest was a rotting black corpse. There were vampires with warmer hearts than she had. Did he not know how entwined she was with the resistance? Every single uprising since, there were rumors of her in the periphery. She might be fucking the leader, or he was just using her as a dipshit front-woman, but she was in deep and had more blood on her hands than the local butcher after a two-for-one deal.

Now the cold little princess was my problem. If the phone lines could be trusted, I would've called Donovan at least twenty times already to truly express how deeply he owed me for this favor. Unfortunately, the vampires were sneaky fucks who couldn't be trusted not to listen in. They tapped phone lines more often than Lonzo tapped the drunk broads at the bar.

"Cole?" Lonzo asked, waiting for directions.

Maybe if I ignored him this would all go away, but that was unlikely. It was too much. I was going to have to step up and get her in hand before she ended up dead.

I'd turned a blind eye too many times in an effort to avoid seeing her. Now there were dead vampires, pissed vampires, upset vampires, every damned flavor of vampires. I'd never liked the happy, pleasant vampires—not that you ever saw many of those—let alone the ones who kept spreading rumors that the werewolves were behind this.

"Cole?" Lonzo repeated, as if I hadn't heard him the first time.

Of course he wouldn't take a hint. He'd probably stand in front of my desk, repeatedly calling my name. Might as well hear him out, because I wasn't getting rid of him until he got it out.

"They didn't touch the shifters, correct?" Maybe I could look the other way, just one more time.

"No, but it's getting real sticky," he said, referring to the tensions that were boiling up.

"I know."

If I'd gotten my objective handled, I wouldn't care if they built up like a powder keg. But once things went to shit with the werewolves and the vampires, that door would be closed for good.

Not to mention every time this happened under my watch, it made people start questioning my control of the district. Turning the other way was making me look weak. The vampires were still chasing their tails on the resistance, but this side of the street had a little more know-how, and everyone was wondering why I hadn't done something yet to get them in line, including me. If the vampires linked Sassy to the resistance, her connection to the pack would make it all come tumbling down on us. She was on the verge of screwing the lot of us.

"If something isn't done..." He shrugged.

Lonzo wasn't great with words, but he got his point across.

How many times had I warned her now? But she just kept going. I was really losing my edge. First, I let Donovan get one over on me, and now this little chit was ignoring my orders in front of everyone.

And I kept letting her.

Why? So I didn't have to see her again? So what if I saw her? For what possible reason did I keep avoiding her?

That one had an easy answer. If I saw her, I'd want to

fuck her, and I was not getting involved with her for many reasons, including that I didn't particularly like her. That wasn't always a deal breaker, but it was when the list was a mile long.

"You're sure? Absolutely sure it's linking back to her?" Even if there was a crumb of doubt I could hang my hat on, it would be better.

"We've got people on her, as you instructed. She loses them more often than not, but we're sure. We saw the building blow, and she was one of the humans running from the blast." His eyes sank a little deeper and he scratched the back of his neck, looking more beast than man as he held something back.

"*And*?" I asked. I didn't want to hear this crap in the first place. Having to drag out the details was making me want to smash my glass against the wall. I wouldn't, because it was good alcohol, but the desire was there.

He took a few more steps forward, looking puzzled. "Well, from the way the story unfolded, it sounded like she might've been the one to set the blast off."

I slammed my glass down, the whiskey splashing all over the desk. Fucking idiot. Tell her to keep her shit clean and tidy and she dives headfirst into a pile of manure.

"And still no word on the higher-ups of this resistance?" I asked. "You have zero idea who's pulling the strings?"

If I could find the guy banging her and kill him, problem solved. Still wouldn't have to see her and the situation would be resolved nicely. Very nicely. That solution was ideal. The leader of this group was probably of the lowest common denominator, taking advantage of a stupid girl with more balls than brains.

"Other than the alias Ghost, we've still got nothing. It's

pretty fitting. No one has a description, a name, any kind of lead on him. It's like he doesn't exist."

Whoever was running this rebellion was good. They knew she had some protection and were putting her in the lead while they fucked her.

Maybe I sit back and let the situation handle itself? It was only a matter of time before she got herself killed. She was dying anyway. What was the difference? Did it really matter if it were a few months earlier? I'd made a promise, but there was a limit to what I could do if she continued to throw herself in front of the firing squad.

Just let her kill herself. Easy enough. Right?

"Cole? What do you want us to do?" Lonzo asked after a couple minutes of silence ticked by.

I leaned back, looking at the ceiling, wondering why this was so fucking difficult. Because a fellow alpha had asked for a favor? So what? It was an old-school mentality that was not serving me well. The girl was a spoiled asshole. *Let her get killed and be done with it.*

"Do you want me to go talk to her again? I could try a different tactic," Lonzo said, taking a step toward the door with a pep in his step that gave me the strongest desire to get out of my seat and punch him in the face. His tactics were well known. *Bed them into delirium.* Did he have to bang every piece of ass walking by? Had he no control?

"No. Bring her to me."

Lonzo glanced around the office before he asked, "Here?"

"Yes. Here." Humans weren't typically brought to the club for myriad reasons, but mostly because werewolves didn't want them here. I didn't want her here either, but the messages weren't getting through. It was time for us to have this conversation again in person, and damned if I'd go to her.

Lonzo took a few steps and paused, turned halfway back to me, and paused again, rubbing the back of his neck.

"What?" I asked.

"I'm not sure it's going to go that smoothly. I don't know if I can get her to—"

"Shove her in your trunk if you have to, but get her ass here."

Sarah walked in without knocking.

You could practically hear the drum beating to the sashay of her hips. The beat had initially called me to attention. Lately it was giving me a pounding headache. She perched on the corner of my desk with a familiarity that was born from sleeping with someone. She hadn't realized she'd worn out her welcome.

"Who's Lonzo bringing here?" she asked as she crossed her legs and leaned a hand on the desk.

"No one important." I nodded at Lonzo.

He shook his head before leaving. The night I first fucked Sarah, Lonzo had given me that same shake, trying to warn me. The whiskey in my blood had a powwow with my dick, and they'd told Lonzo to fuck off. In hindsight, Lonzo might've had the better judgment that night.

Ever since I'd banged her, she walked around the place like she'd been anointed by God, expecting favoritism from all those beneath her. Even if I was into her for more than a fuck, I still would've hated it. Unfortunately, she was also the best shot we had in the pack, and not by a little. She was a natural-born sniper. If I'd realized it at the time, I definitely wouldn't have fucked her.

She was too annoying to keep around and too valuable to dump.

There was only one set of lips I kept thinking of, and they weren't hers. My cock grew hard from my thinking of Sassy's mouth wrapped around me, and Sarah mistakenly thought the invitation was for her.

When she tried to take me up on it, I stood. "Have an appointment coming in. Maybe another time."

8

S *assy*

Cole's men approached my back door. They walked toward the house like men who were walking toward a grave that they'd yet to dig, with a reluctant acceptance of the shit job before them. In today's scenario, I was the corpse about to stink up the joint if they didn't get a handle on me. They should probably invest in some nose plugs.

I knew them both because they used to be Donovan's men. I knew them even better now because they'd been coming by weekly to deliver their warnings. When they didn't stop by, they lingered around the neighborhood, stalking me. They were worse than the damned tiny fairies that hid in the bushes to spy on you. At least their wings got tired after a while.

Might as well see what they were bothering me about this time. It was probably another warning. They'd bluster and tell me how I was in such big trouble. I'd acknowledge the warning and they'd be on their way.

They might just drop a note. A couple of those had shown up, and they were much better. I didn't have to listen to them, and they didn't have to hear me lie. Plus, the notes were always on nice cardstock that was great for kindling. Made me want to start a regular correspondence.

They hit the front porch with empty hands. No letter to add to my kindling. Guess that meant we'd be talking today. I was supposed to be at headquarters in an hour, so I'd have to look submissive and repentant in under five minutes.

Lonzo looked through my backdoor window, waiting as I walked over.

I swung the door open.

"Sassy, we need to—"

"I know. You have to warn me. I get it. I've been warned. Tell Cole I'm so sorry and I'll never do it again." I put my hands up in a sign of surrender to hopefully sell my bullshit. I gave them a lame smile and then inched the door shut.

Lonzo put a hand out to stop it. "Not that easy this time. We need to bring you in." He looked like he'd slept less than I had last night, exhaustion nearly pouring off him at the idea of having to haul my ass over to Cole's. If possible, he sounded more dejected at the idea than I had, which couldn't be possible. I had a schedule they were about to screw up.

"For what? What travesty did I commit now?" There

was actually a long list, but I was only concerned about the ones they were aware of. Odds were it was the bomb last night. If it wasn't, this was *really* strange timing.

My people still hadn't gotten word if we'd managed any fatalities, but if they were here...

Don't smile, you dumbass. Gloating wouldn't get rid of them, and I really needed them to leave so I could go pop a couple of bottles open with my people.

"You know what you did, and he said he wants to see you at the club," Lonzo said like a chiding nanny.

"If he wanted to see me so badly, he should've come here. I've got things I need to do tonight. Tell him I'll stop by in the morning." Wait. I might want to sleep in after tonight's celebration. "Or afternoon. That might work better."

They took a step forward in unison. "That's not the way this works," Lonzo said. His buddy Derek shrugged beside him.

"I just don't have the time right now." I went to shut the door again.

Lonzo added his boot to the bottom. "Look, neither of us wants to be in the middle of this. It's a lose-lose for us. You know we're all in a spot with Donovan, but Cole is the alpha now."

Derek slumped against the doorframe. "Can you please make our lives easier and come peacefully? Donovan will kick our asses from the other side of the ocean if we have to rough you up."

Once my sister left, there had been a fleeting delusion I'd be done with having to appease both sides. Somehow it had gotten worse. The goons were now laying guilt trips on me.

Lonzo was a hair beyond a Neanderthal. Instead of working to my benefit, I constantly felt as if messing with him was like kicking a dog. Because literally, there were some dogs that were smarter than him.

Derek's awkward smile of hope was painful to see. He was nearly pleading with his stare, begging me to come peacefully.

"What did that dick say to do if I didn't?" I asked, knowing it was something unpleasant.

"Toss you in the trunk," Lonzo offered with zero hesitancy.

That jackass. Was I surprised? No. Not with Cole. That guy's heart was so cold he could give Jack Frost a case of the chills.

Derek was nodding. "We really don't want to do that. Donovan ever finds out, he'll come back to kill us. But if we don't bring you back with us, Cole will kill us. Please just come? You can sit in the front and have complete control of the radio."

"You know we don't want to do it," Lonzo said.

Lonzo might be a goon, but I'd always gotten the sense he was more about a roll in the hay than beating someone down into the dust. Derek was just a softie.

Talking about soft—getting friendly with these guys was making *me* soft. It hadn't been intentional. You got to know people when they showed up at your door all the time. They were here so often that it got awkward not to offer them a cup of coffee now and then. Shoot the shit while one of them used the bathroom. Small talk happened. Even in this messed-up world, it was unavoidable.

I blew out a breath and then grabbed my jacket. "So,

Derek, since we've got a little bit of a ride ahead, what's up with the new girl?"

He groaned. "You're never going to believe this bullshit. Turned out she was fucking that other wolf. Unreal, after all the shit I did for her..."

I barged into the office to see Cole sitting at the desk that used to be Donovan's.

"You might think you're in charge, but you don't get to order me about and threaten me with the trunk if I don't comply."

He leaned to the side, looking past me as if I hadn't spoken, and said, "Get out and shut the door behind you."

Derek had followed behind me.

I gave Derek a nod, letting him off the hook. He gave me a smile as he exited. The smile morphed into a scowl as Cole nailed him with a look.

I kept smiling as he shut the door.

"Don't try to get in my guys' heads. It won't work," Cole said.

"Wouldn't dream of it." *Already accomplished, idiot.*

"You just can't cut the shit out, can you?" Cole asked, looking as annoyed as I was about me standing in his office.

"I can't imagine what you're talking about," I said in a sickly-sweet voice.

He tilted his head, letting his stare simmer on me for a couple of seconds.

"You and your sister, you share the same mother and father?" he asked.

"Yes, but I'm sure you already knew that."

I'd seen that look: the brows pulled closer together, mouth in a flat line. It was so familiar that I could tell him what he'd say next.

I'd been hearing it my entire life. *Why can't you act like Pen? Why can't you behave like Pen does? Pen got all A's. Why can't you study and try harder, like Pen does? Pen is going to medical school. What are you going to do, Sassy? Why can't you be more like Pen? Why are you so stubborn? Why can't you be good and try harder like your sister?*

It wasn't that I hadn't tried. I'd idolized Pen my entire life. She'd done everything right. She always acted right, said the right things, did well at everything, and everyone loved her. My sister was so undeniably perfect that even when the world fell apart, the top monster in charge fell in love with her because that's just who she was. You couldn't *not* love her.

Me? I was a mess. Always had been and always would be. I did nothing right, no matter how hard I tried. When I did homework for school, I fell asleep on top of the book. When I tried to not race my skateboard downhill, somehow I'd find an even steeper hill. No matter how much everyone, including myself, wanted to be like Pen, I was cut from a different cloth.

The day Pen was born, there'd been fine silks, lace, and pearls. The day I arrived, there'd been hemp, leather, and chains. I'd never be her, or like her, or even a distant runner-up. I was the exact opposite, and I'd given up long ago. Now I needed the rest of the world to figure it out too so I could get on with living what life I had left. That life happened to be rough and bloody because it turned out I was good at one thing, better than almost anyone: war.

"It's amazing you're related at all," he said, taking a puff of his cigar.

"Yeah, well, I guess genetics are a fickle bitch, kind of like the girls you fuck, huh?" I smiled.

He sat there staring at me as if I hadn't spoken.

Seeing as he didn't seem to be in a rush, I looked about the room and found a comfortable spot on the couch. I kicked my boots up on his table. "Let's get to the point. I've got a full day. What do you want? What's so important that you couldn't jot down a note on that nice stationery you have?"

His gaze went to my boots but then traveled up my long, tan legs. I hadn't bothered to change out of my kick-around clothes before coming.

I crossed my long, muscled legs, giving him a nice display of something he would never touch. Then I smiled.

He leaned back and took another puff of his cigar, as if he weren't interested.

But he was. There were a couple of areas I excelled at. One was making a man want to fuck me. Normally, I had a very high success rate. Combined with my other talents, it worked to my benefit more often than not. He might be repulsed by my sickness, but part of him still wanted me.

Cole took another puff on his cigar, the haze filling the air. "Who are you working for?"

"I work for no one." I yawned.

"You want out of this office? Give me a name." His eyes were leveled on me as if he'd do some damage if I didn't speak.

He had a little problem with that. I'd been ignoring his rules for a month and he'd done nothing. Would he at some point? Maybe, but odds were there was still some leeway.

"Don't have one to give." I looked around the place. Not a single throw pillow on the couch?

"Really? What about Ghost?"

I had the urge to laugh. Did he really think it would be that simple? Throw out a name and I'd be shocked and dismayed? Crumple in a ball and spill my guts?

"You mean like...spirits?" I twirled a blond lock around my finger, looking as stupid as he seemed to think I was.

"I know the leader of your group is called Ghost. You know he's using you, right?"

He almost sounded indignant, as if he were ready to duel on my behalf. I wanted to laugh. No one used me.

"I don't know what you're talking about."

"Are you fucking him?" He shoved up his shirt sleeves, and the cords in his arms were bunched, as if he was ready to beat someone.

The balls on this man... Was it an alpha thing? Did they think they were entitled to know every detail they wanted?

"Who I fuck isn't any of your business." I got to my feet, done with placating him.

"For a few seconds there, I thought you had a lick of sense. I guess I can't be right all of the time."

"What do you want? Because I'm done with this meeting." With my heart doing jumping jacks in my chest and my hands in fists, I gave him one last chance to say his piece before I walked out on him.

He rocked back in his chair, sizing me up again, as if there were something he couldn't quite understand about me. Then the curious look disappeared behind his veil of blankness.

"You don't want to be here, I don't want you here, so

cut the shit. I don't want to hear about all your little adventures. They end now." He sounded as if this might indeed be my last warning. It didn't matter.

"Sure. I'll show myself out."

He stood as I made my way to the door, and my pulse jacked up again as I wondered if he was going to stop me. He didn't. He followed me out instead, all the way to the parking lot.

"My truck is over there," he said, pointing to a large black pick-up.

"Good for you." I continued to walk. No way was I taking a ride home from him.

I got to the end of the block, and he pulled over beside me, rolling down the window. "Get in."

"No need."

He gassed the engine. Instead of taking off down the street, his truck jumped the curb and blocked the sidewalk.

"It wasn't a request." He leaned over, and the door swung open.

It was getting late, and I did have other plans. Taking a ride home wouldn't be the worst thing ever, even if it did mean tolerating him for a few more minutes. Plus he seemed to be willing to make a thing over it.

I climbed into the truck. He said nothing, which was exactly the way I preferred it.

It only took me a few minutes to notice he wasn't asking for directions. Obviously, he had my address, since his men came there to watch me daily. But did he know it by heart? Knew exactly where my street was? That wouldn't be so odd, except it wasn't even really a street but a little offshoot of a road with three houses. Even people who'd lived in this town their entire lives didn't know my street.

I might have to move.

I kept my attention on the road ahead, watching as the gleaming black truck caught the eyes of passersby, humans who'd had their own vehicles at one point, before war came. Before *they* had come and taken everything and made everything left illegal.

He wanted me to stop what I was doing? Then his people needed to stop what they were doing. When they all packed up and crawled back under their rocks, that was when this would end.

"You think you've got carte blanche because you're connected to Donovan, but that won't save you," he said.

"Understood." As much as I'd like that to be the end of things, it was unlikely.

We were only halfway to my house. I had a whole half a ride left with him. I should've walked.

"You keep saying that, but I'm not sure you do." He drove with his wrist leaning on the steering wheel, his gaze focused on the road almost to the point that it seemed he was trying to avoid looking at me.

Cat-and-mouse games had never been my thing. They got boring after a while. Putting it all out there might be a bad play on my part, but I was ready to call it curtains on this back-and-forth.

He might not want to look at me, but I had no issue staring him down. "I'm sick. I'm so sick that I'm going to die soon. As someone healthy, you're unfamiliar with some of the perks of that, but believe it or not, there are a few. One of them is losing my fear of anything you could threaten me with. Like I said, your threat has been heard and understood. You do what you need to, and I'll do the same."

He pulled the truck over in front of my house. I went to open the door, and he reached past me and pulled it closed. His body was so close to mine that the fabric of our shirts brushed.

His hand was still on the door, his body angled toward mine. My gaze shot to his mouth. The man had good lips. Or maybe it was just the perfect square jaw that made them look so good. Or the eyes that pulsated energy and were trained on my lips.

"You think there's nothing left to fear. That's how little you actually know. Don't make me show you otherwise," he said.

My heartbeat ratcheted up a notch, the way it did when I was either about to kill someone or die a small death of my own.

It wasn't like I wanted him. My adrenaline always spiked my libido.

My chest rose and fell, seeming to fuel a heat in his eyes. Then he leaned away, moving back to his seat, as if he suddenly remembered he didn't like me either.

If I moved, would he lean over again? What might happen? The truck was parked in front of my house, but I was finally afraid of something. What if we both forgot we hated each other? How would I live with myself if I fucked this man? It was one thing if I was drunk. Sober? No. Not him.

I had to get out of the truck, but I seemed to be frozen.

"What are you doing?" he asked.

I turned toward him, at a loss for words but knowing something had to be said. "Are you...done?"

"Yes. Get out." He didn't bother looking at me as he

pulled his phone out of his pocket, reading something on the screen.

I didn't need to be told twice.

I shut the door to my house, refusing to look back, knowing his truck was still sitting there. Why wasn't he driving away? He needed to leave, and I needed to never see him again.

9

C *ole*

"If I'd known how you were going to handle this pack, the reason you agreed to come out here, I would've stepped up," Huddy said, pacing the area in front of my desk at the club.

As tedious as he might be at times, it was still better than what was sitting in front of me. Donovan had failed to mention this position came with a stack of paperwork and a territory line negotiation with the neighboring pack to the north that was still in the works.

I tossed the map with territory lines on the pile, preferring to handle Huddy's *sensitivities*.

"That's bullshit. You never would've stepped up because you'd hate the job. You would've hightailed it over to Denmark or Norway or wherever the fuck those two were last seen. The one thing you wouldn't have done was step up."

"I walked into the club tonight and one of the guys was banging someone in the booth, in front of everyone."

He was waving his hands in the air, sounding like a politician pointing out a blunder by his opponent.

"Was it Hector? Who was he with?"

Hector would stick it in anything that moved, but most of the female pack members wouldn't be on board for a show. Had he brought a human in? That probably wouldn't have gone over well either.

Huddy was about to give me a name when he stopped himself short, squinting in my direction. "Are you asking because you care and you're going to do something about it? Or do you just want to know?"

"What do you think?" I asked, and then laughed at his horrified expression.

"You're an animal. Do you know that?"

"Of course I do. I'm a shifter, as are you."

"No, you're an *animal*. I don't know what Donovan was thinking when..."

I didn't hear the rest of what he had to say as I was laughing too hard. This was the problem with Huddy. He was too civilized for his own good.

For all my harsh words, I actually liked the guy. He had the balls of an alpha. His downfall was that he didn't have the stomach for the hard calls. He made a damned good second, though. I wouldn't tell Donovan this, or Huddy himself, but I wasn't altogether upset to have him here.

He didn't look any happier, but he stopped pacing. "And I heard Sassy was brought in. Donovan isn't going to be happy—"

"Donovan isn't coming back, and we both know it. My sources say he's in the process of switching all his accounts out of the U.S."

Huddy didn't blink, but then, I assumed he'd known that was a possibility. Too bad no one had bothered to tell me. It was going to make it a lot harder to extricate myself once I was done with my business here. Huddy might have to find himself an iron stomach and finally step up.

Lonzo burst into the room.

"What now?" I asked, even though I didn't want to hear the answer. It was going to be something with *her*. She was turning into a perpetual pain in the ass, but at least I hadn't fucked her.

Lonzo's gaze flickered to Huddy for a second before he said, "You know the assignment you gave me?"

"Of course I do, and so does he. What's she doing now?"

Huddy's attention became riveted on Lonzo.

"She's about to do something *very* bad," Lonzo said.

I groaned and then reached for my drink, but only took a sip. Shifters metabolized alcohol quickly, but I might need all my wits for this one. Lonzo didn't rattle easily.

"How bad? Is it going to get her killed or just roughed up a bit?" Sassy probably had more than a few beatings coming her way. I should just stand back and let her take her hits the way anyone else would.

I stood anyway, grabbing my keys, not because I cared but because there was a promise.

By the amount of whites showing in Lonzo's eyes, it was worse than roughed up.

Huddy stepped forward. "When?"

"Soon," Lonzo said. "She's about to blow Tony's, that little restaurant the vampires took over a few months ago."

"Hold down the fort. I'm not sure how long this is going to take," I said, turning to Huddy.

Huddy was already heading toward the door. "I'm coming. If they get her, I know more of the vampires than you do. I might be able to work something out."

This was why Huddy made an excellent second, at least for me. He immediately thought of negotiating, while I'd already been contemplating where I'd burn the bodies.

"Lonzo, you stay here. I don't want to draw notice with too many numbers if there's any chance of slipping in and out."

"Fine. Sure," Lonzo said, shooting Huddy a dirty look like a kid who got his toy stolen.

"We'll take my truck," I said when we were outside. "Park a few blocks away and figure out the situation from the ground."

"Agreed," Huddy said, climbing into the truck. "I don't care what she did. She doesn't get touched."

He was staring at me, and I realized he wasn't referring to just the vampires. I was flooring the gas to go save her ass, and he was worried about me? Huddy being a decent guy and an asset would not stop him from getting punched in the face.

"I don't take orders from you."

He dropped the subject, falling quiet. We'd never know if he'd have stepped up because I had no plans on hurting her. Scaring her into not killing herself? Yes, all day long, if that were even possible. She had a reckless gene that was more dominant than the craziest of my pack members.

There was an empty lot, close to where she'd been spotted last. We'd barely gotten out of the truck when the blast shook the ground we were standing on. Lonzo had said time was of the essence. He wasn't wrong.

I took off in the direction of the blast, Huddy right beside me. We hadn't gotten fifty feet when I spotted her running in the distance, all in black, with a cap on and a blond braid swinging loose.

She'd be heading to her group, or at least a few of them. The blood pumped through my system. The chance of ripping Ghost's heart out of his chest might finally be upon me. Even if Sassy wouldn't speak, one of the crew would. Someone would turn. I'd make them.

We were running, but Huddy was getting too close. I dashed ahead, cutting him off.

"Keep your distance. She's going to make you."

"No, she—"

I put a hand on his chest. "She's made all my people and she already knows you. She's going to make you, and I'm not losing this chance to get to Ghost. Stay behind me or go back to the club and wait there."

He glanced ahead toward where she'd disappeared. "Fine, but let's not lose her completely."

"That's not going to happen."

I'd follow her through the gates of hell if that was what it took. I wasn't losing my chance to wrap my hands around Ghost's throat and finish this off.

10

S *assy*

It took a few extra blocks of running to lose Cole and Huddy, but I'd finally shaken them off.

I ducked into the abandoned building, of which there were many at this point. We never went to headquarters after a mission, just in case. I walked past the abandoned printing presses, from when this place used to be a small local newspaper, before all news outlets were either converted to propaganda machines or shuttered their businesses.

The stairs to the basement smelled musty, but I could already see the glow of lanterns.

"Where were you? We thought you got nabbed," Mattie said, greeting me at the door.

Vickie and Harlow were close behind. Neither of them

were good at getting in and out of a tight spot, but they liked to travel as close to the final destination with their product as possible.

"I had to lose a tail." I pulled my cap off, pushing the loose strands of hair out of my face.

"I have to tell them we found you before they freak out." Mattie dialed a throwaway phone.

"You told the rest of the crew?" I said, reaching for his phone.

"You were late. They called at a bad time." Mattie turned away slightly as he hit send and brought it to his ear. "The specter has been located. Fill you in later."

He hung up while I rolled my eyes at Vicki and Harlow.

"Did you feel that shake?" Harlow asked, patting himself on the back for an especially good bomb. The louder the boom, the happier that man was.

"Who followed you?" Vicki asked, ignoring Harlow, who would want to discuss bomb making for another hour.

I grabbed water from the emergency pack on the floor. "You're not going to want—"

"I did." Cole's voice filled the basement.

All eyes shot to a spot behind me. I didn't want to turn around. Didn't want to deal with him at all, because this was going to be an epic disaster.

How had I missed Cole following me? I thought I'd lost him. I wasn't sure which was worse—being followed or being followed and not knowing.

Cole might've already blown up my situation. He might've called Donovan and my sister before he even got here.

Donovan had always known I was mixed up in the resistance but hadn't really wanted to know all the nitty-gritty details. He'd been easy to hide from. Not Cole. He had to chase me down himself.

"Whose bright idea was it to send Sassy to ignite the blast?" Cole asked.

In the end, it didn't matter how he'd gotten here. He *was* here, and he wasn't leaving without answers. I took a deep breath, steeled my expression, and accepted that I had a very large problem on my hands. It was time to figure out how to get rid of Cole, and that was going to be harder than blowing up a thousand vampires.

I turned to find a raging man in front of me. I'd seen enough werewolves to know when one was on the cusp of shifting. After that happened, there was no telling where things might lead. Some lost all semblance of humanity, had little more control than a rabid animal. Some, like Donovan, were as calculating as they were in their human form. Hopefully it was an alpha thing that helped them keep it together, or my crew might be dead in minutes. There was no getting rid of Cole now. It was time for damage control and appeasement before someone ended up dead.

"Speak up. I need to know who to kill—or are you afraid to do your own fighting?" Cole stepped to my group, his ire seeming to narrow in on Mattie. Figured he'd assume *he* was Ghost and the one I was sleeping with.

I'd done enough runs with Mattie, watched as he'd run unflinching into a vampire lair, to know he had backbone. But staring down this particular shifter who was about to turn? Couldn't blame the guy if his hands were twitching. Cole was a sight to see. I'd known Donovan wanted someone tough, but this might be overkill.

In a flash, Cole's clothes were shredded as he shifted. Before the world had turned upside down, people used to think that werewolves looked like the fuzzy and beautiful creatures that they saw in zoos. The old-school flicks had been much more accurate. There was fur, fangs, lots of muscle, but nothing cuddly about them.

I stepped in between Cole and Mattie, afraid that if I didn't, Cole's fangs might end up in Mattie's flesh. Mattie wouldn't last more than a few seconds against Cole in human form; forget about this creature. I wouldn't last any longer, but I was the one who'd led him here. I'd never been afraid of him until right this moment, and his anger hadn't even been directed at me.

"They didn't put me up to anything. I did it. I insisted on doing this," I said in a calm monotone.

Cole's gaze shot to mine, and even in this form, I saw the intelligence and doubt in his eyes. Okay, he was still in control. All wasn't lost.

"I did it. No one tells me what to do," I said.

Cole started shifting back, and I could see the battle it took as he slowly forced himself to regain human form. Unlike the rapid change into his werewolf form, this took long, agonizing minutes until he stood there naked and nearly as muscled as his shifter form, as confident as he'd been when clothed.

I forced my eyes to his face, and not the rest of him, but it wasn't easy. It was like walking around the Louvre and not admiring the art.

"Get out of the way," he said, his eyes nearly glowing as he looked beyond me. "Who's Ghost?" he asked my crew.

"You don't understand the situation," I said, moving in step with him as he went to walk around me. "It's not their fault. *They* don't tell me what to do." I forced myself to get in front of him again as he moved, knowing he could toss me to the side and snap my neck without breaking a sweat.

Cole ignored me as he sized up the people standing behind me, lingering on each one.

"Really? No one has the balls to stand up?" Cole asked.

The fear coursing through me began to mingle with insult and turn into something different that hardened my spine.

"I call the shots," I said, my inflection making my position clear. At least if he killed someone, it would be me. I was dying anyway. What was two months of my life worth compared to years of theirs? It was a fair swap.

Cole looked past me to Mattie. "You take orders from her?" he asked, still not believing me.

Fear was beginning to dissipate altogether. What the hell was his problem? Was it beyond his imagination that I could be the one in charge?

Mattie's eyes darted from Cole to mine.

"Tell him. I *want* him to know," I said, because clearly my words didn't have any weight.

Something about what I'd said to Mattie, or how I'd said it, finally clicked in Cole's head. "This is *your* group?" he asked me.

Mattie said, "It's hers. We follow her orders, or I wouldn't be telling you shit."

There was a spasm or something in my hands. It couldn't be nerves. I didn't get those. Knowing you were going to die a slow, messy death removed the fear of a fast and quick one. Actually, that wasn't accurate. It didn't just *remove* it. It obliterated it. I craved a fast end. So why did I feel this trembling building inside of me as Cole looked me over like he'd never seen me before?

My veil had dropped. My dirty secret was out, and now he was going to blow my situation up. Because if Donovan and my sister found out, she'd try to force me to follow her. When that didn't work, she'd come back to this hell-hole. She was one of my biggest weaknesses, and there was nothing I could do to stop her from blowing up her life to save me.

Cole was still staring at me, as if in shock. "You're in charge of them? You're Ghost?"

"I'm Ghost," I said, and the reality of those words carried more blast power than Harlow's best bomb. I could already hear the haranguing coming. Pen wasn't going to stop. An avalanche of worry would head my way. I'd probably be alive to hear it, too. I didn't think Cole would kill me, but only out of a promise he'd made to Donovan. I might be better off if Cole took me out than if I were bludgeoned to death by guilt.

Cole was going to run back and tell Donovan that I was in charge of the resistance. Then Donovan would tell Pen. Then I'd have to hear them carry on until the day I died, which I might hope was sooner rather than later.

"The attack on vampires, the 'Night of a Thousand Deaths,' that was you?" Cole continued to stare at me as if he were mentally running through my resumé, which was longer than I was planning on admitting to. It would only be more for him to bury me with.

He was going to walk out of here and be on the phone with Donovan two seconds after. Dammit. For the brilliant leader I was rumored to be, I'd blown it.

There was only one thing I could do: buy him off somehow. But with what? He had more money than I did. I couldn't use my looks as leverage because he didn't want to sleep with the sick girl.

"You gotta be fucking kidding me. You're Ghost?" Huddy asked.

My attention shot to the newest arrival. I was so off my game that I hadn't realized Huddy was over by the door until he'd spoken. The way I was operating tonight, I was lucky I was still standing. No wonder no one believed I was Ghost.

Huddy was a whole different problem. Even if I could buy Cole off somehow, and he was way more corruptible, Huddy didn't have a price.

There was only one option left. I'd get Cole to promise silence and use him to keep Huddy quiet. Cole was the alpha. This was doable.

"What's your price? What do you want? Everyone needs something, and I'm a lot more resourceful than you realized before tonight." I stretched my five feet, four inches as tall as I could, standing toe to toe with an alpha who'd just shifted into the scariest beast I'd ever seen. In all the possible endings for tonight, no one would have predicted this. He finally had me. He knew *my* price.

Cole scanned the group again before looking to me. His face was made of granite, and I didn't know if I was going to die in the next two minutes or if there was a way out of this mess.

"Perhaps there's something," he said.

There was something he needed, but relief was not coursing through me. I was in the worst bind I'd ever been in. He could ask me for almost anything and I'd agree.

"Whatever the deal is, it needs to include his silence as well," I said, nodding toward Huddy.

There was a slight gleam in Cole's eyes as we both settled into our new relationship. He pretty much owned my ass, and I knew it.

He smiled down at me, because he knew it too.

"I'll be in touch."

11

C *ole*

I topped off Huddy's glass before doing the same to mine.

"I can't believe she's Ghost," Huddy said, shock and awe still audible in his voice. It was the first thing either of us had said in the last thirty minutes. He was rubbing his jaw like he'd taken a fist to it and was only now coming around.

I didn't respond, my brain still replaying her admitting to being Ghost. How had I missed it? As she stood there in the center of the group, they'd all looked to her for permission to speak. My guys were half taking orders from her already. Why? Because she was a natural leader. It had been so painfully obvious that I could only wonder if I'd been half-awake the past month. How had I *not* seen it?

It wasn't like I hadn't met her, hadn't seen how savvy

she was. Every time there'd been something going on, her name would pop up. She wasn't getting used by anyone. She wasn't the puppet but the one pulling the strings.

As I sat there and thought over all the accomplishments of the resistance, I nearly wanted to laugh. She'd pulled off things I hadn't thought possible. She'd achieved other things she didn't even realize. Every time the resistance took out another vampire, but the shifters went unscathed, it had driven even more suspicion between the uncomfortable alliances of the two races. Did she even realize she was breaking down the pact between werewolves and vampires that was holding this entire fiasco together?

Huddy threw back the last of his drink and turned to look at me, as if he still couldn't register the reality of the situation. He dropped his glass to the desk and then slapped his hand on his leg.

"*She's* Ghost. Sassy is *the* Ghost?"

"Yes, she is." I sipped my drink as Huddy was busy refilling his.

At least one thing finally made sense. This was why I hadn't been able to stop thinking about her. I'd known something was off and ignored my gut. Not that I wouldn't mind fucking her, but this was the cause of her constantly leaking into my thoughts. It was my subconscious trying to tell me I had my solution, if I'd only see it. It wasn't some strange draw she had on me.

"Donovan is going to lose his shit when he hears." Huddy grabbed the bottle and drank from it, giving up on the glass.

Oh no, he wasn't blowing the leverage I had. "He's not going to hear. We need to keep this quiet."

Sassy had known Huddy would be a problem. She

also knew I was the way to control him. How had I missed how slick she was?

He lowered the bottle. "We *have* to tell him."

I always knew Huddy had stayed behind to be Donovan's eyes and ears, but he'd proven useful enough to ignore the reasoning. Now that looked like it might've been a mistake. *Another* mistake. I was racking them up lately. But that would be changing.

"Why would we? Donovan's trying to make a new life for himself. Telling him isn't going to stop Sassy. It's only going to drag him back here, where he doesn't want to be. No. We're going to be loyal and handle it for him so he doesn't uproot the new life he's building for nothing. Now that I've got leverage, I'll get her in line."

Huddy was the type to eat up bullshit about how being quiet would be better. Even if he didn't totally buy it, he'd give it a shot if he thought there was some merit. God forbid the man didn't do the right thing for once in his life.

His honorableness made it so easy that I almost felt a twinge of guilt. Not quite, but almost. Bottom line: I was doing Donovan and his wife a favor. Everything I'd said was true. Sassy was nothing but trouble, and their coming back here would be a waste of everyone's time.

It would also screw me. I might've found someone capable of what I hadn't been able to accomplish in the past year. I wasn't walking away from her that easy, not even for her brother-in-law, now that I had a use for her.

"I don't care what you have. She's not going to be easy to control," Huddy said, as if I didn't know the woman I was dealing with.

I hadn't. I did now.

"I'll get her in hand."

Huddy rolled his eyes. It was a new look for him, but one that was warranted, considering the subject matter.

"She's headstrong, stubborn, and smarter than almost anyone I know. She's not like the usual brain-dead bimbos you typically get involved with." Huddy waved the bottle at me before he drank some more.

"I might have something she wants enough to toe the line on top of giving her silence." I leaned back in my chair as the pieces came together.

"Which is?"

"I'm going to give her hope."

"Hope is dangerous if you don't have something to back it up. Not to mention cruel." He was eyeing me like a true alpha.

"Smooth your hackles. I'm not looking to bullshit her." He didn't need to worry. I'd make sure I could deliver first. I might be called ruthless, but I wasn't a liar.

It might be dangerous and expensive, but if it got me what I wanted, it would be worth every dime. *If* it worked. That was still a big if.

12

C *ole*

Considering her current line of work, Sassy needed to do a better job protecting her house. The tripwire in front of the door was laughable. The motion detector lights didn't light. Even the stuff she seemed to put a little more work into, like the alarmed wire, was faulty and easy to short.

I'd made a cup of coffee and been sitting at her table for fifteen minutes before she walked downstairs and found me.

She walked into her kitchen as if she weren't in the least bit surprised to see me. At least she still had her hearing.

The thin t-shirt she wore fell right below the top of her thighs, revealing legs a thoroughbred would envy. She shoved a handful of tousled blond hair over her shoulder, her nipples poking at the shirt.

I adjusted my seat, trying to keep my focus on her face. She had a purpose to serve, and it wasn't in bed, no matter how fun that might be. That road was blocked off with yellow warning tape.

"Don't you know how to give someone space? I swear, you're going to be barging into my nightmares soon." She walked over and grabbed a yellow coffee mug. It had a happy face with "Have a Good Day" printed underneath. It was the last thing in the world I'd imagine her using.

She caught my gaze and looked down at her mug. "I know. My sister gave it to me."

That made more sense. That mug was Pen all day long.

She took a sip of coffee and made a gagging sound. "This stuff tastes like tar. You show up at the crack of dawn and you don't even make good coffee. Have you no manners?" she asked, and then took another sip, scrunching her face as she did.

I pointed to the other chair across from me. "Sit. It's time to talk."

She leaned against the counter instead. "I've got some errands to do today, so if you could make this quick..." she said, pushing me like last night had never happened.

There wasn't a single werewolf that didn't scare the hell out of humans when they shifted, and I was among the worst of them. Now she woke to me sitting in her kitchen and hadn't even bothered to throw on a pair of jeans.

The girl really did have some balls on her. All that fluffed up blond hair and tight dresses—it was all to mislead. The more I thought about it, the more absurd it was that I hadn't realized who I was dealing with earlier.

The need to establish dominance was something that

pulsed through my alpha blood. I was about to kick the chair in her direction before she coughed. Her eyes looked glassy and her skin had the flush of a slight fever. Not much was understood about the Sucking Sickness, but typically it got worse at night. She didn't look like she was doing that well this morning. I might be an alpha, with all that entailed, but I wasn't a total dick. Plus I needed her alive for what was to come.

"I've got a deal to offer you," I said, ignoring all her bluster. I leaned back in her kitchen chair, the thing creaking like it had come from someone's front corner on garbage day.

"Let's make one thing clear—even if I agree, you aren't going to rule my life because you happened upon a meeting with a few friends." She eyed me like I was the thing found in the trash.

Did she really think she could pull that off? With me? No. She wasn't nearly that stupid.

"We both know I can, so let's move past the bullshit," I said. "I have things to do today as well."

She sipped her coffee for a few moments, weighing whether she had a shot of pushing the issue. She didn't.

"Fine. What do you want in exchange for your silence?" she asked, coming to the only logical conclusion: I could do whatever I wanted.

"I have a target I've been trying to get to that's causing me difficulty. You might be able to get to him for me."

"By 'get to,' I'm assuming you mean kill?"

Looking and sounding so arrogant while wearing a stained t-shirt, and standing on worn linoleum, was a true skill.

"Yes."

"What race? I don't kill humans."

That she hadn't included shifters on her refusal list didn't go unnoticed, as she'd probably intended.

"Vampire," I responded coolly, not taking her bait.

She nodded, as if at least that checked off a box. Figured it would. Her resumé indicated as much.

She hopped onto the counter, crossing her legs and leaning forward. She gave me a slow once-over before raising her brows. "You don't look averse to getting your hands dirty. You can't get the job done yourself?" she asked like a woman talking to a man about his whiskey dick.

I couldn't decide what I wanted to do more—kill her or fuck her. She'd probably be sensational in the sack, but that wasn't a smart option. I couldn't kill her, either. That left me in the unfortunate predicament of having to discuss these things with her.

Of course a human wouldn't realize the details of why I might have a harder time, but only because they didn't realize how strained the situation between vampires and werewolves was.

"Vampires don't feel threatened by humans. They're waiting for an attack from us. They're more on guard when we're around than a hundred humans because, as a whole, you're all pretty fucking useless."

Even now, the vampires secretly blamed her kills on shifters. She had no idea that she was single-handedly driving an even larger wedge into the divide, and I wasn't sharing it with her.

"Give me a name."

She let the insult roll off her shoulders as if nothing said could make a dent in her armor. I might want to kill her, but I couldn't help admiring her as I contemplated digging the grave.

"Pavro." The name dropped like a cement block onto a priceless crystal vase, all crash and then stunned silence.

She had a half-decent poker face as she wrapped her head around what I'd asked for, the rumors and tidbits, all the information she'd ever heard running through her mind. I could see it in her calculating eyes. It was a lot to contemplate. Pavro was one of the oldest vampires around, with all the wisdom that came with age. He never left himself vulnerable and was considered untouchable.

"That's a big ask, way bigger than your silence," she said before sipping some more of the coffee she claimed was so horrible.

I met her glare. "I'm aware of the difficulty of getting to him. I'm willing to sweeten the pot if you can get it done."

"Really? How so?" She leaned to the side, reaching for the coffee pot to top off her mug.

"I know someone who says he can fix you." When I discussed it with him last night, he'd said it was going to cost a lot, but he could do it. He better be right, because I didn't like promising things I couldn't deliver.

"This discussion is over. I don't deal in fairytales. Show yourself out." She jumped off the counter and walked past me.

I grabbed her wrist, stopping her.

She looked down her outstretched arm, where my hand was detaining her. Her lips parted; her chest rose. I knew fury when I saw it.

"I've been down this road. You're wasting my time. No one can fix me."

"I know people who can do things that aren't circulated or talked about." Some things had to be seen to be believed, but as scary as the people of this world thought their new reality was, they hadn't seen anything of the true darkness that existed. The things that hadn't crawled out of their caves yet.

"And what are these things?"

I shook my head. "Not yet. Not until you live up to your end." And not until I had to tell her, because no one would be ready, not without some preparation first. But she'd do it. I knew this girl like I knew myself. She'd take whatever deal I laid in front of her if it gave her a chance to keep living.

She yanked at her wrist. I let her go after a moment longer.

"And if this can be done, what's his price?" She spoke like someone who'd been around long enough to know there was always a possible screw job with every negotiation.

"Will be paid by me. An eye for an eye, a life for a life."

She nodded slowly, crossing her arms. She was still thinking it through, but she'd take the deal. Her thirst for life was too voracious.

"You really think you can get me a cure?" She was gripping the mug from her sister with both hands like it was a security blanket.

"I think if you're willing to pay a high enough price, you can get anything you want in this world."

She sucked in her lower lip, the way I'd seen her sister do at times, but that was where the resemblance ended. When Sassy did it, all I wanted to do was drag her to bed. Doing a deal with her was going to be dangerous indeed.

She met my gaze and nodded. "Yeah. I'll do it. I'll look into the details and give you a timeline."

It was like talking to another alpha, except in a small, tight female package. This was why I wanted to fuck her.

She was a novelty. But it still didn't mean we were doing things her way.

"That's not the way I work. I want to be involved, every step of the way."

She actually scoffed. "I don't work with outsiders."

"I've seen some of your team. You should be begging for outside help. It's amazing you've accomplished anything at all, but it was probably in spite of them. You need more capable backup." There was no way I was leaving this up to the bunch I'd seen. Not a chance. Not even with her as the lead.

"If your people are so capable, you wouldn't need me," she shot back.

"My deal. My call."

She let the silence hang in the air for a few moments.

"Fine." She walked over and leaned on the counter, putting some distance between us. "Is that why you came here and took the alpha spot? You've got a thing for killing Pavro? I bet it is and Donovan has no idea what you're doing or getting his people involved in."

"I don't run my plans past Donovan. And to be honest, I don't give a fuck."

Instead of getting her back up, she laughed.

"As long as you realize you don't get to back out if it gets uncomfortable. I hold people to their word," I said.

"When I give my word, I don't take it back." She crossed her ankles, the shirt riding up her thigh a little too high for me to ignore. "I'm going to need some things. The person you want is a tough target."

"Make a list." I headed toward the door, knowing it was time to get out of here before other matters clouded my judgment. "By the way, you need to secure this house better."

"The tripwire is for idiots so they think they've gotten past my defenses."

I stopped at the back door. "I'm not talking about the tripwire. I'm talking about the one you hid along the frame. It's faulty."

"If it's shit, it's because I can't get good stuff on the black market because your people take everything."

I ran a hand along it again. She was right about that. It was crap. "Add it to the list. I can't have my top assassin getting murdered."

13

C *ole*

After an hour of debate, Sassy had finally agreed to hold the meeting at the main hub of the resistance. The club had too many eyes and was too dangerous. I wasn't going to have it at Donovan's, where I was living. I'd already dragged him in enough. She didn't want to have it at her house either, for obvious reasons. Eventually it became clear this was the only safe place.

Her headquarters were on Davey Street, the border between the vampire and werewolf territory, not that you'd find that in the pact or written anywhere. The unspoken tension between vampires and werewolves didn't exist, according to the official record. It was one of those open secrets.

The location made sense—easier to keep an eye on everyone and somewhere neither of the races liked to be.

It was another notch on her belt. She had the kind of balls that were usually reserved for people too stupid to know better, but the girl was smart.

"Are you sure about this?" Huddy asked. "It's one thing to have a single human who's a brilliant planner doing your dirty work, but you really want to deal with the rest of them?" Huddy was looking at the building in front of us as if someone were asking him to walk through a field of dog shit.

"I thought you were one of those humanitarians? You're the one who likes these humans," I said.

"I like Sassy. I feel bad for a lot of them. Some of the others aren't horrible. Do I want them covering my back? No," Huddy said.

"Fuck no," Lonzo added.

I looked at Derek, the only one who hadn't chimed in yet. "I like the chick but can't say I feel all that good about them as a race," he said, shrugging.

I focused my attention back on the building. "Doesn't matter. We aren't actually working with them. We're making sure they do what I want and don't fuck things up."

I walked up to the rusted door of what appeared to be an abandoned building. It had char marks along the old brick face and plywood on the windows.

Scanning the facade, I saw there was a small hole in the peak of the roof that gave off a glare. There were probably more on the other sides. This was definitely the right place.

I knocked twice and waited a few seconds before knocking three more times faster. The knock was for our benefit, but I went along. They'd already seen us with their surveillance cameras.

A few minutes later, Sassy swung open the door. She stood there, hair in a messy bun, ratty sweatshirt, and snug jeans that had been worn so many times they'd molded to every curve. She didn't have a lick of makeup on and was one of the hottest women I'd ever seen, human or shifter.

She eyed my group, gave a nod, and then waved us in to follow her. Everyone with me eyed her ass, even Huddy, who prided himself on being a gentleman.

My attention was quickly back on my surroundings as I realized that there was a building within a building.

She stopped in front of a shiny steel door, blocking entry to the next layer. "Before we go any farther, I need some assurances," she said.

Those balls weren't bigger than mine, but they might crowd out Huddy's.

"You know everyone here. Are we really going to do this?" I asked.

"I need to protect my crew," she said, her eyes never leaving me, making it clear who she viewed as the real problem.

"What do you need to feel secure?" Huddy asked calmly.

His pants didn't need to drop to prove that my earlier prediction was spot-on.

"I want a blood oath," she said, as if a human requesting that from a shifter wasn't outrageous.

"Blood oaths are only between shifters. We don't do them with humans," I said.

"You'll do them with this human if you want to continue."

I'd turned to leave, ready to call her bluff, when Huddy spoke.

"Do you have a knife?" he asked, stepping forward, hand outstretched.

I stared at Huddy. It was as if those balls were shrinking by the second.

Sassy reached down, pulled out a knife tucked into her black combat boots, and handed it over.

Huddy sliced it across his palm, and a welt of red dripped to the ground.

"I swear on the blood I shed, I will not do you nor none of yours harm."

"If you're going to ask for the vow, you better back it up yourself," I said.

She took the knife without a second's hesitation and ran a line down her palm without flinching. "I swear on the blood I shed, I will not do you nor none of yours harm."

Fuck it. I held my hand out for the blade. If I was going to do this, I had no interest in getting my knife all bloody.

I repeated the same gesture and then handed the knife to Lonzo. "Just do it and let's move on."

When he and Derek finished, she nodded. She rapped on the steel door, and it opened.

The interior building didn't have a window in sight, but there was the hum of a ventilation system. The walls looked like coated cement and could withstand some heavy artillery.

There was a large table in the center, lots of chairs, and a couple of couches off to the side. None of that was interesting. The wall lined with monitors was the thing that caught my attention. There were too many and too high-tech. This place was much more than I expected.

I continued to size the place up as the humans sized us up. Sassy made introductions: Mattie, Harlow, and

Vicki. I'd seen them all before on the night they blew up Tony's.

Four and four, as agreed upon. I half heard mine do the same. They were all still on the introductions stage when I pointed at the screens, losing my patience with the niceties.

"Where's this surveilling?" I asked Sassy as I moved closer to the dark screens.

Mattie edged closer to Sassy, as if he thought she'd need protection and he'd be the one doing it. He didn't realize she was a lot safer than he was. She wasn't the one irritating me right now.

She walked closer, Mattie tailing her like a shadow.

"I'm discussing this with Sassy. Not you," I said.

Mattie's brow furrowed, but Sassy waved him off. He retreated to the other side of the room, where the others were making awkward conversation, but didn't stop watching us.

"Just places of interest. Nothing important," she said, not making a move to turn on the screens.

"I'd like to see anyway." I eyed the dashboard beneath it, trying to get a handle on the control system.

Sassy glanced at her group. "Vicki?"

"Yeah?"

"Did you fix our glitches earlier?"

"Yep," Vicki said, walking over. "We should be good. Was just about to load the system up."

"Could you do it? Cole wants to take a peek at our wall of eyes." Sassy smiled.

Wall of eyes? This should be interesting.

"Of course," Vicki said. She sat in the rolling chair in front of the desk that ran the length of the screens, rolled to one end, pressed a button, and then rolled back to the center before typing in something else, then deleting it and retyping.

It would've been a good act if Sassy played it solo. Her team member couldn't stop her hand from shaking long enough to enter the right information.

The screens went live. Some were outside this building, others in crowded areas of the city. Each scene had a number in the bottom corner. The one at the park was numbered 127. Another one facing a cafe was 198. The ones outside of this place were single digits. Why? Because they were the first cameras set up. Vicki was staring up at me, as if to say, *See? It's all good here. No secrets.*

"Change the channel." I pointed toward the controls.

"Huh? No. There aren't anymore. This is it." Vicki rolled slightly away and then made a show of fidgeting with a dial.

"What's on forty? Or channel fifty?"

"Go ahead, Vicki." Sassy leaned a hip on the dashboard as if she didn't care what I saw.

Vicki nodded then typed in some more numbers. Different places popped up, more bars and local hangouts, most of the areas that vampires frequented. How had they gotten these up? I leaned closer, looking at the screens. And yet no shifter hangouts?

If they had the vampires under surveillance, it didn't take a mental giant to take the next leap. We were here somewhere.

"Which camera number is my club?" I asked, looking at the scenes.

"Why would we watch the club my brother-in-law used to run?" Sassy lifted a brow.

As if I'd believe she wasn't.

Vicki was twitching. Even the fucking club?

"You might as well cut that feed." That camera would be gone by tonight if I had to go over every inch of that area myself.

Sassy smiled. I could read her thoughts as if I'd had them myself. *Fuck you. Go ahead and cut it because there'll be a new one up the next day.*

I didn't know if I wanted to strangle her or fuck her. That was bullshit. I definitely wanted to fuck her. The more I knew her, saw her in action, the more I couldn't think of much else. It was getting out of hand, too. I used to just want to fuck her for her looks. Now I wanted to fuck her for her mind. That was some scary shit. I didn't usually care what a woman was thinking. Now I seemed to be as turned on by her thoughts as her body.

"Let's get to business," I said, walking back to the group waiting by the table.

There was a file on the table laid open with all the details the werewolves had on Pavro. I skimmed through it, catching up.

"This is a suicide mission," Mattie said, maneuvering so he was next to Sassy. "Pavro runs this town."

I ignored Puppy. I already knew he didn't call the shots. Sassy leaned back, meeting my gaze.

"Not a suicide mission, but I'll agree it's difficult," she said.

She wanted Pavro too, and badly. She wanted this job. I was realizing I might've been able to drop the name into her lap and gotten her signed on without any other payoff.

"Well? Is this something you can handle or is he too big?" I asked, wording my question in a way that would put a nice ding in her ego.

Sassy was a lot like myself, and I instinctively knew

what made her tick. The more I doubted her ability to do that job and told her she couldn't, the more she'd rise to the bait. I caught Puppy giving me looks across the table, like he wanted to use his baby teeth to gnaw on my leg. I guess he'd figured her out too. Puppy wasn't stupid, just several shades of green.

"We can do it." She tapped a finger on the paperwork. "Do you have any more information?"

"Anything in particular?" I asked.

"Every little thing you can get. I want to know if he eats, drinks, if he still fucks and with whom. The more information, the better to find the soft spot."

"I'll get you more." I pointed toward her wall of TVs. "Do you have a visual on him?"

"Some, but not much. He's tough to get close to."

"We'll get it done, though," Mattie said, already assuming he'd be by her side and making sure I knew as well.

"That should do it for now," I said, calling an end to the meeting before turning to Sassy. "I want to talk to you, alone."

My people nodded and headed for the door, catching the signal. She gave a nod of her chin, and her people did the same, except for Mattie.

"Alone," I repeated, staring at the man.

"I'm fine," she said to Mattie, making it clear she didn't take orders or bend for anyone. She would, for me, though. She just didn't know it yet.

The room emptied and the door closed.

"Whatever happens, whatever plans come up, I have direct say on who goes where and does what job," I said in a tone that brooked no argument.

"Your job. I'll let you have some say."

She took a seat and kicked her boots on to the table, grabbing the papers and reading over them again.

I walked over and sat on the table beside her boots. "Not some say. Final say."

She dropped the papers to her lap. "Are you backing out on the agreement? *Equal* say." She lifted the papers in between us.

"I'm doubting some of your team's abilities. I don't want Mattie backing you up."

Her eyes narrowed, and I could taste the irritation welling up. "Why? What if he is?"

"You might've started this group with him at the helm when you were running little gigs, but he's not ready for the big time. He's not your backup. I am. He'll get you killed." I could smell weakness, and Puppy was pissing and shitting himself with it.

"You don't tell me how to run my team. Who do you think partnered with me for the Night of a Thousand Deaths? Because that would be him. I've worked with him for years. We know each other's ins and outs. You might think you're the stronger partner, but there's also familiarity and human dynamics at play."

Familiarity. If I hadn't banned him before, I would've just for that.

"That's my problem. He wants to fuck you. It's making him soft and stupid. Or, at least, I hope so for his sake. I'd hate to think he was born like this."

"What if I don't agree?" She tossed the papers on the table beside me as she got to her feet, getting ready to do battle.

"Then we don't have a deal." Lucky for me, I was a much better liar than Vicki was.

I'd seen too much death. I was realizing lately that it

might've fucked with my head a bit. I could walk through bodies piled around me and not blink an eye, but every now and then, I'd stumble upon someone like Sassy. Someone so much bigger than what her small frame should've allowed, so much brighter than the rest that she shone like a beacon in any crowd, and the idea of seeing that light go out was like seeing the sun set for the last time.

The idea seemed unbearable, and if there was something I could do to stop it, I would. Of course, I wouldn't have that discussion with her. One, she'd get a bigger head than she already had. And two, why the fuck would I?

"You're really going to do this, even if it screws up my head going into a job?" She had her hips tilted at an angle that made my mouth water and my dick hard.

"You're tough. You'll get over it." I walked over to the wall of monitors, punching in some random numbers as Vicki had done and watching the screens change.

Sassy followed me, leaning against the desk to get a better view of my face. She ran a hand through her hair before crossing her arms. She licked her lips as she stared down.

"You don't get it. I've got a system, and Mattie is crucial to me."

Crucial to me. Those words slid like flesh over pavement. Besides how offensive I found that, her little boy was too soft. Let him get someone else killed, but he wasn't taking down Sassy.

"No. I get the final call on the plan. And to be honest, it's not good for him either. The guy thinks he's got a shot at banging you."

"Maybe he does have a shot."

Oh no, that was not the right thing to say if she wanted me to back down. Not that she could.

"Darlin', let me enlighten you on something. There are two types of women in this world. Some want your man Mattie, all soft and considerate and mushy inside. Some want me. You're one type of woman or the other."

I stepped in front of her, grabbing her to haul her up to my height while I wrapped my other hand around the back of her head, her gorgeous hair threading through my fingers and adding to the burn inside. I wasn't sure what had lit the initial fire, or why it had gone from a small light to a blazing heat that would wipe out an entire city, but it wasn't extinguishable.

My lips clashed with hers, my tongue diving into an unresisting mouth, as I showed her how thoroughly I wanted her. A hint of how I'd claim her if the time ever came.

By time I was done, her spine had curved to mine; her breathing was beating to the sound of my heart. She was mine. She just didn't realize it yet.

"I think we both know which type of woman you are." I dropped her to the ground. "Now cut the little puppy loose before you fuck him up."

She finally spoke as I walked out the door. "He's not a puppy," she called out after me.

14

S *assy*

There was someone standing over my bed. I would've reached for the knife under my pillow, except I already knew who it was. Some part of my brain, the same part that liked to get up close and personal with Cole, had filed away his scent in my permanent memory. If I knew exactly which part, I'd would've given myself a lobotomy.

I looked over at my clock. Five in the morning! The day ahead needed a sharp mind, and I'd be as good as an old, rusty butter knife now.

I sat up, shoving the hair out of my eyes as he walked about my room, taking in all the details, from my pile of folded sweaters that never made it to the drawers, to the dress hanging by my door.

"Don't you sleep? What is *wrong* with you?" I stared at

him with all the annoyance I could muster, but it was dulled by the morning light. Dawn and I had never jibed.

"If this place were more secure, I wouldn't be able to wander in here. I told you, you need to do something about that."

Figured he'd go back to that. "Yes, and I told you I needed supplies. By the way, you like to make a lot of demands. If you narrowed down your list a bit, I might hear you better. Now why are you here?"

I shoved the covers off me and looked for my slippers while he stared at my feet.

"Why do your socks have holes? You're telling me you can afford to outfit your headquarters to the teeth with tech and you can't buy new socks?"

He was looking at my toe poking out as if it were offensive. I thought it was quite cute with the pink nail polish I'd used.

"My feet go in slippers or shoes. A little hole here or there doesn't make a difference." That was why I could afford to tech out my place. I didn't waste a dime where it wasn't absolutely needed.

The way his eyes were working their way up my legs to the t-shirt that barely covered my ass might've made me blush if I were a weaker girl. Internally, it still had the same effect. I never should've let him kiss me yesterday. Working with someone you wanted to fuck, even if you hated them, was not good for business.

He could say whatever he wanted about Puppy —*Mattie*. That situation was under control. A little crush never hurt anyone, and at least Mattie was the loyal type. He wouldn't abandon me for some drunk down the street.

And why the hell was Cole still looking at me like that,

anyway? If he kept it up, he was going to start kissing me again, and we all knew how well I rejected those advances. I put my hand to my mouth and forced out a cough to remind him I was the sick girl who was beneath fucking.

He smiled. He'd been repulsed by my illness and now he found it amusing if I hacked up a lung? The fucker was crazy, and I was the idiot who'd ended up in a partnership with him.

I grabbed the robe draped over the chair and wrapped it around me. "I'm still waiting to find out why you're here?"

I went to move past him. He didn't move, like that would stop me. I shoved past him anyway, my elbow accidentally landing in his ribs.

He laughed as he followed me downstairs, toward the kitchen.

I went to the pot. "Let me guess, you want coffee too?"

"I'll take a cup. Thanks."

I flipped on the lights and saw the boxes piled by the door and froze.

They couldn't be. I'd just given him the list yesterday. None of what I'd put down was easy to find, or not for me. For him? I guess it was easier.

"That's not..." My tongue got twisted, still frozen in shock.

"It is. Are you going to make me coffee?"

I spun on him. "That's the list I gave you?" I pointed, waiting for him to say yes. This was going to need confirmation before I'd believe it. I wasn't getting my hopes up, ripping open those boxes, and then having them crash to the ground.

"Almost all. There are a couple items that won't come in until tomorrow."

"You mean I'm getting *everything* on the list?" That list had been worse than that of a spoiled five-year-old with Santa's ear. I'd thrown everything and the kitchen sink on it in hopes of getting a handful of items I could use.

"Yes," he said.

Don't act surprised. Act as if this is an everyday occurrence. Be cool. Definitely don't jump up and down like a fool, at least until after he leaves.

"Are you making that coffee? I'd do it, but mine's horrible, remember?" he asked, showing a little self-deprecating humor for once.

I turned, grabbing the pot and trying to not show my enthusiasm by ripping open the box in front of him.

"Did you get the Vamp 1000?" I asked as I casually scooped grains.

No way was that in there. That was cutting-edge vampire surveillance technology. It had night vision, body temperatures, facial recognition. That was probably one of the things missing. He didn't realize he couldn't get it. Nobody could get their hands on that.

"I told you, if it was on the list, it's either there or will be tomorrow."

The Vamp 1000!

Don't jump. Don't even jiggle a little. Get the smile off your face before you turn around. Be cool. Do not let him know how amazing this is. He'll use it against you. Tell you that you have to partner with a hedgehog or something insane.

I turned, staying beside the coffee, waiting for the stuff to fill the pot, all while trying to not look at the boxes by the door.

"You want to look at the stuff?" he asked, as if he knew how much it was killing me.

I shrugged. "I'll get around to it."

He nodded.

I glanced at the pot. It was a third full. That would have to be enough. A person only had so much patience, and he needed to drink his coffee so he could get out.

I shorted his coffee, taking a couple sips and a few minutes off his departure time. He leaned against the counter, as if he were in no rush.

I sipped my coffee, watching him. Did he have to drink so slowly?

"I hope you checked the boxes before you paid," I said, sipping coffee, while actually eyeing up the size of the boxes again.

"No."

"How do you know you weren't ripped off?" I loudly sighed and grabbed a knife from the drawer. "You always check."

"People don't rip me off," he said.

"You can't know that," I said, even though he probably could. Still, it was as good an excuse as any.

I tore into the boxes with more excitement than some women opened their engagement ring boxes. Piece after shining piece was reverently pulled out, examined, and set back.

One piece didn't go back in, and I had to stop myself from petting the packaging, which was much larger than what lay inside. It was a tiny machine the size of a gnat. No one would see anything. It was supposed to be quieter than fairies. The only catch was it couldn't be that far from its base and transmitter.

"Where were you planning on using that?" Cole asked, eyeing the prized box.

"Outside Pavro's estate for starters." After that, everywhere else. That little beauty was going to be working until it dropped from exhaustion.

"Where, exactly?"

"There's a big old oak tree in his backyard. I should be able to plant its base somewhere in there."

"How close have you gotten to it?"

I'd been so enamored with my new toys that I missed the lead-up to his disapproving tone.

Cole was enough to give anyone whiplash. He wanted me to help him go after vampires, but now he was going to judge what risks I took doing it?

"Just admired it from afar." Last night I'd lain awake, thinking of the perfect spot if I ever managed to get one of these.

"When are we going?"

"Huh?" I felt like someone had grabbed me by the hair and yanked me from my dreams.

"If you're going to plant surveillance on his property, you're not doing it without backup. I'm going with you."

I swiveled my ass on the cold tile floor. "Oh no. *You're* not coming."

There were sparks shooting from his eyes. "You forget the agreement already? I make the final call."

"You're too noticeable. You're too"––I waved a hand at him––"much! How am I going to get in and out with you attracting all sorts of notice?"

"Which is why you should want me. I'll pull attention from you as you go ahead and plant it."

Oh. *Hmm*. I leaned my back against the cabinets. That wasn't the worst idea. He wasn't actually going with me. He was acting as a diversion. Clearly, he wasn't used to planning these things, or he would've specified that in the first place.

"You'll keep your distance?" I asked, nailing him down, not that I could guarantee he'd stick to the agreement.

"Of course. I'm aware I draw attention."

I gave him the once-over, as if I'd have the last say-so, no matter what he might think. Because the truth of it was that I would. Come hell or high water, we'd be following my gut instincts, the ones that had kept me alive this far.

I gave him a skeptical look but said, "I guess it could work."

His look said he saw right through my bull.

"Get dressed. We've got another errand to handle," he said, and then helped himself to more coffee.

"Where to?"

"The one who's going to fix you wants to examine you."

The *one*. Something about that choice of words didn't sit right.

15

S *assy*

"Where is this...*one*?" I asked, using his word as we entered Kalorama Heights. It was one of the highest-priced neighborhoods in D.C., or had been before the war. I wasn't sure how real estate was priced these days. Most of these houses were occupied by vampires now, and I doubted any of them had paid a fair purchase price. There were certain perks to living in a small shack on the wrong side of town.

"Here," he said, pulling in front of a townhouse.

"The person that's going to cure me is here? Right smack in the middle of vampire territory?"

"Yes, so act natural," he said.

He didn't move for a minute, eyeing the townhouse.

"What is it? Why aren't we going in?"

He turned to me. "It might not be that pleasant, but it won't be lasting." Then he got moving.

"What's that mean?" I managed to ask before he got out of the truck.

"Don't worry about it. You don't have to do anything you don't want." He shut the truck door and headed toward the front of the townhouse.

It was either follow him and find out what was waiting for me inside or sit here looking obviously out of place for all to see.

That wasn't really my fear, though. This mysterious *one*—whatever he was—was probably my last frontier. This was it. If this couldn't fix me, I would die, and soon. I'd never turn thirty, or even twenty-five. I'd never see my nephew grow to be a man. Never have children of my own. The next few months would be all I had left. Maybe I'd make another dent in the vampire population, but it wouldn't be enough to take them down. I wouldn't see the grand revolution.

I got out of the car and caught up to Cole.

Whoever this person was, they were powerful if they had a townhouse here. Or they had powerful friends. They had to be doing something right.

Or very wrong.

"He's going to want to take your measure. Stay calm," Cole said.

"Really?" Had he missed that I was the head of the resistance?

I didn't get the chance to remind him before he knocked on the door.

The door opened, and in front of me was something that might've scared me worse than death. It wasn't the way he looked. As far as appearances go, he was quite handsome. Clean-cut and with a pretty-boy appearance. What screamed inside me to run was instincts, and mine were saying to choose death over anything to do with this creature. This thing might've resembled a human, but everything, from his smell to his skin, screamed monster.

The monster's eyes ran over me, but it didn't feel sexual. It was some other sort of measurement I couldn't quite figure out. I wasn't sure I wanted to, either.

"Come in," he said. He held out his hand, gesturing us in.

I walked in, Cole right behind me.

"You are Sabrina Abbot, more commonly known as Sassy," the monster said, staring dead into my eyes.

"Yes."

"You may call me Merlin."

Merlin? I doubted that was his true name.

"I don't have all day. Run your test," Cole said, standing nearly shoulder to shoulder with me.

For someone of Cole's choosing, he didn't seem to like Merlin any more than I did.

Merlin looked at Cole for a moment. It was unclear what was running through his mind, whether he was contemplating killing Cole or simply asking him to leave. Whatever payoff Merlin was getting must've been big enough to swallow his inclinations, because he nodded.

"I'll need to sample your blood," Merlin said, holding out his hand to me.

I didn't want to touch him, but I took his hand, letting him lead me wherever we needed to go for this sample.

Merlin wrapped his fingers around mine, and it felt like a million little pricks on my skin. *He* was taking a sample, through his skin.

That wasn't the worst. As soon as his hand touched

mine, I was swallowed by a darkness that felt as if it were swallowing me whole, so thick and bleak that I didn't think I'd ever be the same.

Cole stationed himself behind me. I didn't know if he was there to support me or to hold me in place if I tried to run.

Merlin released his grip seconds before I was about to make a run for it. As soon as he let go, the darkness eased, but not entirely. It was if a bleakness hovered over me.

What the hell kind of creature was he? Ideas flitted around my mind, but I wasn't sure it was something I truly wanted to know.

Even if Donovan knew this person, I wasn't sure he would've brought me here. It wasn't clear what this Merlin dealt in, but it didn't feel right. Donovan would respect that some lines shouldn't be crossed. Cole wasn't of the same mind. As I stood there knowing this was my last chance, I realized I wasn't either.

Merlin smiled, as if reading my every thought.

"I can see your soul, dear little Sassy," Merlin said.

His gaze, words, tone—it all added to the slithering feeling down my spine.

"You're done, correct?" Cole asked, as if he'd better be.

Merlin stared long and hard at me before a slight smile came to his lips. "I think that should be good. Now it's just a matter of price."

"We'll discuss that later," Cole said.

Whatever this man was, he didn't need money.

I took a short step back before I caught myself. The urge to run from this...*person* was just too strong.

"We're leaving. I'll be in touch," Cole said, an arm around my waist, steering me out of there.

I walked from the townhouse like my feet were tied to

cinder blocks and there was nothing but storm clouds above. I made it into the truck, hoping the distance from Merlin would help. As we drove away, the only thought I could conjure was crashing into a ball of fire.

I shook my head, trying to dislodge whatever Merlin had done to me. Cole was staring forward, but he was watching my every move.

By the time I walked back into my house, I didn't have much energy left. It felt like all the sunshine had been robbed from my life.

I walked into my kitchen, turning around as I realized Cole was shadowing me.

"What did that thing do to me? What is he going to do to fix me?" I leaned against the counter.

"He doesn't explain his ways, but those who do know of him say he delivers." He moved closer, taking in my slumped form. "This feeling you have now, it'll wear off."

I would've slumped in relief if I wasn't slouched already. "How long?"

"You'll feel better by tomorrow, almost normal by the day after that. A few days and it'll be gone completely."

I nodded, still wondering what that man was. "What *is* Merlin?"

Cole leaned on the counter beside me, a heaviness about him that I didn't typically sense. Or maybe it was me and what that thing had done to me already.

"No one who knows him is entirely sure. There are rumors he was a vampire at one point, or one of the larger breeds of fae, but no one knows the truth. It's all rumors."

There was another question I couldn't get past. Before I could talk myself out of asking, the words slipped out.

"How much does a life go for?" I should have the balls

to at least look him in the eye. What could I live with, knowing the alternative was not living at all?

He took his time answering. "I guess it depends on the life."

"How much is *my* life worth?"

I'd told myself not to ask that question, to let it lie with the rest of the foul things in life that were better off not knowing about. And there were plenty.

It was true that knowledge was power, but only to a point. Too much knowledge, about too many dark things, left you insane. Before the takeover, I hadn't understood that. Even after the takeover, I hadn't completely grasped the idea that some things were best left unknown. Not until I set up eyes and ears all over this city did I truly understand how information could sometimes cost you pieces of your soul, your sanity, the person you thought you were.

In the later stages of the resistance, after the wall of eyes went up, sometimes I'd sit and stare for hours, making lists of atrocities that needed to be avenged. I filled page after page until I had a notebook full. Then several notebooks. Eventually I had boxes full. One day, I stopped writing it all down. I stopped watching every free moment. The day I stopped watching was when I realized the cost of knowledge. That was the day I became who I was now. Sometimes to make the world a better place, you had to harden your heart to the atrocities you saw, or you'd be swallowed whole by the travesty.

But if I let Merlin save me, I wasn't so sure who I'd be after.

"I can't say. We haven't finished negotiating yet," Cole said.

"I want to know," I said, knowing when someone was holding out on me.

"I told you, it doesn't matter."

I didn't know why Cole was intent on saving me, but I could feel it, see it. His eyes would burn when I coughed. When I had a fever, and he looked upon me, I could feel his rage.

He leaned back, and I saw someone the devil would run from. The rage and fury I'd seen hinted at before was boiling to the surface and was capable of taking out this entire place and everyone in it if he didn't get his way.

But it didn't matter. I had to know.

"But there's the rub—it does matter. A lot. I don't think—"

"Don't say it." He straightened, as ready to do battle as I was.

"I can't—"

"You can and you will," he said, walking toward the door.

"Why does it matter to you? I'll do your dirty work. I'll still hold up my end either way," I said before he walked out.

"Make sure you use some of those supplies to batten down the hatches over here. I'm not known for my patience," he said, making it very clear the other conversation was finished.

The door shut, and I slumped to the ground.

I jerked my gaze up as Cole opened it one more time. "And we're not planting that droid at Pavro's for at least a few days, if you haven't figured that out."

I dropped my head on my knee. Yeah, that last part I'd realized.

16

S assy

My bike nearly toppled as I hopped off it at the club. Every single time I started to trust Cole a tiny bit, he'd screw me up somehow. Every single male I'd ever come into contact with did it. Every damned guy I'd dated, my father—the lot of them were a bunch of jerks.

The shifter at the door didn't try to stop me as I marched into the club. Derek was a handful of steps away from the door.

"Where is he?"

His mouth gaped open as he scrambled for a lie. "He's not available right this—"

"Then I'll wait in his office." I brushed past him, refusing to hear no.

Derek darted in front of me, trying to block the

hallway without physical contact. "I don't think that's a good idea. He doesn't like people in his office—"

"I know you're afraid to touch me because of Donovan. So do you plan on standing here all night?"

He rested a palm on the wall, as if needing every ounce of strength he had to deal with me. It was an effect I seemed to commonly have on people.

"Sassy, don't give me grief. You know he'll be pissed."

"He'll be pissed at me. Cole isn't delusional enough to think I'd listen to you."

I placed a hand on his chest, steering his body closer to the wall and away from me. He moved as if my touch would cause anaphylactic shock.

The door to Cole's office was unlocked.

Cole's head was leaned back as he sat in his desk chair, eyes closed, fingers pinching the bridge of his nose.

"This isn't a good time," he said, not bothering to turn in his chair or open his eyes.

What the hell? I was supposed to wait because he wanted to nap in the middle of the day? Cross town and then come back again? No. There couldn't be a better time for me.

I marched to his desk. "Do you have to be in a particular mood to be able to speak? Do you need someone to tickle your back or something?"

"It's *not* a good time," he said, spinning around to face me.

"Do you want me to make an appointment for an hour from now? Is that a good time?"

"Yes, but I don't see that happening." He sighed and said, "Leave," looking past me to the door.

I leaned my palms on his desk. "I just told you, I'm not—"

"Not. You."

There was some rustling coming from behind me. I spun and realized there was a woman getting up from the couch. She straightened her dress lower, making me wonder why it had been rucked up. Her shirt was still half-open, and she was shooting me daggers as if I'd interrupted her show.

She looked to Cole. "Should I come back..."

"Go," he said.

Well, I guess that answered that.

The woman froze for a second before there was an infinitesimal straightening of her spine. She gathered the last tattered shreds of her pride and walked from the room, only pausing long enough to shoot me another dirty look on the way out, as if I'd been the one to eviscerate whatever was left of her self-worth.

The door closed with a heavy thud.

I didn't know the woman who'd gotten the boot in the most degrading way imaginable, but some feminist streak within me had to take a shot at Cole's ego, just for fair play. Or maybe because he shouldn't be running around trying to fuck everything that walked. That was a fine reason too.

"I can't imagine why women put up with you. Is it the alpha thing? I don't get it," I said with a shrug.

"Really? You can't imagine why?"

Of course he'd remind me of how I'd nearly been one of the women who slept with him.

"I'd only been around you for a few minutes," I said. "Trust me when I tell you I would've come to my senses before I made a horrific error in judgment."

He laughed. "I've seen the way you live. I highly doubt it. Your life seems to be full of bad judgment calls."

As much as I wanted to hang around here trading insults and explaining where he'd gone wrong in life, there were other pressing problems. There were people he was about to screw over that had to be handled.

"You stopped my supplies. Where are they? Why did you stop them?" Every first and third Sunday of the month, I showed up at an old factory on the fringes of town and handed out foodstuffs. The bulk of it was "donated" by a network Pen and Donovan had put in place. Tonight, for the first time in over a year since it had been in operation, I'd gotten a call that the truck would not be arriving.

When I asked Devon, the driver, why, he'd told me it was on Cole's orders.

"It was drawing too much attention that we can't afford right now," Cole said. "I want it to look like I'm running a tight ship, and you're walking the line. You'll get your supplies, but you need to find a different way to distribute them. You shouldn't be running around right now anyway."

He shifted his attention to a map with bright red lines, as if dismissing me.

"I'm going to give you the benefit of the doubt and assume you don't quite understand the consequences of what you're doing," I said. "People depend on those items to survive. They're going to show up, have budgeted what they had for the last two weeks, expecting more. What do you think? I can send a newsletter."

He dropped the map and stood. "Whatever people you are referring to aren't the people I'm in charge of keeping alive. There's word that your situation is being watched. You can't distribute anything if you're dead. You're not responsible for feeding the entirety of D.C. They need to start taking care of themselves."

If the desk wasn't between us, I might've tried to kill him. I might anyway.

"There are kids out there that aren't getting enough food to eat, that go to bed with their stomachs cramping at night. How are they supposed to take care of themselves? This has to happen tomorrow. You don't have the right to cancel this."

There might've been a flicker of shock on his face, but it was hard to tell behind all that righteous alpha *you'll do as I say* rage.

"Oh, I have every right. I'm the alpha of this territory and I'll do what I want. Feel free to call whoever you want and see if anything changes. I'm not screwing up our situation or risking your life when I'm the only one who seems to give a shit about it. I'll get them the supplies, but it's not happening tomorrow." He grabbed his phone off the desk, holding it out to me. "Go ahead. Call your brother."

I'd never get Donovan involved in this, not that Cole would realize that. He seemed to be under the impression I used Pen and Donovan as a get-out-of-jail-free card. Not sure why, when I used to keep them as far from my plans as possible. The only thing they had known about was the food drives, and mostly because my sister, who wasn't a heartless bastard, was the first to start funneling food to the people hurting.

Now I was stuck with this heartless asshole who was going to starve them—and no backup plan.

"When will you get me the truck?" I asked, knowing I was in a losing position. I might not eat crow for myself, but I'd eat it so others wouldn't go hungry.

"I'll get it done this week. That's the best it's going to get. Not to mention you're not up for anything. You should still be at home resting."

Fuck him and his "this week sometime." He wasn't the one who wouldn't eat. He didn't know these families by name, when their birthdays were, who'd lost a tooth last week. They didn't cry to him as they thanked him, at the same time as their cheeks burned from humiliation at having to take handouts.

I wanted to leap over the desk, grab him by the collar, and shake some sense into him, but he wouldn't get it. He'd probably never had to take a handout or had a growling belly. He didn't know what it was like to have to rely on others to make it another day.

I shook my head as I gave him my best look of disgust and then turned my back on him and walked out. He probably assumed I was going to go home, as told. Not likely.

17

S *assy*

I coughed out the last lungful of water, straining my arms that were tied to the pipe above my head.

"You think you can steal from me?" Louis wasn't an altogether ugly fellow, but the sneer did something awful to his looks. Plus, this close and personal I could see every pockmark scattered across his face. I'd heard about that. He'd been a late shifter. Sometimes when they didn't start shifting soon enough, it threw all their systems out of whack, including their skin. It was rare for an alpha to shift late, but it added up with his need to project invincibility. He was probably still trying to make up for his late turn.

"Wait until you see what comes next," he continued. "You think this is bad? Wait until my guys get a chance at you."

He had two goons behind him, one holding the fire hose and the other by the water valve. Considering they'd already been torturing me as a team, my mind went to the worst place.

"No one is above paying the price for stealing from me. I don't care who her sister fucks."

Louis lifted his hand.

I took a deep breath, knowing he'd be making a point with this next session.

It seemed to go on forever. I twisted this way and that, trying to get whatever air I could steal.

When the hose finally shut down, I was coughing water out of my lungs, knowing I'd be paying an additional price for this later, if I made it out alive.

He grabbed a hank of my hair, pulling my head back. "You don't bend easy, huh? Well, we'll see. Normally I kill people who steal from me, but you might have other uses. Maybe I'll just make you one of my whores."

I didn't know if he was expecting an answer, but I stayed quiet. I'd kill anyone who tried to touch me, so we'd see how well that worked out. Plus my people would get me out of here. They knew where I was. I just needed to endure whatever he was going to dish out first. How bad could it be? This wouldn't be the first beating I'd taken.

"What's wrong? Nothing to say? Maybe you like the idea of being my whore? Your sister certainly enjoys the position."

I saw red. If he wanted to kill me, fine, but I wasn't going to let that stand and die anyway.

"Fuck. You."

"Spray her again. Make sure you get her face this time so she can wash out that dirty mouth of hers."

The hydrant hose was lifted again.

"If Don—"

"I told you, I don't give a shit about him," Louis said. "He's gone."

I couldn't hear anything after that because the sound of the water blasting drowned out all other noises, along with nearly drowning me.

The shifter wielding the hose wasn't as reckless as Louis. He seemed to be angling the hose so I could get air on and off, not wanting to pay the price for following his idiot leader's orders. I might be able to work something out with that one. He was definitely a weak link.

As the water stopped, I coughed and noticed a new face in the room. He was standing beside Louis, his head bent as he spoke softly.

Louis' stare remained on me the entire time he listened, nodding slowly as his eyes narrowed.

The newcomer finally stopped speaking, and Louis continued to stare, finally saying to the newcomer, "You can go."

The newcomer hesitated for a moment, as if wanting to stay for the show, but slowly made his way out.

Louis walked closer to me, stopping a couple of inches shy. The burning rage so clear in his expression before had shifted into something more calculating as he scanned me again. This was more of an appraisal of worth than of how to abuse or use me.

"I've heard something very interesting," he said.

A smarter person would hear him out, play into anything that bought them time or a respite. Listening might buy my people some time to get a plan together to get me out. I'd always been more stubborn than smart, especially when I really disliked someone, and boy did I not like him. I gave him a once-over and then looked to the far wall without speaking, making my appraisal of his worth crystal-clear.

He tilted his head back and laughed. "I understand why you'd be a bit miffed at me, but I think you and I might be able to come to some arrangement after all, a way you can pay me back." He circled me. "That is, if you are who they say you are." He lifted the strand of pink running through my platinum hair then grabbed my chin. "I'm thinking they're correct."

I jerked my head away from him. He didn't seem to care anymore.

"Cut her down and bring her to my office."

The man who'd been wielding the hose was all too quick to slice through the rope that held me, looking more relieved than I was.

"You know I was only following orders, right? That I was trying to take it easy on you?" he asked in a hushed tone.

"You can relax. I don't even know your name."

But I would.

There was a sigh of relief.

Donovan must've really scared the shit out of these people on his way out.

The man waved his hand to follow after Louis.

I followed him through the warehouse to an office that overlooked the main floor where I'd just been tortured.

"Fernando, get her a change of clothes," Louis said to the man who'd just cut me down.

Thank you, Louis. One less name I wouldn't have to hunt down.

Fernando hurried back with a t-shirt and sweatpants and waved toward the bathroom. I didn't ask if I could use it. Louis had decided to play nice for a bit, and for once, I wouldn't be so stubborn as to shoot myself in the foot. Even if that gun looked really tempting right now.

Louis was alone in the office when I came back out. There was something slightly cooler about his demeanor that jumped out at me right away.

"Have a seat," he said, with none of the flamboyant act he'd used when he spoke to me downstairs.

I took a seat on the couch, almost stunned into agreeableness.

"I'm a businessman. I can't allow an attempt to steal from me and let it go unchallenged. It would breed more attempts." He picked up a pack of cigarettes off his table, lit one, and held it out to me.

I shook my head.

He shrugged and dropped the pack in front of me. "It's business. You can be annoyed, but you'll understand. From what I've heard, you're savvy enough to get what has to be done."

Perception was everything in this world. It could make or break you before any transaction even unfolded. Whether I liked it didn't matter—he was right.

"What do you want?" I asked, placated enough to lower myself to speaking to him.

"Did you kill all those vampires?" he asked, nothing but calculation in his gaze.

"I'm sure I don't know what you're talking about."

He smiled, too cool to laugh.

How the hell was word getting out that I was Ghost? I'd managed to keep it under wraps for so long. It couldn't be a coincidence that I'd met with Cole's group and now they had a description of me.

"From first glance, you don't seem very lethal, but

there's strength in you." He leaned on his desk, crossing his arms. "Yes, I think you killed every single one of them —and probably a few more you're not getting credit for."

I kept silent. He could think whatever he wanted. I wasn't confirming anything.

"Can I make you a drink?" He waved toward a small bar along the wall.

The chill from the hose was already doing nasty things to my lungs. This guy would probably have his mother shot if she had a bad day. I'd rather drink my way through this than start looking weak.

"Bourbon, neat."

He walked to the bar then came back and handed me a glass.

"What do you want?" I asked.

He settled onto the other side of the couch. "At the moment? Nothing. But I'm sure you know there are problems brewing within our alliance with the vampires. Your unique abilities might come in handy at some point in the future if things devolve."

What was the deal with these werewolves? Couldn't anyone do their own killing? Seemed they all wanted a vampire dead these days but no one wanted to do the dirty work. *We're so tough, but let's send in the human.*

"I'm not looking for trouble," I said. He didn't know the mountain of it I already had.

"You tried to rob me. You already found trouble. I can't let you walk out of here without payback." His threat was delivered so calmly that it was clear he didn't really care what way this went down. He'd use me if it worked out or kill me just as easily.

"You took a fire hose to me just for the attempt. I'd say

that was payback enough." It went against my nature to roll over that easily.

"Why don't I make this beneficial for both of us? I'm going to offer you a deal that I think you'll be hard-pressed to walk away from. I'm going to load a truck with the supplies you want. In return, you're going to agree to a favor in the future."

"Can you get it delivered by tomorrow?" The guy had me, and he knew it.

"Yes, wherever you want."

"Deal."

18

C *ole*

"Why's Sarah walking around all bent out of shape now?" Huddy asked as he walked in and helped himself to one of my cigars.

"Things didn't go the way she planned this morning." As bad as the timing had been with Sassy walking in, if she hadn't, Sarah might've continued to insist we could be a great pair. She seemed to be under the delusion that we'd ever had a chance.

"Really? Is that what we're calling it? Because she's telling anyone who will listen that you can't get it up anymore. Although that's typically the course with her relationships, so no one is paying it any mind." He laughed before he added, "Lonzo did try to warn you."

He took a sip of his drink, settled onto the couch, and then laughed some more.

"This is almost as funny as when I spread the same rumor."

My head jerked up. "What are you talking about?"

"The night you shot Sassy down—you didn't think in a house frequented with werewolves and shifter servers that you weren't overheard, did you?" This seemed to make him laugh more.

"Actually, I did."

"Well, you were. I heard some of the servants talking about how you rejected her, and I told them you couldn't get it up."

He was laughing the hardest yet, and I didn't even mind. Somehow that little nugget of information sat better than what I'd thought happened.

So the rumor hadn't been spread by Sassy. I'd rejected women who'd done much worse, so I hadn't made a thing of it. But it was nice to know that wasn't who Sassy was. Considering the situation, at least I was becoming obsessed with someone who hadn't spread lies about me.

If Huddy knew the extent of it, he wouldn't be able to leave this room for laughing fits. Sarah was right: I did have a problem. I couldn't seem to get it up for anyone unless they were Sassy, the one person I was determined not to fuck.

I'd been trying to prove a point with the kiss the other day, but the only person I'd proven anything to was myself. I couldn't touch her. It had taken long enough to force her out of my every waking thought, and then I had to go and touch her.

My God did she burn as hot as she looked. This one wasn't all fizz and steam and then flat. She was a handful in heaven, which was why I couldn't touch her again. She was also stubborn, a headache and a half. I'd have to be mental to get involved with her, and if I touched her again, it wouldn't stop at kissing.

I got up and grabbed a bottle of bourbon, holding out a glass to Huddy.

"Why not?" he asked.

I was beginning to think I was corrupting him.

We hadn't taken a sip before the sound of Lonzo's footsteps sounded in the hall, his pace way faster than his typical stroll. He might as well be ringing the alarm bell.

I slammed the glass down, sloshing the liquid all over, knowing my day was about to take a nosedive.

Lonzo burst into the room.

"What did she do now?" I asked.

Huddy's brows dropped. "Are we talking about Sassy?"

Lonzo nodded. "She got caught trying to steal food from a neighboring district."

I'd told her I'd handle it. She couldn't give me a few days to do so? If she wasn't already dead, I was going to kill her.

"Whose district?" If it was Jack's, this would be an easy fix. Greg might be a pain in the ass, but he was easy to buy off. Anybody but Louis. That jackass had an ego the size of an elephant and was stubborn to boot. Constantly had to put on a show so everyone knew he couldn't be rolled over.

The pause told me it was the worst-case scenario before he spoke.

"Louis," Lonzo said, grimacing.

I groaned. Huddy was covering his face with his hand.

Lonzo continued, "Someone inside knew she was connected to us and put out a call. I told them she was under our protection, but he said he's not releasing her unless you come and get her personally. I don't think he's hurt her."

"He's going to need an offering to salve his gigantic ego." I drank what liquid was left in the glass.

"Did the new delivery of phones get here?" Huddy asked.

"Please tell me you don't mean the ones not even on the market yet," Lonzo said, knowing he'd just lost his booty too.

"That's a good call." This was why Huddy made a great second.

The better phones were tough to come by these days, with all the trade issues going on. Technically, trade hadn't officially stopped, but there were suspicious shortages that only affected the U.S.

"Load them onto to the truck," I said, heading for the door.

"Do you need backup?" Lonzo said.

"I should come," Huddy said, grabbing his jacket.

"No, I'm going alone." I didn't want anyone there telling me not to kill someone this time.

I'd told her to go home and rest. I knew she wasn't physically up to doing *anything*, let alone something as crazy as this. She could coordinate killing all those vampires but couldn't manage to steal a loaf of bread if her head wasn't on straight. And she'd probably be a wise-ass when she got caught, too. I pressed the gas a little harder. Not that I cared if she got roughed up. Why should I? It was only that I'd get screwed in the process.

They better not have touched her. She was technically

mine, or my responsibility, anyway. They had no right to touch her.

My truck kicked up gravel as I swung into the lot outside the warehouse that served as Louis' hub.

I pushed open the door, not bothering to knock.

"Where is she?" I asked the shifter who was on guard. I'd seen him at enough gatherings to recognize his face and know he wasn't someone typically looking for issues.

"In the office." He nodded to his right and didn't follow me as I went.

She was curled up on the end of the couch in Louis' office, a throw blanket over her legs and a drink in her hand. I'd raced over here imagining her being tortured, and she looked like she was on a date.

Louis sat on the other end, his arm along the back of the couch, outstretched in her direction. He gripped the back as if he wished he was grabbing something else.

I wanted to rip his arm off his body.

"Cole." Louis unfolded himself off the couch and walked over to me before I had to do some reconfiguring. "Your girl is ready to leave."

He gave me a nod. That slight deferment to me was just enough for the werewolf inside to settle down.

"Let's go," I said, turning to Sassy.

She was already walking toward me. If she'd hesitated, Louis might've still lost an arm just for the hell of it.

She walked out in front of me, and I sent a silent message to anyone who dared look at her that they better avert their eyes.

She climbed into my truck like she'd done it a thousand times before.

"Did they call you? Apparently, I'm now considered part of your pack or something."

She bent her leg, resting an arm on her knee as she looked out the window.

I scanned her again, making sure everything was as it should be. "Not your usual attire."

"Am I not allowed to wear sweatpants occasionally?" she asked.

They were bright fuchsia and looked like they were two sizes too big. She wasn't stupid. She wouldn't have gone to raid a warehouse dressed like that.

She hopped out of the truck before it stopped rolling. She didn't turn around or acknowledge that I was following. I stopped for half a second to see the woodpile on her porch was once again depleted before I kept going.

She stopped in the kitchen, glaring at me. "Thanks for the ride, but I have some things to do tonight."

I leaned against the counter. "I told you I was handling the food situation."

"Yes, whenever it was you were going to get around to it." She shook her head and then climbed the stairs two at a time.

"You're seriously going to follow me?" she asked as she walked down the hall and into her room.

"Until I get some answers. What happened at Louis'?" The scent on the clothes, the wet hair—none of the pieces were fitting.

She had a pair of jeans in her hand. "Do you mind?"

I gave her my back so she could change, but only because I wanted her out of the clothes she'd gotten from him. If she thought I was leaving before I got some answers, she'd started drinking too early this morning.

"What happened over there? And don't tell me 'nothing,'" I said.

"The question/answer portion of the day is over; check back tomorrow," she said.

I spun on her. "Are you ever not a smart-a—"

She had her back to me as she pulled off the t-shirt. There were bruises all along her torso.

My entire body seized. What had they done to her before I got there? A burst of adrenaline shot through me. My skin started to change.

I turned back before she caught me looking, my hands fisted and my heart thudding out of my chest. I had to leave, and now.

"Don't leave here," I said, walking out.

"Finally," I heard her say as I left.

I barged into Louis' warehouse and strode up the stairs to his office. I walked across the room and punched him in the face. He fell flat on his back, and I followed with a kick to his ribs.

"Get up," I said, watching him at my feet just lying there, holding his nose as it spurted blood.

"I couldn't let her attempt to steal from me and not send a message. As an alpha, you know this." He finally sat up but didn't get off the floor. "For the record, I had my softest guy wielding the hose so she wouldn't take too much of a beating."

"I don't care what she does. Don't touch her."

"Man, you've got it bad for this one, huh?" He had the audacity to laugh as he sat on the floor bleeding.

"In case you think you made some kind of deal with her, it's off. You contact her again, you're dead. You touch her again, you're dead."

19

C *ole*

I was sitting at the table, drinking coffee, watching her as she walked downstairs, her hair all over the place with another pair of those shorts she wore to bed that she seemed to have an endless supply of. Her t-shirt was hanging loosely on her form, a tattered old thing that should've done nothing for her. And yet the way it draped over her breasts, the thin fabric doing nothing to hide the shape and form of her nipples... It was as if she were trying to seduce me in the rattiest clothes possible. It was so idiotic that I couldn't even mention it to anyone.

What was worse—I wanted to lift her shirt to see how her bruises were healing more than I wanted to fuck her. What the hell was happening to me?

She stopped on the bottom landing, finally noticing me in the kitchen.

I got up and handed her a cup of coffee in her favorite mug, the ridiculous yellow one with a smiley face.

I moved to the door. "I want to show you something."

She sipped her coffee, looking mostly comatose. She used to jump to alertness as soon as she saw me. Then she'd be a little groggy for a few minutes before snapping to attention. Now I was finally being treated to the way she normally spent the first half an hour after waking. She followed me outside onto the porch at a slow shuffle.

She looked over the lawn, sipping her coffee, not paying attention to the issue. I took her by the shoulders, turning her toward the side of the house, then I let her go like she was a burning coal. With her eyes half-shut, her expression right now reminded me of exactly how relaxed I wanted her to be.

"Do you know what this is?" I asked, pointing to the new stack of wood.

She continued to sip her coffee, looking like she was trying to decipher if this was a trick question.

She finally looked at me, a little wrinkle on her forehead. "Wood?"

"Almost correct. This is *your* wood."

She stared at it for a few more seconds. "Sure. Okay. This is *my* wood."

She made a little face, as if I were acting quite ridiculous about wood.

"Do you know what that means?"

"That I can do whatever I please with it, because it's mine?" She smiled as she spoke.

"No. It means you have to use it for you."

"But if it's mine, shouldn't I get to choose what's done with it?"

This shouldn't surprise me. This woman had probably

come out of the womb difficult. Always the challenge. That was probably why I couldn't stop thinking about fucking her. I was so used to easy at this point that it would make sense I'd crave anyone that didn't simply spread their legs and ask to be used.

I waved a hand. "Forget what I said. This is *my* wood."

"You're taking it back? You gave it to me. You can't give something and take it back two seconds later." She took another sip of coffee before wrapping both hands around the mug, like her hands were cold.

"I can and I did. My wood has rules. My wood only gets burned here, in this house. Is that clear?" I said, then steered her back toward the door.

She sipped her coffee, a little crinkle forming on her forehead as she absorbed my words and decided she didn't like them.

She tilted her head slightly, giving me a vague acceptance. I knew where this led. She was going to do whatever she chose.

"Sassy, if this wood goes missing, I will beat you. Now go back inside."

She outright laughed at me. I'd never threatened someone with physical violence and gotten laughed at. What the hell was happening to me? Thank God my men weren't around. I'd lose all credibility.

"I'm serious."

"Yeah, sure. I hear you." She walked through the front door and went straight to the coffee pot, topping her mug off as her soft laughter continued.

She had zero fear of me. How was I going to keep her under control with absolutely no threat left? I needed something, or she was going to run roughshod over me.

"Sassy, don't push me on this. I won't have this house freezing every night."

"I know, I know. You'll beat me. I heard." She was actively trying to suppress her laughter as she took eggs out of the refrigerator. At least she was keeping the groceries.

A smile lit my face as an idea occurred to me. She glanced over and froze, her laughter dying.

"If you push me on this, I will take all of your things and move you into the mansion." She hated Donovan's house. I did too. I crashed in the club office more than I slept at that place.

She gasped. "I'm not going there, so get that out of your head right now."

"If you give that wood away, I'll drag you there. You know I'll do it." To keep her from freezing every night, damned straight I would. "Either use the wood here, or it's the mansion."

She put her coffee on the counter and climbed the stairs.

"Sassy?"

"Fine. And you can make your own eggs," she yelled before the door slammed.

I walked to the bottom of the stairs. "I want to plant the droid today. Can you be ready soon?"

There was nothing but dead air for a few seconds. "I'll be down in five. Don't put too much pepper in the eggs."

20

C *ole*

Sassy was standing down the block, wearing banged-up jeans, a cap, and a jacket with threads hanging from the hem as I pulled in front of Pavro's.

I hopped out of my truck and walked to the front. "Dammit," I said, loud enough to draw all the tiny fairies that acted like watchdogs for his residence. Fairies were great for security because they were nosey. That same trait also made them horrible for security because they were easily distracted by everything and anything.

They all came buzzing over, which drew the attention of Pavro's security.

"Get back here," one of them said.

The fairies didn't listen and swarmed around my truck.

"I blew out my tire. Do you have a jack?" I yelled to the security guards trying to wrangle the wayward fairies.

The first security guard looked at his partner. "We have one of those around here?"

They were arguing back and forth about whether they had something as Sassy slipped through the open gate and into the back.

Before they could come to a conclusion, I swatted around my head at one of the fairies that dipped low.

"How do you stand to work with these little fuckers?" I said, sending the swarm of them into a tizzy of buzzing tirades.

The two security men didn't say anything, but they didn't have to with the expressions on their faces.

The fairies were buzzing past all three of our heads like dive bombers.

Like clockwork, Sassy slipped out of the gates and headed down the street.

I swatted at a fairy before moving toward the truck door.

"Forget the jack. I'll drive on the flat," I said, swatting again. The security guards nodded.

Sassy was a few blocks away. She glanced around before hopping in the truck.

"You got it planted?" I asked once we were on the road. She was efficient if nothing else. Why should I be surprised that she'd been fast?

"Yeah, of course. I'll watch it for a few days and see if there's a way to get in," she said, her eyes never leaving the road. "Pull over here? I've got some errands I need to get to."

I pulled in front of the food store, expecting her to go in. Instead she kept walking.

I got out of the truck. "Where are you heading? I'll give you a ride," I said, catching up to her.

She kept walking. "Nah. I'm good."

I followed her. I could smell a secret from a mile away, and this girl left a trail of them twenty feet wide.

"What are you doing?" she asked when I continued to walk beside her.

"Walking with you. Is that a problem?"

She kept trying to enlarge the gap between us, but I walked faster.

She looked about. "Yes. You draw too much attention. I don't want to be seen with you."

"Then let's take the truck."

She looked ahead, where the streets got more congested, and then behind me, where we'd left the scene of the crime.

"Where are you going that's more top secret than your headquarters and what we did?" I asked.

"I have personal matters that have nothing to do with you. My life is not all business." She took a few more steps, and I followed.

The road ahead had more people standing around, and we were starting to draw notice. I was used to it. She was fidgeting.

"No you don't," I said. "You have your nefarious work, and that's about it. You breathe, eat, and sleep the resistance."

"And how would you know that?" she asked, planting a hand on her hip.

"I've had eyes on you for months. You've been pretty good at losing them. Some things slipped through the cracks, but not many." Like her trying to steal food from Louis and getting banged around. My blood boiled every time I thought about it. I shouldn't have beaten him. I should've killed him.

She kept looking down the street at the people looking back our way.

"Fine. Drive me, but you're dropping me off and leaving."

She went back and climbed into the passenger seat. Her arms were crossed, she was biting her lower lip, and she wouldn't look at me as I got in. Where the hell did she have to go?

"What's the address?" I asked, half wondering if I was going to get turn-by-turn directions.

She rattled off a place across town instead.

"What is this place?" The area wasn't somewhere you typically saw humans. I started the truck and threw it in drive.

"Why do you always ask so many questions?" She turned to look at me. She wasn't biting on her lip anymore, but she looked like she wanted to bite my head off.

My brows dropped. Not once in my life had I been accused of prying. Or caring, for that matter. Why did I want to know this woman's secrets? When had I started giving a shit? She was trying to hold up her end of the deal. That was all I should care about.

"You're right. I don't give a fuck."

If I hadn't forced her to take a ride, I would've let her keep walking. The less time I spent with her, the better.

"Thank you," she said, legitimate relief in those words.

It was the worst thing she could've done. Now I wanted to know even more. Why I wanted to know was beyond me. Why should it matter? I needed two things from Sassy: I wanted her brain for this assignment, and maybe her body for a few afternoons after our business was concluded, so I could prove it wouldn't be anything special, that *she* wouldn't be. Maybe a couple nights, too, if things went well. Whatever else she had going on didn't matter to me as long as it wasn't going to get her killed between now and then.

I pulled up outside of a dreary strip mall.

"Thanks," she said, getting out. "You don't need to stick around." She shut the door and then waited for me to pull away.

There were no numbers on it, but it was sandwiched between sixteen and twenty. This was definitely the place. The windows and the door were blacked out.

None of my business. I threw the car in reverse, watching what door she entered in my rearview.

21

S *assy*

I knocked on the door, waiting for someone to let me in before Cole got curious and turned his truck back around. There were certain moments in life that were hard to forget. The one where he'd rejected me because I was the sick girl was up there. This was the last place I'd ever let him come—not with me, at least.

I'd been coming to this place for almost a year now, ever since Donovan put me in touch with the doctor. Cole could say whatever he wanted about a cure. Prance me in front of all sorts of strange beings. Until he produced, I'd continue to come here, mostly because I was afraid to stop. This place had already bought me time.

One of the techs opened the door and gave me a nod. I didn't know his name, or anyone else's, and I had the feeling that was intentional. It was frowned upon to have shifter doctors treating humans, no matter what the connections.

There was one large room taking up the front half of the place, with equipment lining every free inch. The back half was broken into different offices. There were other techs or nurses, whatever they were, working, but I'd never seen another patient. I was fairly certain my appointments were buffered with a healthy amount of time before and after.

"Sassy," Doc called from the back like he was greeting an old friend.

"Hey! What's cooking today?" I asked, not as confident in our relationship as he was.

I was never a fan of delusion. The only reason he'd helped me was because it helped him as well. What the werewolf doctor was getting out of this arrangement wasn't clear, but it went beyond the Donovan connection. If there was something that could wipe out a vampire with just a taste, it was in their best interest to know what it was. Even if he couldn't cure me, I didn't mind coming here if it might help kill more vampires.

I'd decided a while back that the human's biggest threat was the vampires, and that was even before my sister fell in love with a werewolf. It was really simple in my mind: if you were the race's food supply, a race that could expand exponentially at any point, they took top billing, no contest. Hell, a busy Thanksgiving could wipe out half of us, and it was rumored their numbers were growing.

"Nothing much. Same old grind," he said with a smile.

It didn't look like that with the way the techs were hopping around and whispering to each other. It proved my point. After a year, we still weren't any closer to being friends than the day I'd walked in. We said the same greetings, same limited conversation. We were exactly where we were a year ago, and that was fine with us both.

"Are you ready?" he asked.

"As ready as I ever am." No sane person would enjoy these treatments, but it was better than dying.

"I'm guessing you're not going to let me do the epidural again." He took my wrist in his hand, feeling for my pulse.

"I told you, I don't need the epidural."

He took his stethoscope out, putting it on my back. "A spinal tap will be—"

"Painful. I know. Had it many times before, remember? You know what's worse than that pain? Getting chewed on by a vampire when I can't run because my legs are too numb."

"You can stay here until the anesthesia wears off."

This was where that pesky little problem of not being friends came in. I couldn't afford to totally trust anyone, and definitely not a shifter, not even one masquerading as my doctor.

"Except that I don't want to. I understand it's not your thing to hurt people, but you know you're going to lose this fight. Can we skip the five minutes of arguing and get to it?"

I hopped onto the table, getting ready for what was to come.

"Why won't you take anesthesia?" Cole's deep voice came from near the door behind me. Of course he'd come in. Why wouldn't he? I'd told him to go, so that meant come. Nothing else would make sense to him.

"This is a bit of a delicate matter," the doctor said, clearly recognizing Cole and treading softly.

I shook my head and looked over my shoulder to Cole filling the door. One of the techs was on his tiptoes, trying to look over Cole's shoulder, shrugging as if he was powerless to stop him.

Doc turned to me. "Are you all right with this?" he asked, clearly wanting the answer to be yes.

"It's fine," I said. No one got rid of Cole unless he was willing, certainly not the doc.

Cole walked around and then stopped in front of me, staring down at me where I leaned on the table.

"Why won't you take the anesthesia?" Cole repeated.

"Because I don't need it. Why are you here?" I asked, while Doc was trying to make himself look busy.

He wasn't supposed to be here. Not him. Anyone else wouldn't have been as bad. Anyone.

"Because I wanted to know what you were doing," he said, looking around the small examination room as if he weren't seeing the sick girl at her most vulnerable.

"Oh, well, that makes sense, then." I dropped my head, as if it was the most comfortable position. It had nothing to do with not wanting to look at Cole.

Doc stepped beside him and said, "The procedure would be easier if she took anesthesia."

If these two thought they were going to decide what I needed without me, this wouldn't be happening at all.

Cole looked at Doc. "She said she didn't want it, so do it without. She knows what she can handle."

It was the last thing I'd thought Cole would say.

Doc sighed and threw up his hands. "Fine." He pulled a rolling tray over. "I'll be right back."

I shot the doctor's back a dirty look. "Thank you for that," I said.

"For what?" Cole asked.

"Not siding with him."

"Why would I have sided with him over you?"

I didn't know. He was a fellow shifter? Why wouldn't he side with anyone else but me? He didn't like me most of the time, and here he was being reminded that I was damaged goods. He'd made his feelings about that crystal-clear. Most importantly, when had he ever turned down an opportunity to boss me around?

"Because in the short time I've known you, it's clear you like to tell me what I should be doing," I said.

He had the gall to laugh. "*I* like to tell you. That doesn't mean I enjoy other people trying to tell you. Plus, how can I side with him when I agree with you?"

He was looking around the place, fiddling with the dispensers like he'd never been in a medical office before. He probably hadn't. Most shifters were pretty resistant to disease. Maybe that was why he couldn't stand being with someone sick?

"You agree?"

"Of course. No sane person should weaken themselves to avoid a few minutes of pain."

Figured he'd be the one to understand.

"What's the deal here, anyway? Donovan told me you were seeing a doctor." Finished with his perusal, he leaned on the counter and turned his full attention to me. "You don't need to do this anymore."

"I also met the person you said will cure me. I think I should keep all options open until the last possible moment."

"Again, not sure I can disagree." He smiled wide, followed by a throaty laugh. "Just so you know, if you did want the anesthesia, and this place was overrun, I could handle things."

If there was anyone that could, he'd be where I'd put my money. It wasn't the way Cole looked—not that he had an overwhelming amount of polish. There was an air about some people who'd gone through tough times. It was hard to put your finger on it, and you couldn't quite describe it, but you knew from being around them that they'd been to hell, shaken hands with the devil, and made it back in time for dinner. This was not a man you wanted on your wrong side. Right now, we had a partnership of sorts. When that changed, he'd probably be firmly with the doc, on the other side of the line.

Somehow, imagining him staring back at me as if I were the enemy burned a little deeper than when I imagined the doc doing it. I was also spending a lot more time with Cole, so it was only natural. If I saw the doc every day, it'd probably bother me more. Either way, I'd deal with it when the time came, if I were still alive, the same way I dealt with everything else coming down the pike.

"Thanks, but I don't need anyone watching my back," I said.

Cole folded his arms as he stared my way. He tilted his head slightly as if he knew some great secret I wasn't privy to.

"What?" I asked. I might've sounded defensive, but how could I not, considering? This was why I didn't want him here.

"You have one glaring weak spot. You're almost too cut off. Leaves you vulnerable when you've got no one to watch your flank." He was speaking like an alpha.

I wasn't looking for a pack leader.

"Really? I thought it was that I was dying?"

"That can be fixed. It's your stubbornness that's the issue. Everyone needs someone to watch their back."

"In case you don't remember, I have quite a few people watching my back, but thanks for the pro tip." He spoke to me as if I were green on the vine. This wasn't my first season, or second. I'd been around enough, and had the scars to prove it.

"That clown crew you have? They'd be lost without you."

"You don't know them," I shot back. "You haven't seen them put their lives on the line for me, so please don't tell me about my crew."

If I did have a weak spot, it was intolerance for people talking shit about *my* people. Typically I didn't have this problem because no one knew about us. Live and learn.

He shrugged, staying quiet but clearly maintaining his low opinion of my crew and, worse, my weak spots. It shouldn't matter. I should be able to brush it off, like I did with everyone else's opinion. Yet somehow he managed to wriggle under my skin, as always.

I leaned back and raised my brows. "Do you sit around dreaming of ways to try to aggravate me?"

"Try? I think I accomplished it," he said, smiling as if this were a joke I was in on.

I tried not to soften, but it was like he had the blueprint to my psyche. He'd annoy me and then charm me. God I hated him sometimes.

The doc walked back in with more items I tried not to look too closely at. He put on his gloves, picked up one large-ass needle, and said, "Last chance—"

"Just start already." I leaned forward again as the doc moved behind me.

I let my head drop forward as the needle worked its way in, focusing on my breathing. I tried to let the pain wash over me, forcing my body to stay relaxed.

Cole moved closer, laying his hand right above my knee.

"How long does this usually take?" he asked. "I'm going to need to leave soon so I can work on tomorrow's plans."

Even with the pain, I couldn't help but laugh a little.

"I knew you worked at it," I said.

He squeezed my leg slightly. I found myself focusing more on his touch than the procedure.

Then it was done. Doc was pulling the needle out. I got off the bed, a little stiffer than normal, pulling my waistband up.

Cole smoothed down my shirt as if it were his job, standing beside me, almost hovering.

I should've moved away. But I stood there. So did he.

"Before you go, I need a word," the doctor said, jarring me out of the moment.

I took a step away from Cole, realizing that not only was I getting a little too comfortable with him but that we had someone watching us as well. "Yeah, of course."

Cole moved toward the door. "I'll wait outside for you."

I nodded.

The doctor shut the door.

"What's up?" I asked, knowing whatever it was, it wasn't good.

"Your numbers don't look good. We've been doing everything we can, but we're losing ground faster and faster. Your body is starting to lose this fight. Might be time to get your affairs in order."

How was it that my body would give up when I wasn't anywhere near ready? Why couldn't I will it to keep trying?

I bit my lip and nodded, holding all the frustration back. I'd been telling myself that the increase in coughing recently was a cold or a nasal drip from allergies. I'd gone through several explanations, excuses, and lies to myself. I'd become an expert on explaining things away, but every time I felt that familiar burning in my chest, I knew.

It wasn't the end of the world anymore, right? There was Merlin, whatever that might entail. When push came to shove, I knew I'd take any chance. I'd never been a quitter, and that would be the ultimate forfeit. I didn't have it in me.

"Thanks for the warning."

Cole was leaning on his truck when I came out. He walked around, opened my door, and gave me a boost into the seat.

He got in and began driving to my house without asking. He didn't stay silent for long.

"It doesn't matter what the doctor thinks," Cole said, driving a little faster than normal.

Doc had pretty much broadcast his intentions all over his face when he asked to speak to me. Still didn't make me want to talk about it. My possible looming death didn't make excellent small talk.

"You're going to be fine," he said.

"I'm not concerned." Or I was attempting not to be, and damned if I'd cry on his shoulder. When had Cole become my confidant? The one who held my hand at the doctor's? I was letting him in too much, and he was the enemy. This wouldn't lead anywhere good.

He pulled in front of my house.

"Thanks for the ride. I'm good," I said, hopping out before he could follow me.

He wasn't even looking in my direction. Just like that, something else had taken precedent. I shut the door, walking away from the truck by myself, refusing to look back and see what he found so interesting.

22

C *ole*

Sassy walked inside her house as I called Lonzo.

"Who do you have on the assignment? I don't see anyone." I'd already driven through the neighborhood twice and seen no one.

"Frogger and Snooze," he replied, using the code names we used.

"I'm at the location and I don't see them, but there's lots of mosquitos around." Since I'd pulled up there'd were two vampires that I knew weren't from this area, and I could smell the scent of more.

They'd either gotten information on who she was or they were circling because they'd seen her with me too many times. She was officially on their watch list.

It might be a coincidence, but I didn't believe in those. I'd been raised by one of the strongest, fiercest alphas to ever live. He'd drilled many things into me as a young man, and one of them was to treat everything as a threat until proven otherwise.

"How many?" Lonzo asked.

"Enough to stink up the place."

"I'll have a talk with them and put different people on tomorrow."

I pulled my truck around the corner, out of sight of Sassy's as I spotted the two idiots heading back. "Don't bother. I'm going to handle it myself."

I got out of my truck, and they spotted me instantly. They'd been laughing about something a second ago, but all the humor was gone now.

"How many vampires have walked by here since you were on watch?" I asked. These were two of our younger pack members, but that didn't mean they were allowed to act like idiots.

"Just a couple, but not on her street," Frogger said. He'd gotten that code name because he was hooked on the old video game.

"Her house is on a dead end with one other house. No one is going to be so obvious as to walk right up to it."

Frogger turned so red that even the tips of his ears were crimson. Snooze was looking at his shoes. There were muffled apologies.

"What about yesterday?" I asked.

"None," Frogger said.

Too bad I didn't trust their information. "I want every single vampire that comes past this house logged."

"We got it. We're sorry. We just went for a quick coffee and a piss," Frogger said.

"You don't need to hold hands for that, do you? Next

time, go alone, or you're going to find yourself without a pack. I need people I can rely on. Not this crap."

"Got it," Snooze said.

"Yeah, sorry."

I left, but I'd be back soon. It was clear this wasn't a job I could trust anyone with. If there had been a problem, what then? Would they have noticed? There were only two ways I'd feel comfortable going forward: Sassy would either have to move to my place or I'd be moving to hers.

I dropped my bag by Sassy's back door and started unpacking the groceries. If I was going to stay here, I didn't want to have to call out every time I wanted a drink or a snack. Wouldn't kill her to eat a little bit healthier, either. The woman existed on caffeine, protein bars, and the occasional egg.

I unpacked the groceries and started dinner, knowing she probably hadn't eaten. She was walking around upstairs for a few minutes before she decided to greet me, even though she knew I was here. The new wiring was rigged up.

She stopped just inside the kitchen, her brow furrowing as her gaze shot to where I was cooking, a bag of still-unpacked groceries on the counter beside me. The lines grew deeper as her attention shifted back to my bag by the door.

"Why are you in my kitchen cooking, and why does it look like you don't plan on leaving?" She was pointing at my things as if she couldn't quite put everything together.

"Safer."

"Safer? Safer than what?"

"Safer with me here than not."

"I installed all the new surveillance already."

"It's not enough." The truth was that she wasn't capable of safeguarding her home from what might be coming.

"This is *my* house. You can't just move in."

"For the next few weeks, it'll be our house," I said, using the fork I was cooking with to emphasize my point.

She marched over to me and shoved my shoulder but didn't budge me.

"You are not moving in just to give me a hard time," she said.

"I'm cooking over an open flame. It's not safe to get physical." She was right about one thing. I did like to poke at her for no reason I could quantify, other than enjoying when her feathers got in a fluff.

"We have a deal. That doesn't mean you get to barge into my place whenever you want. I won't have it."

"We *do* have a deal, and I now have an even bigger vested interest in your well-being. This place, alone as you are, is not safe." Especially with the vampire traffic passing by lately. No way was that a coincidence. I didn't believe in them.

She was staring at me like she wanted to run me through with the knife on the cutting board. It might've been easier to tell her about the vampires, but she didn't need any more stress than she was already under, especially being sick.

"I either stay here or you can move into my place."

"I'm not moving in with you." She took a step back as if that were a worse fate. It was. Her place might be smaller, but it was much more comfortable. There was nowhere to go in Donovan's house where there wasn't a servant stalking your every move.

"Which bedroom should I take?" I asked.

"Did you not hear me? None."

"Top room to the right should work out fine." I flipped the scallops and added a little more butter and oil to the pan. "You hungry? I made you some."

The anger on her face flickered to interest as she took a glance at the pan. The scallops were caramelized perfectly. I wasn't much of a cook, but I did have specialty dishes.

"You really think this is going to work out?" she asked. "You really want to piss me off and then sleep under my roof?" She lifted a brow as if she were a serious threat to me.

I smiled and then leaned close, my stubble grazing her cheek. "Come near my bed tonight and we'll see what happens."

She jerked back, her heart thudding, and it wasn't from fear. She took a few more steps back as the anger she was so intent on portraying slipped. "How do you know how to cook?"

"Because when things went to complete shit for a while during the takeover, and everything ground to a halt, I preferred not to exist on protein bars." I put some scallops on her plate and handed her a fork.

She might still be glaring, but she didn't let it ruin her appetite.

23

C ole

Sassy was bent over the table, looking at some of the images that had come in from Pavro's. My attention kept slipping back to her bent head with that pink streak of hair that fell and grazed her chin. When I first saw her, I'd thought she had a thing for pink. Then I'd seen her day after day, almost every day for weeks. Not once had she worn pink, except for what I suspected were loaner sweatpants when I picked her up at Louis'. She didn't fuss with her hair much, either. I watched her take a scissor to her long locks, chopping them haphazardly, keeping them long enough to pull out of her face but not long enough to get in the way.

But that pink streak was always there. It would fade a little and be back bright as ever the next day.

I reached out, feeling the strands between my fingers.

She froze and then glanced at me.

"What's it for?" I asked, letting the lock drop.

"I like pink." She took a sip from the glass of wine next to her as she forced her attention back to the images.

There wasn't a speck of pink anywhere in her house. She never wore pink. Her nails were bare, and her toenails were a shade of purple so dark they looked black.

"You do?" I asked.

She looked up again. "I do."

"You could simply say it's personal."

She leaned back in her chair and took another sip of wine. Along with food, I'd had a few cases of wine delivered. We'd had some with the scallops and she'd been keeping pace with me ever since, as if she were on a mission.

Whatever was going on, she wanted to tell me. I could sense her need.

"Appease my curiosity and I'll get you another case of this wine before I leave," I said.

"I liked you better when you sent your goons out to do all the talking." She smiled at her own joke. She took a sip, leaving me hanging for a minute. "Two cases."

"Done." I couldn't take my eyes off her. The soft evening light made her skin glow and her eyes that much more seductive. She was loyal like a shifter. It shouldn't matter to me that she was dying, that maybe my plan wouldn't work out, but it did. I liked her, and the more I found out, the more I liked.

"I don't *hate* pink, but I'm not a fan. It's a remembrance for my mother. It was her favorite color, and when Pen and I were little, she used to put us in matching pink dresses all the time. Some people get tattoos. I dye a lock of hair. It's a little bit of pink for her." She grabbed the bottle, filling her glass again and staring over the rim, a haunting look in her eye. "Today is the anniversary of her death."

"I'm sorry." I wanted to drag her into my arms and fix everything, but that wasn't possible.

"If he'd drunk from me first, she'd still be here. I tried to get him off her, but..." Her voice was shaky as she tried to finish and then gave up.

She sat still for another few seconds, drawing in a long breath, and then another, getting herself back together.

"I don't know why I'm boring you with this." She put her glass down, getting up from the table, looking to retreat to lick her wounds.

I grabbed her wrist, tugging her down onto my lap, and not because I wanted to sleep with her. Well, that wasn't completely true. I always wanted her. It was as if I had an on button when she was around and no off option. All I wanted to do right now was comfort her, and the feeling was more intense than anything I'd ever felt.

She shifted, tense.

I pulled her against me, not saying anything. Her chest heaved unevenly, but she was too tough to cry in front of me, or probably anyone. How many times had I seen a woman's tears and cringed? Wanted to get away from them as fast as possible? Yet here I was, refusing to let this tough but fragile human woman leave, wishing she'd cry and let it out if it helped her. I did the only thing left I knew how to do: I kissed her.

I feathered my lips over her cheek, leaving a trail of kisses until I got to her mouth. I traced her lips with mine, softly sucking on her lower one until her eyes opened.

Her gaze held mine, silently asking what was happening, because whatever it was, this wasn't leading to fucking. This was something altogether different.

The realization seemed to frighten her more than the idea of fucking me when we first met.

Her eyes dropped to my lips, her heart beating fast before she pulled away. "It's been a long night. I'm going to get some sleep."

She stumbled off my lap. I didn't try to stop her, stunned myself. What the fuck was wrong with me?

"Yeah, that's a good idea."

24

S *assy*

Mattie walked into headquarters at eight a.m., saw me at the planning table, and stopped short. "When did you get here?"

"Not that long ago." If an hour wasn't that long.

After last night, it had become very clear that if Cole was there, I needed to be out of the house as much as possible. The proximity was beginning to do strange things to our relationship, like making him seem as if he weren't ultimately the enemy, which he was. Making me think that he was perhaps a decent guy, which he wasn't.

Mattie walked over and looked down at the photos and notes spread out. Pavro was as untouchable as they said. No one got close to him, ever.

He moved some photos around, leaning over the plans, shoulder to shoulder. I'd never noticed how close he stood to me until Cole brought him up. Getting involved with Mattie would be so easy, effortless. Unfortunately, as Cole had pointed out, it wasn't going to happen.

"Any ideas? This looks pretty bad to me, but you see things I don't," Mattie said.

I rested my elbows on the table, leaning my chin in my hand. "Only one. The option of last resort."

Mattie shook his head and straightened away from the table. "There's no other way?"

I turned toward him, wondering how he could ask such a thing. The risks were high. The only time I suggested something like that was when it was the only way to take a vampire out.

"I don't see another option, or I'd say it."

"Your new *partner* isn't going to like it either." There was an edge to his pronunciation of "partner" that I wasn't going to address.

The door opened, and Cole walked in, followed by Lonzo and Derek.

"What aren't I going to like?" Cole asked. "I'm assuming he was referring to me, unless you have some other new partnership I'm unaware of."

I'd come here to think clearly, and now he was here too. Plus, I was going to have to defend a decision that I wasn't ready to tell him about, especially not with this group.

Cole walked across the room as if he already owned this place. It was as if he had some innate ownership of everything around him. Like the universe decreed it all should be his. Mattie, on the other hand, was looking like the kid on the playground who kept getting his toy stolen.

"Oh shit." I turned to Mattie. "I forgot I told Vicki I'd

run wiring over to her place. Can you do it? She's got a side job that's due."

Mattie looked over my shoulder to Cole, clearly unwilling to be the first person to leave the party.

I laid a hand on his arm. "I really need you to do this."

I would've done a lot more to get him out of the room as I laid out the details to Cole. I didn't need them fighting, or worse, agreeing it wasn't a good idea.

"Yeah, sure," Mattie said, with a hesitant nod.

I went to the corner and handed him a box that I hadn't planned on dropping off until tonight.

Mattie was out the door and Cole was glowering in my direction. I couldn't win with these men.

I did the only thing I knew how to do: work.

"If you want Pavro, I'm going to have to lure him out or get him to let me in. I'm not getting a bomb in there. His windows are bulletproof, and he barely leaves his house." I pushed the papers toward where Cole was standing near the planning table.

I crossed my arms and shrugged. He'd probably complain about something, how it wasn't reliable and was hard to plan. It would be all the reasons we didn't do it much but there were no other options. Pavro never left his house, which was set up like an attractive aboveground bunker.

Cole leaned his hands on the table. "How exactly do you plan on doing that? You're just going to walk up and say, 'Hey, follow me to your death'?" He added a falsetto giggle.

"Not quite like that. More along the lines of 'hang out with me for a few minutes. I've got something you might be interested in.' I've done it before, and from the intel we do have, he's susceptible to that kind of bait. I can get him, or at least get an invite in."

"You're going to lure him out with you or willingly go in there alone, and then let him feed on you? That's what you're saying? That's your great plan that you've had weeks to figure out? You're going to act like a hooker and then hope he doesn't kill you before he dies?"

The lower and calmer his voice got, the more apparent his anger became. Derek and Lonzo stepped back as if afraid they'd somehow get pulled into the fight.

Anyone with a brain would know it wasn't a good idea, but it was all there was.

"I'm not saying it's ideal, but I agreed to kill him. This is how I have to do it." I threw my hands up.

"And you think letting him feed off you is the way to do it?"

"Yes." It wasn't like I enjoyed it. But sometimes it had to happen.

"You become dinner then watch him drop dead?"

Talk about beating a dead horse. If Cole wasn't crazy about the plan so far, he was really going to hate this part. "Ideally. With the really strong or old ones, it might take a little longer."

"How often have you done this?"

"I don't know. If I'm going to die of a disease, though, it's a pretty good one to have in certain circumstances."

"How many times?"

"I don't keep count."

"I want a number."

"Well, you're not getting one." I didn't know myself. After the first few times using that method of killing, I'd focused on not thinking about it at all. After a while, I'd lost count.

The best I could do was guess, and that wasn't a figure I'd admit to anyway. "If that's what it takes to get the job done, then I do it because I'm not feeding them. I'm killing them."

He crowded me back until we breathed the same air and the chill in the room turned to boiling heat.

He was going to be a real handful to work with if he had a fit every time things didn't go according to plan.

"Look, part of this business is pivoting when things take an unexpected turn," I said. "I thought you'd know about this type of thing."

"It's not happening this time."

"You wanted me because I'm good. Why bother if you're not going to listen to me and let me do the job?"

His jaw twitched. "No."

It didn't matter. I didn't need him to get it done. He'd hired me for a job, and Pavro was going to die.

Cole's eyes locked on to mine like he could read my every thought. He probably could. I wasn't hiding them well.

"You try to do this and I'll send my guys to level your place tomorrow, and put you under lock and key at the mansion, until I can get you shipped off to your sister."

It was such a ridiculous threat that it was hard to fathom. Not to mention his guys wouldn't do that anyway. I glanced at his two *enforcers*.

"Yeah. Because we will," Lonzo said, puffing his chest out.

"Fuck yeah we will," Derek said, trying to look stern when Cole glanced behind him.

Cole was their alpha, and even *he* wasn't sure they'd follow his orders.

"You will do it," Cole said.

"Of course! That's what we said. We'll go do it now if you want," Lonzo added.

Derek nodded so hard he looked like he was going to concuss himself.

This was just getting out of hand. Did we really need to pretend? I should let Cole know that if he wanted to raze my place, he'd have to go do it himself. These two weren't going to.

What if he found another two that would? He had a large pack. Not all of them knew me, and some knew me and hated me. That wouldn't be good either.

Not to mention that he'd probably give Derek and Lonzo tons of shit for not doing it. Would he kick them out of the pack? That would be horrible. They'd be devastated, and I'd have had a hand in it.

Cole turned back to me, and Lonzo put his fist to the corner of his eye, like he wanted me to pretend to cry or something. Fuck that. I was not going to cry.

Derek was making a praying motion with his hands, as if that man believed in a god to pray to.

Cole's bullying might not get me to cave, but apparently I was highly susceptible to guilt.

I guess I didn't *have* to try to kill Pavro that way. It wasn't exactly my best plan. It was the only thing that I'd come up with, but if I was going to tank Derek and Lonzo, I could keep thinking for at least a few more days. It wouldn't change much.

"Look, I don't agree with you, but I'm not completely opposed to compromising. I could definitely think it over for a while longer. There may be another way."

"Good, because I'd prefer not to have to level your house," Cole said.

I looked down at the pictures I'd stared at for hours

already while Cole took the opportunity to view the wall of eyes.

Derek and Lonzo made their way closer to me, thanking me with their eyes. I waved them off, silently telling them not to worry about it. The whole time, I could feel Cole's attention on us.

Wait a minute. I was getting duped.

"Guys, can I have a minute with Cole?"

They looked at each other as if saying, *She wants to be alone with him?* Derek shrugged, and then they hightailed it out of there.

"You ass. You're using my sympathy for them to control me." He was using the guys to keep me in line. He was playing us all.

Cole turned from the screens and smirked. "And?"

"It's not happening anymore. That was it, your last freebie." I piled my photos, ignoring Cole as he crossed the room to me. He stopped next to me at the table, his arm nearly brushing mine. He was standing almost as close to me as Mattie had, but with Mattie I barely noticed. With Cole I couldn't focus on anything else.

"See, you're misunderstanding something here. I don't deal in idle threats. If they won't do what I order, I'll kick them out of the pack and replace them with people who will."

"You're going to leverage your people against me?" I asked, turning to face him and using that as an excuse to gain a few inches of separation so my brain could think of something other than him.

"Why not? It works so perfectly."

"Don't you feel a little bad about what you're doing to them?" This was why I couldn't let myself get involved with him. Heartless to the core.

"No. They should toughen up. If they weren't so soft, I couldn't do it," he said, like someone with a burned piece of charcoal in their chest.

I shook my head, shifting my attention back on the papers in front of me as something in his stare became unsettling. Sometimes I imagined I had Cole in this neat little box that was a few steps away and safely locked. Then he'd look at me like he was now and make me remember exactly who I was dealing with. Someone utterly unpredictable, with very few lines he wouldn't cross.

"How many times *have* you let them feed off you?" he asked, his voice soft and utterly alarming.

I shrugged him off.

He took a hank of my hair, tugging my head back, forcing me to look at him.

"That's none of your concern," I said, giving as good as I got.

This wasn't about answers, or not *just* about that. For someone disgusted by my sickness, he still wanted me.

"What do you plan on doing, fucking the answer out of me?" I asked, goading him as his gaze went to my mouth.

I wanted him more than I'd ever wanted something in my life, but I couldn't forget how he'd walked away from me that very first night, left me standing there like an idiot. How he'd paraded his floozies about after he rejected me.

"You don't want me, remember? I'm the *sick* girl."

He released me immediately and stepped back. "It's not what you think," he said, coldness creeping into his eyes, the burning heat gone.

"You mean my being sick had nothing to do with that

night? Because I would've bet a million bucks it's the very reason you walked away from me."

I moved to the wall away from him, and his arm shot up, blocking my path.

"Nothing in life is that simple."

"Well, guess what's really simple? You had your chance and didn't take it. I don't give seconds." Not even for men like him. He'd nearly stripped me of my pride the first time we met. I wouldn't let him finish the job by taking all of me. I had very little left to my name, and what I did have, I protected.

25

C *ole*

The sound of wheezing drifted into my room. My body tensed as if I were about to go to war. Sassy had already been sick, and then that asshole Louis hosed her down, leaving her hanging and freezing. It was the last thing she needed. I shouldn't have beaten him. I should've killed him. I should go find him now and finish him off.

I turned on my side, away from the noise, as if that did anything. I could've heard her a block away.

My promise to Donovan didn't cover sickness. This wasn't my issue.

I got out of bed, making my way down the hall. The house was freezing. I'd put some more wood in the stove. That was all I could do for her, and then I'd go crash at the club, away from here. I'd send one of the guys over to watch the house. It would be fine for the night. I never should've moved in here in the first place. There were more reliable men in the pack that could handle this.

The porch was bare. There was no wood. I'd had a bundle dropped off yesterday. Why was there no wood? Where did it go?

Did I need to ask? It was scattered to a dozen different homes already, with Bobby and Betty and the kid with no front tooth. I'd have to get more delivered in the morning with the threat of death if she gave it away, stubborn ass that she was.

I grabbed my phone from the counter and called Merlin. "How much longer?"

"I'm working on it. Every chemistry is a bit different. It takes a while to figure out what tweaks need to be made," Merlin said.

"Figure it out soon, or there won't be any tweaking to do, and there won't be any payment, either."

"I'm going as fast as I can. It's not that I wouldn't prefer a—"

I hit end. The more time he had to complain and justify it, the likelier he'd start believing it, not that it wasn't true. It just didn't matter. She didn't have that much more time.

I'd done what I could. It was time to put some distance between us and let it play out however it would.

I went upstairs to grab my truck keys, and made it almost past her room, almost past the wheezing. My steps slowed.

This was not my problem. I couldn't *will* her to stay alive. I'd find another way to kill Pavro. Odds were she wouldn't be able to get to him anyway. Lately I was finding myself more obsessed with keeping her alive than killing him.

Keep. Walking.

I made it to my room. If this place wasn't so damned cold...

Her wheezing filled the house. There was no getting away from it. I grabbed my keys and headed back down the hall.

This was not my problem.

Keep. Fucking. Walking.

Her wheezing grew louder.

Fuck. Why wasn't I walking? I needed to get out of here, not crack open her door quietly to not disturb her sleep.

She was curled on her side, her face barely visible in the cocoon of covers. I padded across the room, not making a sound. Not that she could hear anything over the racket she was making struggling to breathe. I stood over her, watching her small form, not used to seeing her look so vulnerable. If she were awake, she would be mortified. She'd puff out her chest and declare she needed no one. She was so good at it that she fooled almost everyone, including her sister.

I wished she could fool me.

I walked to the other side of the bed, crawling in slowly, not looking for a fight. If she woke, her claws would surely come out.

Inch by inch, I settled in closer, until I was sharing the same blanket and filling her space with my heat.

She shifted, a soft moan escaping her lips, making me wonder what she sounded like in bed.

No. Don't think of that. She's sick.

She shifted toward me like a heat-seeking missile, still on the edge of sleep. Her cheek found my chest and her hand fisted on my shirt as her leg hooked over mine.

I didn't cuddle, wasn't in my make-up, but something about her curled up around me felt right, probably because I hadn't fucked her. That's all this was.

Sassy sank further under the covers, cuddling into the warmth behind her because it was freezing in the room. The sun streamed into the windows, and her lids flickered open.

Then she froze. She turned around with a fist to my chest—not that she had much fight in her.

"What are you doing in my bed?"

"It was the only way to shut you up last night when you were wheezing as loud as a damned diesel engine. You're welcome," I said, getting up and noticing how red her cheeks were getting. "I'll go put coffee on. We've got errands to run."

I made it downstairs, listening to her breathing smooth out. She never got right out of bed after a bad night. The exhaustion weighed her down for half the morning, and last night was the worst I'd seen her.

I grabbed the eggs out of the fridge and then picked up my phone.

"I'll be out this morning. Handle the business at the club and tell the crew I'll be with the assignment, so no need to go until later."

"Everything okay?"

"Fine."

I finished the eggs, poured some coffee into the smiley face, and carried it back to her room, afraid she wasn't going to make it down.

I put the plate down on her nightstand and handed

her coffee before I moved to her dresser, digging out a pair of jeans and a sweater.

"Do you need help getting dressed?"

"Most definitely no," she said, dragging herself into a sitting position. "Where are we going?"

"I have a couple places to run by today and want you to tag along."

She nodded without pressing me for details or giving me a hard time about dictating her day. It said a lot about how sick she was.

I tossed jeans and a sweater onto the bed beside her.

"Get dressed," I said, and left her room.

26

S assy

Cole pulled in front of the darkened doors and windows in the strip mall, also known as my doctor's office.

"I thought you wanted me to see something at the club? Why are we here?"

"Because you could barely breathe last night, and your cure isn't ready yet. We need a stopgap measure."

"Cole, he can't do anything for me." A fresh surge of humiliation was building. How bad was I last night? I wanted to jump out of the truck and run. When I'd woken and he was in my bed, I thought for a second it was because he wanted me. I'd been indignant, at least outwardly, even as something inside grew warm and excited. That was before he told me he'd heard me breathing.

And now this. I was having a hard time even arguing past the lump growing in my throat.

"And yet he's going to do something anyway," he said.

I was still sitting in the truck as he walked around and opened my door.

I didn't budge. "I get it. You're afraid I'll die before I take care of things, but there's a limit to what he can do." My eyes were burning at the thought of Cole dragging in the poor dying girl to get a short-term fix.

"We don't need a lot more time, just a little. Now are you getting out of the truck, or do I need to carry you in there?"

He would, too. Make a spectacle in front of all the staff, as if I were too weak to walk. He wouldn't budge, waiting to drag me out of the truck. There was no way out of this. He was going to force this scene. The quickest way to be done was to let him hear it for himself.

"I will come of my own accord, but don't throw a fit when he says he can't do anything." I waited to hear him answer, barely able to bring myself to look at him.

"I don't throw fits. I *kill* people. There's a marked difference," he said. "And he's doing something."

That might be funny if he was kidding. Nothing about the steeliness of his eyes or the set of his shoulders gave a humorous impression. He looked more like the ax man walking over and looking for a couple coins to make it a clean death.

I slid off the seat before Cole decided he would drag the doctor out here and chop his head off for the wrong reason. Anything was possible with him. I knew because, after all, he'd shown up and moved in with me.

"Whatever your preferred terminology, don't do what you do to the doctor," I said.

"As long as he falls in line, it'll be fine."

The psycho grabbed my arm, steadying me when I wobbled even as he threatened the doctor with death.

"Sometimes I think there's something wrong with you," I said.

He brushed that off like a man who'd heard it one too many times.

He tried to open the door, which was locked. Then he took a fist to it, rattling the structure.

"Can you not break the door?" I leaned against the building.

"If they answer soon, sure," he said, pausing to look at me. Then he banged even harder.

Cole was about to take his fist to the glass when the door opened.

A shifter I'd never spoken to but seen as one of the nameless faces swung it open.

"Did we do something?" he asked breathlessly, as if he'd run across the building.

"It's me," I said, leaning over so he could see me.

"You're here for the doctor? We weren't expecting you." He was white-knuckling the side of the door, and there were a few more of the familiar unnamed staring behind him.

"We are. Get out of the way," Cole said, wrapping an arm around my waist and dragging me along with him. He placed a hand on the door, and the nameless shifter skidded back like he was a paper doll.

"It's okay, Roger," Doc said as he walked over.

The doctor sized us both up, taking a little longer on me.

"Come in the back," Doc said, leading the way.

I wasn't going to take a seat on the table, and then Cole lifted me and put me there anyway.

"You know, you can be exceptionally pushy," I said.

"You haven't seen anything yet," he replied, smiling.

"So what's going on?" Doc asked. "I wasn't supposed to see you for another few weeks."

"She needs a treatment."

The doctor was already shaking his head before Cole finished. "I can't. It's too soon."

"Do it anyway."

"Cole, he said he can't," I said.

"Why not?" Cole demanded.

"Because it could make her sicker," Doc replied. "I'm transplanting bone marrow into her. The more I do it, the more her body is likely to reject it. It's already rejecting it to a certain degree."

"She's getting sicker. Do it anyway."

"I'm a doctor. I can't knowingly harm her."

"I'm fine," I said. "I don't—"

Cole stepped in between me and the doctor. "She's not fine. Do. It."

"Cole..." I grabbed his arm because nothing I was saying seemed to make a difference.

Cole turned on me. "You were barely breathing last night. What happens tonight?" He leaned closer. "We need more time. Just a little. Without this, you might not have it. It's worth the chance."

I swallowed hard, nodding. Whatever his motivations, Cole wanted to keep me alive almost as much as I wanted to be alive.

"Okay." I nodded and turned to the doctor. "Do it."

Doc shook his head again. "I'm not sure what it'll do. It might make you worse."

He didn't get it. Any worse and I'd be dead. "He's right. Do it."

"You heard her. Do it," Cole said, looking as if he were ready to get the needle and load it up himself if needed.

The doctor hesitantly took a step toward the door. "If this goes bad, I'm telling Donovan you forced me."

"Tell him whatever you feel like, but get her medicine now." The doc was halfway out the door when Cole said, "And bring the epidural."

The doctor walked out, willing to do just about anything Cole said, it seemed.

Cole turned to me. "Let's face it, you can barely walk. Skipping the epidural isn't doing anything for you today."

I might not be able to put up much of a fight today, but without the epidural, running was still an option. With it, I'd be a sitting duck.

"I'm giving you my word that I won't leave your side until it wears off," he said.

I felt myself nodding before I'd even given it serious thought, as if my gut answered for me. When had I decided Cole was trustworthy? My gut was obviously tanking along with the rest of my body.

He'd probably keep me alive for an afternoon. He needed me, after all. Instead of fighting over it, I let myself slump against the doctor's table with Cole standing watch, knowing I was going to have to rely on him.

ole

I glanced at my buzzing phone.

Need to talk. ––Sassy

Ever since the other day, I'd been leaving early and getting back late. I wasn't avoiding her so much as putting some much-needed distance between us. I'd never met someone who was more trouble in my life, and I had enough of that without her. I couldn't afford to get pulled further into her issues. I'd gotten her to the doctor, and she was feeling a little better. I'd hold up my end and get Merlin to finish the job. But emotional involvement was not on the table. It complicated way too many things, and what we needed right now was space.

If whatever she had to say was important enough, she'd wait up tonight.

You want your job done, then WE NEED TO TALK. —Sassy

Did she not realize that they might be monitoring the messages? I grabbed my phone and hit her number.

"Do you not remember the conversation about communication?"

"And how would you like me to do that when I don't see you?" she asked. "We need to speak."

It was three in the afternoon. If I went to the house now, it would be the two of us there alone for hours, awake.

"Fine, but I'm busy. Come here. I'll send a car for you."

"I don't need a ride. I have one."

That beat-up hunk of metal she called a bike was far from a ride, especially when it was cold and sleeting.

"I'll send a—"

"I'll be there in a few," she said, and then the phone went to dead air.

I went to call her back and then stopped. There were guys stationed outside of her house. I went to call them but stopped again. If she wanted to ride that metal clunker and kill herself, that was her choice. Her every move was not my responsibility.

Lonzo walked in the office, eyeing me as I poured a drink. He'd been wondering why I was here so much but hadn't figured out how to ask yet. I sipped my bourbon, ignoring his interest.

"We expecting trouble today?" he asked, leaning over, checking out the monitor I was watching.

"No."

He looked from the monitor to me, then back to the monitor, before giving up and walking away.

Lonzo was still snooping around twenty minutes later when Sassy rode up on her clunker, her cheeks red from the wind.

The guys at the door opened it before she got close enough to knock, and then stared at her ass as she walked in. I was going to have to have a talk with them.

"Sassy just got here," I said. "Go disable her bike and don't make it obvious you screwed with the engine. Have Derek offer her a ride when it won't start."

Lonzo cleared his throat. "Got it," he said, heading out.

Sassy strode into the office. She gave Lonzo a smile as she walked in. He returned it in an invitational way. I had the urge to punch him in the throat before he shut the door.

She dropped onto the couch, her jeans snug and her shirt clinging to all the right spots. I needed to get her out of here fast.

"Well? What did you need to discuss?"

There was a slight furrowing of her brow before she smoothed it out. She probably wasn't used to getting rushed out of anywhere by a man, not the way she looked. It was the exact reason I wanted her gone.

I'd finally come to the realization that I was going to either have to avoid her or fuck her to get it out of my system. If I was sure it would evict her completely from my thoughts, I might just opt for fucking her and be done with it. One thing was becoming clear: as far as Sassy was involved, the outcome was never a foregone conclusion. She had a way of shaking things up in the most volatile of ways.

"I've looked over my notes, plans, details, everything I could get on Pavro," she said. "You didn't like my idea of luring him out, but I need more access. You didn't pick an easy target."

I shook my head. "You said you needed a list of equipment, thousands of dollars of surveillance. I got you what you needed. Now you're saying you still can't produce? I'm starting to think I overestimated you." I turned, looking at the monitor on the floor of the club, knowing how bad that last comment would sting. But we weren't friends or anything else. She was an employee, and I'd treat her like any other. If she couldn't handle it, she could go cry to her sister.

"I can handle it fine if you'd get the hell out of the way. You're the one that needs everything done *just so* for whatever reason I can't comprehend," she shot back, with the bluntness of a mallet.

I wanted to laugh. The bourbon must be blurring my judgment if I thought she'd shrink away from a little criticism. No, if you threw a punch her way, she'd swing back twice as hard. Made me want to her that much more.

"I'm assuming you had some idea when you came here?" I asked.

She got off the couch and perched on the corner of my desk. "I need to get inside. It's the only way, and Pavro never leaves the house. You want him dead? You need to get me in."

"And how do you think I'm going to do that? Or are we back to marching you up to the door like a whore again? I nixed that plan for a reason. It sucked." And fuck Pavro. If I wasn't going to touch her, damned if anyone else would get to, not even for a few minutes.

She was staring at me as coolly as I'd received her. She really did give as good as she got.

"There's word out he's having a party, and there'll be shifters invited. I know humans are sometimes taken as dates. You need to get me in with one of the shifters attending. I'm going to bring a vial of my blood and spike his drink if I can."

She didn't want to be Pavro's whore or meal anymore, but she thought she was going to prance in on the arm of another shifter? Hang all over one of my fellow alphas all night?

"No," I said.

"No, you can't, or no, you won't because that doesn't meet your standards either?" she asked, her voice growing sharper by the second.

"Do you know his parties tend to be orgies?" I asked.

"Yes. I'm not saying I have to stay for the festivities. I just need to get in. Do you want this Pavro guy dead or not? Because if you do, you're going to need to start working with me. You talk a big game about being a team as you sit on your ass and shoot down every idea available. I need to get close if you want him dead." She stood up and walked away, her hands on her hips. She'd clearly had lost all patience with me.

"Your plans are all reckless and idiotic. Give me something good and we'll discuss it."

"It's not reckless. There's nothing that's going to be smooth with this target." She walked toward the door. "Let me know if you ever want to get anything done. Otherwise there's no point in this."

The door slammed into the wall as she left. I turned the monitor back onto the shot of the parking lot as she was trying to get the bike running. Derek was walking over.

Lonzo entered the office, shutting out the noise from the club. "She left in a huff, and she didn't even know her bike wasn't going to start yet."

"We aren't seeing eye to eye on a few things."

He took a few seconds before he added, "Like how to get to Pavro?"

"Yes, that does seem to be a problem."

"Are her plans that bad?"

"Yes."

I leaned back, rubbing my jaw, the stubble longer than usual, since I'd been leaving her house as early as possible. Were her plans *that* bad? Maybe not, but somehow when she suggested those things, they seemed outlandish. If it had been anyone but her walking in here today suggesting that, would I still have said no?

Of course I would've.

"What are they?" Lonzo asked.

I shook my head, brushing off the question. Why? Because maybe they weren't so bad.

I *knew* they weren't that bad. They might be the only way to get to Pavro, and I'd wanted to get to him for a long time.

She wasn't going without me, though.

"Do we know anyone going to Pavro's party?" I asked.

"I'm sure I could dig up some names. You want me to get an invite list?"

"Yes. I'm going to need to tag along with one of them."

Lonzo let out a long laugh. "This should be interesting."

28

S *assy*

My phone rang, Cole's name flashing on the screen. He *never* called. Everything with him was said in person, or relayed from him by a different person, but still *in* person.

It had been a little tougher lately, since he seemed to be avoiding me. He came in after I was asleep and left before I woke. Besides our meeting at the club at my insistence, I hadn't spoken to him at all. Ever since I got sick that night, he'd been putting as much distance between us as possible. He'd remembered I was the sick girl and someone to steer clear of. Well, fuck him.

I didn't answer.

The phone rang again.

I muted it and then turned on the *do not disturb* option.

Five minutes later, Derek pounded on my back door.

I opened it. "What does he want?"

"Can you answer the phone?" he asked, the begging face forming.

"For him? No." I shut the door on him before I got sucked into another guilt trip.

Half an hour later, Cole strode into the kitchen. He walked over to the counter and put a new phone down.

"Your phone seems to be broken. I brought you a new one."

I stared at the new phone like it was a poisoned apple. "I don't need a new one. It's not broken." I coughed into my fist. "You should leave, because I feel a hell of a coughing fit coming on."

He leaned on the counter, looking at me with a bored nonchalance that didn't match the heat in his eyes. "So I guess that means you won't be able to go to Pavro's tonight?"

My internal record skipped off its track. "You're getting me in? How? Who's taking me?"

"I am," he said.

"You couldn't get someone else to take me?" I asked, not one to let anything go. He'd been avoiding me like what I had was catchy, and now he was going to escort me?

"I didn't try. You're not going in there with anyone but me."

"You don't trust anyone else to get the job done, is that it?"

"I'm going to handle the vial of blood, if that's what you mean. You don't need to come if you don't want to," he said. "Because it's your plan, I felt it was only right to give you the option of escorting me."

He didn't need me there, but he was going to take me anyway? He was treating me like a full-on partner in this?

"You sure you're up to that? You'll have to be with me for hours. That's a long time. What if I sneeze or something?" I asked, pushing at him some more. He was acting like being around me wasn't an issue, when it clearly had been. I wouldn't want him to forget what his problem was.

"I think I can manage," he said sarcastically, as if he'd never had an issue with my sickness. "I'll be back at eight. Dress appropriately." He walked out.

My heart banged around my chest as the prospect of what might happen tonight sank in. Pavro might be Cole's target, but he was very high up in the vampire hierarchy, which meant he was automatically on my kill list. Word was he had a considerable say in steering the policies. If I took him down, it would be a huge strike against the powers that be. It would send a clear message from the resistance, because I'd make sure somehow we got the credit, that it was known we could get to even their highest-up.

My adrenaline was pumping the way it did before a job, but this time seemed even more intense. It was just about Pavro. That was it. That was all I could afford it to be—because if the giddiness had anything to do with seeing Cole, or being with him all night, I might as well let Pavro take *me* out for being such an idiot.

I grabbed my phone, ignoring the new, shiny one Cole left behind. It was already four, and I didn't have an outfit that would be trashy enough to sell me being a legitimate hooker.

"Hey, I need you to forget tonight," I said when Vicki picked up.

She was supposed to be casing a new recruit so we

could get a handle on his possible loyalties. There were a lot of people that thought they wanted to be part of the resistance, but few could handle the stress.

"Sure. Why?" she asked.

"I need you to bring me your trashiest dress." One of Vicki's favorite ways to size up a new recruit was to pretend to be interested in them, ply them with drinks, and see if they'd tell all their secrets. It was the exact opposite of how I liked to handle things, which was to stick a blade to their throat, but we all had our ways.

There was a pause, and then a giggle. "One of mine? Oh, I can't wait to hear this one. Be right over."

"And shoes too, just in case nothing I have works."

She was laughing as I hung up.

I fluffed up my hair a little bit more, burying the pink highlight that had started to fade. Details were leaking out about me, and the fewer identifying marks, the better. My mother would surely rather have me alive than sport a remembrance that got me killed.

I stepped back, taking in the whole picture in the mirror. My wardrobe had provocative clothing for all occasions, but nothing like this. This might be even more than needed.

"Do you think it's too much?" I turned sideways, checking all the angles.

"Oh, it's just the right amount for where you're going," Vicki said. "You know the kind of party this is, right? If you're too clothed, you might get booted." She walked over and fluffed my hair a little more.

"I need to look believable, but this is just..." I put my hand to my stomach, turning again.

"A lot? It's definitely that. If Mattie saw you right now, he'd lose his mind." She backed up, eyeing me. "Can't say I'm not curious to see how Mr. Alpha Man finds the view."

"He's not the objective." Didn't matter what Cole thought. He was too busy with his life and avoiding me to care. I barely saw the man anymore, and it was much better that way. We'd probably do this job and that would be the end of it.

"*I* know that." She stepped back, smirking and crossing her arms.

"You think *I* don't? I have zero interest in him in that way."

She scoffed.

"Fine. Maybe there's interest, but I'm not doing that," I said

The sound of a truck pulling up drew my attention to the window. We both looked at him, and then each other.

Vicki turned back to look at me, all kidding gone. "Don't do anything stupid."

"You know I won't."

"Or at least not until after you get the job done," she said, laughing. She dropped on my bed. "I'll let myself out."

I made it outside before Cole reached the door.

He slowed to a stop, letting his gaze run from the spikes on my feet, all the way up my tan legs to where the dress started, barely a few inches past my hips. The neck was high and the sleeves were long, but the dress was nearly sheer, my bra and thong, the only other clothing I wore, showing through. It wasn't that much less than what I'd wear at the beach, but somehow going to a dinner party, even if it did devolve as the night went on, seemed strange. The thin jacket covering me felt like it was doing nothing.

He looked more annoyed than impressed with my outfit, shedding his jacket and handing it to me.

"It is winter," he said, waiting for me to head to the truck.

"You told me to dress appropriately for the occasion. Considering the occasion, this might be a little *too* much," I said. The fact that he couldn't seem to stop looking at me even as we got into the truck was feeling a little bit like revenge. I couldn't even get him to answer the phone because he didn't want to be near the sick girl? *Well, here you go—now you can see what the sick girl is going to be giving to someone else one day.*

29

C *ole*

I glared at the male servant eyeing Sassy as we stood in the mausoleum now in my care. I definitely hadn't missed this place. From her expression upon our arrival here, neither had she.

"Why are we here?" she asked. "They couldn't pick us up at the club or something?"

"Looks better for Alvin. He's a neighboring alpha who's very impressed with money and anyone who has it. He's been trying to form a relationship with our pack, so he was more than willing to bring us along. He's going to Pavro's to enjoy the festivities and believes we are as well."

A limo pulled up the drive. The servant who was now afraid to look in Sassy's direction held the door open for us.

"Keep the jacket on. It's cold," I said. I didn't care if it was a hundred out.

She nodded, inching closer. The act was on from the moment we stepped outside the house.

The driver walked around and opened the car door, and we joined the other couple in the back.

Alvin was all smiles, as if he'd found a kindred soul.

"Cole, I didn't think you were the type to enjoy these parties," he said. "Thought you only associated with vampires for work purposes. So glad you decided to join us."

His date giggled as if it were her job to laugh at anything that came out of his mouth.

"I've heard enough stories to pique my interest." I smiled in return, pretending that not every single cell of my being didn't feel like doing this tonight.

"Perhaps we might swap later," Alvin said, eyeing Sassy.

Sassy smiled, as if the man had a chance at touching her. He didn't.

I draped my arm across Sassy's lap, tugging her legs closer to me. "We'll see how the night goes," I said, knowing how to play the game, even as I wanted to blind Alvin for even looking in her direction.

Sassy had talked about following her gut. I should've followed mine. This wasn't a good plan. My hackles were already rising, and we weren't even to the worst of it.

Alvin began a tirade about the different problems plaguing the territories, how this one wasn't happy with their boundary or allotment of goods, and this one was hogging. It was like the highlight reel of every reason not to be an alpha in an urban district, but I feigned interest until we pulled up to the stately brownstone building. The house was lit from every angle, guests spilling out onto the front stoop in spite of the cold.

I weaved through the crowd, my hand on Sassy's back, wondering once again what I'd been thinking. This wasn't the way I handled business.

It was mostly a vampire crowd, with only sporadic shifters. They all nodded as we made our way past them, and there wasn't one in the bunch I had any desire to talk with.

Even if I hadn't recognized Pavro from photos, I would've known this was his party by the way he held court in the main drawing room.

I nodded in his direction, and he didn't waste any time making his way over to us.

"Cole, am I correct? You're new to the area, right? Took over while Donovan is on an *extended* vacation?"

"You know your district well," I said. Sassy stood by my side with a stupid look on her face, a much better actress than I'd expected.

"Have to. I'm glad you could join us. I know there's tension between our races, but I believe that there are certain joys in life that help bridge that gap."

"I'm hoping to walk across that bridge several times tonight."

Pavro laughed heartily, believing my crap. Important people usually fell for flattery. They were used to being fed it on their daily menu.

"Beautiful date you have."

"Thank you," I said.

Sassy smiled, playing the part of an object to perfection.

"Hopefully I'll see both of you later." He stepped away to greet his other guests, but not before giving us both a once-over. There was word that Pavro swung both ways, and it seemed that was true.

I wrapped an arm around Sassy's waist, telling her without words to stay close. I had a vial of her blood in my jacket pocket. Now it was time to wait for an opening.

Sassy

Cole was waiting for an opening that wasn't coming. Even at ease, as everyone was supposed to be at this party, there were constantly eyes on him. When he'd said they watched shifters, he hadn't undersold it. There was a couple about to have sex on the couch not even ten feet away, and they still couldn't stop watching him.

"Could you get me a fresh drink? I prefer white." I was holding a glass full of my favorite red but was afraid to take more than the tiniest sip.

Cole cupped my neck as he leaned closer. "I hate leaving you, even for a moment," he said, his voice seductive even as his meaning was clear. For anyone watching, we were just a couple flirting.

"Should I go myself?" I asked. I laid a hand on his chest, right over where the vial was in his pocket.

"No. I'll handle it. White, you said?"

I smiled. "Yes."

Cole walked away into the other room where the bar was, drawing eyes with him. Once he was gone, the interest in me waned. He'd probably pick up another set of eyes in the other room. He wasn't going to want to hear this, but I was the one who needed to figure out where to slip my blood. This night was looking like a total bust.

One of the few shifters at the party walked over to me. "Hello, pretty lady," he said, his hand landing on the swell of my hip. "Why don't you come sit beside me in the other room?"

Telling the man to fuck off because he was being forward wasn't in the cards when you were at a party with a bunch of swingers.

"I'm sorry, but Cole likes to be first," I said, knowing that this shifter had seen me walk in with Cole.

"But so do I," he said, smiling. He wrapped his hand around mine and began to drag me toward a room across the hall that didn't have any occupants.

Making a scene wasn't an option, and it wasn't as if I'd get any help from the other guests in this room. An empty room might play to my benefit. Less people would see if I had to knee this guy in the balls.

He continued to tug me forward until we were alone, pulling me in the direction of the couch.

"I'm really going to have to check with Cole. He gets very upset if I don't ask him before sleeping with other people," I said.

The shifter's eyes snapped toward the door, and then a familiar arm wrapped around my waist.

"She's right," Cole said. "No one touches her without my say-so."

I couldn't see his face, but his voice was deep and soft, the way it got when he was on the brink of shifting or ripping someone apart.

The shifter held up his hands. "Sorry. Most people here don't typically care."

"Well, I do." Cole's tone, or the shifter's slightly panicked face, was drawing some attention as people began to linger nearby.

"Enough said. My apologies," the shifter said, making a move to leave us.

"To the lady," Cole said, stopping him cold.

"What?" The shifter squinted, as if he thought he'd heard wrong.

"Apologize to *her*."

"You want me to—"

"*Yes*. Apologize to her."

"It's not necessary." I could feel all the eyes on us. If there was a chance he could've slipped away unnoticed before, he'd shot that to hell. Still, I couldn't help but try to do damage control.

"I disagree," Cole said, staring down the shifter as if this were going to be his last night on Earth if he didn't.

The shifter pressed his lips firmly together for a moment as he visibly came to terms with having to lower himself to such a humbling position.

He shot a last glance at Cole before he said to me, "I'm sorry if I offended you."

I nodded, wanting him to move along and get all the eyes off us. The last thing we needed was any kind of attention. What the hell was Cole thinking?

The man took a step to leave, testing the waters. Then another, before exiting quickly.

I spun in Cole's arm, reaching up to weave a hand through his hair as I spoke.

"Why did you do that? I don't think he meant any harm, and now you might've made everyone else uncomfortable," I said, trying to couch my meaning in innocent enough words for all who might be listening.

"The guy is a rude asshole, and I don't like him. That's the point," Cole said, not softening his words at all.

"But we are at a party."

"I don't care."

I was in a room full of vampires and shifters, my sworn enemies, and I felt as if no one could touch me. Not since the war, and maybe not even before that, had I felt like someone had my back the way this man did right now. It wouldn't last past this night, but it was hard not to revel in it.

My father had always been a weak man. My sister tried to protect me her whole life, but she'd never been the strong one. Smart, amazingly kind, but not tough enough to survive this world, let alone save someone else. She'd nearly gotten herself killed trying to save me. When Donovan stepped up...it had been the first time in years I could sleep deeply.

"What?" Cole grabbed my hand, his other arm curved around my back.

My eyes traveled up his chest, to where his shirt was slightly open with his tan skin showing, up to his chiseled jaw, pausing at his mouth.

"Sassy..."

My gaze finally met his. My pulse was racing, and my breathing was shallow.

I went to pull back, but his grip held me close, his gaze focused on my lips, making it feel like I couldn't breathe at all.

Job. We were here for a job. This wasn't the time for romantic feelings. There would never be a time with this man. We had worlds between us, and nothing was ever going to change that.

"I need a minute to freshen up."

His expression shuttered and his hold grew lax.

I pulled away from him slower than I'd meant. Every inch cost me more willpower than I possessed.

30

S *assy*

I made my way down the hall, looking for the most obvious place a bathroom might be but finding nothing but locked doors.

A human servant approached me. "May I help you, miss?"

"Is there a bathroom I might use?"

"The ones downstairs are currently occupied, but I can show you to one on the upper level if you would like?"

"If you could just tell me where, I'm sure I'll find it well enough."

"Upstairs, third door on your right," he said with a smile.

"Thank you."

I climbed the stairs, and no one seemed to care. No

one was watching or paying attention at all. It was too good of an opportunity to pass up.

Cole thought he could get my blood somewhere that would kill Pavro, but from the moment we entered, there'd been constant eyes on him. Me? I was another useless human. I walked down the hall, passing a bedroom on my right where a vampire was simultaneously feeding and fucking a girl bent over the back of the bed. The vampire stopped and glanced over at me.

"Care to join in?" he asked, blood dripping from his mouth.

"Maybe later," I said. "Already promised for the first round." I pointed down the hall, as if someone were waiting for me, in case he thought to take things into his own hands.

I kept walking, past the open bathroom and several more rooms, knowing enough about the layout to find Pavro's room toward the back of the house. If I could see it from inside, maybe I'd find a vulnerability or somewhere to slip a drop of my blood. Some vampires kept a bottle of human blood on hand for a nightcap.

I scanned the ornate furniture, but there was nothing. Figured. He probably liked it fresh, which was why there were so many human servants roaming around.

"Can I help you?"

I stiffened. It was Pavro himself, and here I was, in the middle of his bedroom.

Fuuuck.

I turned, smiling like I'd planned it this way. "I was hoping to find you."

I forced myself to take a step closer.

His eyes roved over me. "As was I," he said.

I could scream. Cole would come running. He might

try to kill Pavro or die in the process. If he did kill Pavro, there was a den of vampires downstairs waiting to finish him off afterward. There was only one option left. I wasn't getting out of this room without paying a price. And if I was paying, I wasn't doing it for nothing.

I leaned my head to the side, pushing my hair out of the way and making the invitation obvious. Most vampires would feed before fucking. I hoped it held true.

He smiled, his fangs growing.

My heart was beating erratically.

He dipped his head as his arms encircled me like a steel cage.

"What's that scent?" he asked, hesitating. Did he recognize the smell of sickness the way shifters did?

"Do you mean Cole? Oh, or I was taking care of my mother earlier. She's unwell." I tilted my head back. "Am I not desirable? Most other vampires I've been with enjoyed my taste," I said, laying on the stupidity because my life depended on it.

He hesitated for another moment before sinking his teeth in. I gasped at the feeling that I'd never get used to or enjoy. He drew hard from my vein with no restraint, and my legs grew unsteady. Relief and panic warred inside of me. He'd taken the bait, but would I make it through before my blood killed him?

He jerked back, anger seething in his eyes. He was still alive, and he'd figured out that my blood was poison. Had he gotten enough?

He curled his lip back as if he were going to use his fangs to rip my jugular out, gripping my forearms so tight that it felt like my bones might snap.

"You..."

He didn't finish as he dropped to the ground.

I fell against the wall, trying to breathe, lightheaded from how much blood he had taken in those short few seconds. I slid to the floor, trying to fight past the black spots encroaching on my vision.

That was how Cole found me.

He turned and locked the door to the bedroom.

"I…" I lifted a hand toward Pavro and then dropped it.

"Tell me later. Right now, I have to get you out of here."

I could feel the blood still dripping down my neck as he knelt down, tilting my head back. He disappeared into the bathroom and came back, wiping my neck and throat with a towel before placing it on the wound. He took my hand and placed it on top.

"Put pressure on this." He took off his shirt and put it on me, hiding the rest of the blood. "I'm going to tell them you're drunk and fell, in case they smell the blood on you." He scratched my knee. "You're going to have to walk. I'll help you, but if I have to fight our way out, it'll be easier." He hoisted me up.

"I can do it," I said.

My knees nearly buckled, but his arm around my waist wouldn't let me go down.

"Just lean against me and don't turn your head. When we get downstairs, you lift your head slightly and giggle, but don't turn it toward them so they can't see the blood on your neck," he said, then waited for me to agree before he continued. "If I drop you, stay down and behind me. Don't fight. All it will do is distract me. You got it?"

I nodded.

"You don't do anything else, do you hear me?" He lifted my chin so he could look in my eyes.

"I got it. Just get us out of here."

Vulnerable wasn't a feeling I liked, and being this down and out, surrounded by enemies, it was my worst nightmare.

The place was in full swing as we made our way downstairs. I kept the door in focus, as it took all my effort to put one foot in front of the other.

"What happened to your date?" Alvin asked.

"She seems to have imbibed too much and then took a fall."

I forced a giggle out, as I'd been instructed.

"I like a little fight in my woman, so I'm going to walk her out in the cool air so she knows when I'm fucking her. If there's anything left, I'll bring her back for seconds."

Alvin waved his hand. "My driver can walk her outside. No need to bother yourself."

Cole kept his arm wrapped firmly around me, telling me he had no intention of letting go. "No need. I enjoy a little fresh air myself. We'll be back."

We walked toward the door at a leisurely pace. Cole even stopped to take a drink from a passing waiter.

"Need some help with your load?" one of the vampires mingling outside asked.

Cole laughed. "We're fine. Just walking off some of the booze," he said as he continued to steer us around the block.

The minute we were out of sight, his pace changed. My legs could barely keep up, and they were only going through the motions, as Cole carried most of my weight. Another block and he tossed me over his shoulder, hightailing it out of there.

S *assy*

I woke up on the couch in Cole's office at the club, a blanket draped over me. The place was quiet, which meant it was even later, or earlier, than I'd imagined. How long had I passed out for? The sky was still dark, so maybe not that long.

I ignored my heels, which were beside the couch, and padded out of the office, looking for signs of life.

"Heard you had a rough night. Care for a drink?" Lonzo asked at the main bar.

Cole was reclining at a booth, staring at me like he had a bone to pick.

I turned back to Lonzo. "I wouldn't turn it down."

He was already heading over to Cole's booth with another glass and a bottle.

Cole was watching every move as I took the seat opposite him. "You're looking a little better," he said, as if I never should've been in bad shape in the first place.

"I bounce back pretty well."

Lonzo poured us a round, the room quiet except for the slosh of alcohol.

"You really sealed the deal tonight—no holds barred, either," Lonzo said.

"Did what I had to." I wasn't used to talking outside of my group about my unique ability to kill someone, no matter what it took. I wasn't used to this conversation with other races.

Cole didn't say anything, but the heat in his eyes promised a future discussion.

"Well, you got the job done. That's for sure," Lonzo said.

He was right. It was done. The job was over. I stared at my glass, afraid my thoughts were written all over my face. Cole and I had been enemies, and then tacit allies. Would we go back to being enemies again? I gripped my glass, downing the contents before placing it in front of Lonzo for a refill.

"How long have you been at this little side job of yours?" Lonzo asked, topping off my glass.

I'd been evading questions about the resistance for so long that even when someone like Lonzo asked, it was as if I'd lost the ability to speak about it.

"It's okay. He won't repeat anything," Cole said.

"A few years," I said, finding my voice again, immediately wondering why Cole's stamp of approval had loosened me up enough to get the words out.

I was dropping my guard, the one thing I told my crew to never do, yet here I was, getting sloppy with the...

With whatever he was.

Whatever he was? He was the guy who'd just saved me from certain death. If a vampire had found me beside Pavro's body...

"There might be some heat after this if they figure out what killed him." Lonzo glanced at the two of us, made a low whistle, and downed the last of his drink. "I mean, I'm sure there were a lot of people at that party. I'm not sure if they can trace death by poisoning with vampires. They'll instantly suspect Cole, but good luck pinning it on him. They never think it's humans, though. They're too tough to be laid out by a mere mortal," he said, and then laughed.

No one else did. I was too busy thinking through the ramifications if they did decide it had been a human.

Cole seemed to be busy staring at Lonzo. The deadline to that other discussion I was expecting looked like it would be bumped up.

Lonzo stopped laughing. "Well, it's getting late for me. I'll be taking off." He grabbed his jacket and was gone in the next few seconds.

Cole looked at me like we were about to go to war. I got it. He was pissed. Things hadn't gone to plan, but sometimes you had to pivot. His target was dead. But the way he was acting, you'd think he'd just started in the killing business.

"What happened tonight?" he asked.

The room felt like it was shrinking. I glanced at the door.

He shook his head. "What the hell were you thinking?" he asked, as if I were either the stupidest or most stubborn person alive.

All sorts of possible explanations popped into my head, but I settled for the truth.

"I wasn't. I was looking for a bathroom, and the opportunity presented itself. I got caught snooping and it was my only option." I shrugged. There it was. I'd been winging it.

"You should've yelled for me." He reached across the table, grabbing my arm and turning it over. "I had to have the doctor come by to give you a blood transfusion. He might've killed you."

I looked down, seeing a prick mark.

He let go, settling back on his side of the booth.

"If I'd called you, everyone there would've heard and you'd be dead. We'd both be dead. What good would that have done?" I asked, giving him a dose of judgment he'd been dishing out.

He shook his head, but I could see the anger draining. "You're like a damned shifter sometimes."

I shouldn't be flattered—shifters were still my enemy —but I was anyway.

This might be it. Cole would probably leave my life shortly after this. I shouldn't care, but what I should or shouldn't feel didn't matter. I did.

I didn't even know why he wanted Pavro dead. I didn't know so many things.

"Why did you want him killed so badly?" It was obvious Cole didn't want to discuss it, but seeing as I'd killed Pavro tonight, at the risk of my own life, I'd earned the right to ask.

"He had someone close to me killed."

Was it a woman? Had he come here to avenge her? It must have been a heady kind of love to inspire him. What had she been like? Was she a shifter? Probably, and glowing with health. Not a vulnerable human like me.

"Who was she?"

He swirled his drink in his glass. "*He* was a mentor to me, closer to me than my father."

"I'm sorry."

He nodded.

"I thought there were rules against that, you know, that the vampires and the shifters had some sort of agreement that you couldn't attack each other."

"It happened during negotiations, the night before the pact was signed. Once it was, all fights and disagreements prior to the pact were quashed. All future issues had to be brought to the council." He was swirling his bourbon in his glass as if he were transported back in time for a minute.

"Which you couldn't do because it happened right before the signing."

He gave me another nod, looking up at me. This time the emotions raging in him shone clear as day.

He hated the vampires as much as I did.

"That's why you agreed to come here."

It wasn't a question, and he didn't bother answering it.

There had always been something off, some disconnect, something that tugged at me when I saw him walking through the club. Everyone would watch the new alpha in awe, waiting to embrace him, while he seemed to always keep his arms outstretched fully, wanting his distance. Wolf packs didn't act like that. They were tight-knit groups. He demanded their loyalty but didn't want their adoration. He was here for revenge, and maybe that was all.

It shouldn't matter. I shouldn't want to take him into my arms and soothe his pain, a jagged wound I could feel in myself. He was still one of the oppressors, the enemy.

"Now that it's done, what are your plans?"

Cole was going to leave, or he wanted to. But could he if Donovan didn't come back? And Donovan wouldn't be returning. My sister might think this was a trial run, but Donovan knew the risks to her here, even having borne an alpha. If something ever happened to him, there would be a line out the door of shifters looking to claim her, whether she wanted it or not, to ensure their line. He'd rather bear the risk to himself somewhere else.

So where did that leave Cole?

I sipped on my bourbon, wondering if he'd answer.

He let out a soft laugh.

"Didn't think that far ahead, huh? Couldn't see past the blood of revenge?" I asked, smiling because I was intimately acquainted with that situation.

"Any advice?" His eyes lit with amusement.

Both of us knew I had none worth a damn, and he wouldn't take it anyway. From the way I saw it, he was good and stuck here, and I was a pretty darn good strategist.

"I'm only adept at planning deaths. Planning lives isn't my strong suit. Not a lot of practice." I leaned back, settling in when I should've been leaving.

Dragging out tonight, being alone with him, wouldn't change a thing. It was time to start cutting ties.

"I should probably get going." I slid out of the booth.

He didn't speak, but the heat in his eyes told me he was looking for a different ending to the night.

He was the enemy; the job was done. There was no future here. If I didn't leave, and soon, I was going to let this night end however he wanted, and damn it all.

I might not have a future anyway.

Except we already almost did this once, and I wasn't good enough.

That got me moving toward the door.

"I'll give you a ride," he said,

The heat in the room chilled.

He grabbed his jacket off a chair and held it out to me like a peace offering. I took it and resented every second. When had I become the person who did the right thing? When had he become the one who listened?

Suddenly wearing his shirt seemed too personal, even though I'd taken the offer of his jacket. I grabbed the hem and lifted it off.

"Here," I said, holding it out to him.

His features looked carved out of granite as he stood stone still, staring at my offering, and then beyond.

As still and cold as he was, I could feel the heat pouring off him, the want, as he looked at me.

There was something about the look of lust in Cole's eyes that always had an effect on me. The breath in my chest stuttered, and I had a hard time replacing it.

He reached forward, as if he were going to take the shirt. Instead he wrapped his hand around my wrist and yanked me toward him. He ran his other hand over the place Pavro had torn at my flesh.

"Don't ever let anyone do that again, do you hear me?" he asked, before he nipped at the tendon that ran from my neck to my shoulder with teeth sharper than human, as if trying to remove what was there.

He cupped my ass, lifting me. I straddled his waist right before he dropped me back onto the booth, shoving the table out of his way.

I turned my face away from him, trying to get a moment to clear my head even as he gripped his shoulders. It only gave him better access to my throat.

I knew where this was going to end. I didn't have the

strength to stop it completely, but I could try to limit the damage.

I placed both palms against his chest.

"This can't happen. We're on different sides of a brewing battle and this is going to complicate things."

He flattened his hands on either side of my head, looking intently on my mouth before he dragged his eyes up to lock with mine. "Except we both know it's going to."

I would've told him he was being presumptuous if my spine wasn't arching to get even closer to him.

"This isn't good, for either of us," I said.

"You'd better say whatever you need to say."

I wasn't sure what there was to say. This was going to be a massacre no matter how you sliced and diced it. There was only one shot at trying to mitigate the damage.

"This is fucking, nothing more." Even as the words were said, I didn't believe them myself. Sleeping with someone always changed things. It was inevitable. Static situations didn't exist in real life. It was an illusion.

"Do you know how old I am?" he asked.

"No."

"In human years, I'm fucking ancient."

There was something in those deep eyes that made me believe him. Something in his manner that was almost archaic at times, in the roughness of his person, as if any of the issues we faced now were trivial in the scheme of things he'd seen.

He dipped his head toward mine, nipping at my lower lip and then sucking it into his, before his tongue traced its fullness.

I needed to jump off this booth, run home, and lock the door. But I lay still, letting him push this farther. It wasn't because I liked the feel of his hands on my hips, which I did. Or the way he tugged them forward so that I was snug against a very hard erection pressing through his jeans. I liked the feel of *him* closer. Cole would never be anyone but him, and the rawness of his soul spoke to my own. Of all the people I might've found a connection to, why him?

"Do you know how many relationships I've had?" he said, slowly dragging me along as he got to his point.

"Not too many?"

"I think you're safe from me. Are we done with this?"

I answered him by covering his mouth with mine. Men had always told me I was good in bed. Part of me wondered if it was because I'd always taken the reins early, led them through the act step by step exactly the way I wanted it done.

There was nothing orchestrated about this moment. I could barely keep a thought in my head before it was swallowed up and devoured by a feeling, a need, a necessity. His hands were all over me, gripping my ass, the flimsy fabric of my dress ripping in his grasp; he quickly shed his clothes until we were flesh on flesh.

There was no thinking. It was movement, to action, to feeling. It was as if I'd only been wading in the baby pool and someone tossed me into the rapids. I could barely catch my breath, and I didn't care.

He gripped my head, dragging my mouth to his, growing impatient for more, and I gave it to him. Any idea about resisting him disappeared as soon as he'd touched me, his hands burning me.

I should tell him again how this meant nothing, but then I'd have to hear it myself. For tonight, maybe I'd pretend. I'd be someone different. Someone like my sister, for whom sex did mean something. Who married the man she was crazy about and did all the things so many other women want and dream of. Tonight I wasn't going to be the sick girl who was doomed to die, who killed and struggled, surrounded by blood and doom. Tonight I would be the princess, the cherished queen, a woman I could only pretend to be.

He descended, parting my lower lips with his tongue as he thrust his fingers inside me, his touch forceful and reverent all at once.

"You taste as sweet as you look," he said.

I jerked up, and he wrapped an arm around my hips, holding me there.

I'd never wanted someone or something so completely as I did at this moment. I reached down, grabbing his hair, urging him upward.

He finally moved upward when he was ready, bringing my leg with him, and sank deep into me.

Cole fucked the way I felt inside, all buried rage and excitement and life. When we came together, it was like my soul cried as it met its perfect match, knowing that he would shred my heart apart given the chance. The only thing that would save me was that he wouldn't get the opportunity. I didn't have the tender heart of someone my age. I'd seen too much, done too much, killed too many. It might be as shriveled up and hard as his.

But for tonight, for now, I opened to him like I'd never done in my life. And when I asked for more and he took us over the edge, I bit my tongue to not say the ridiculous things I wanted. I tried to cling to that small bit of reality even as he obliterated my world.

32

C *ole*

Sassy shifted in bed, her back turned to me as she sat up, as if she were already regretting what happened between us last night.

After we'd had sex at the club, I brought her home. I was going to walk her in and then leave to find out if word was spreading about Pavro's death and what the rumors were. Instead, I followed her upstairs.

With the morning light, it was as if she were seeing things a little differently.

I traced the line of her spine, testing the waters, feeling the chill in the air.

"You should probably get going. I'm sure you have a busy day. You can let me know what happens with Merlin...or send Lonzo by."

She stood, still not looking at me. Last night, I couldn't

extinguish the heat she was throwing off. She'd been like fucking live ammo, even better than I'd imagined. Now she was nothing but ice, even as her back arched at my touch.

It was taking all my control to not pull her underneath me and bury myself in her again.

"I have a few more things to do before the day starts," I said—things which included her.

She tilted her head toward me, catching her lower lip with her teeth, her heartbeat telling me she wasn't as done as she wanted to portray. I traced the curve of her hip, and she tilted her head back slightly as the ice melted a little more.

I cupped her hip, squeezing. Her breathing hitched.

I wrapped an arm around her waist, tugging her flat on her back underneath me, like I'd wanted to from the second I woke.

"What if I have things to do?" she asked, but the ice had already melted as she fought a smile.

"You'll have to handle them later." I dipped my head, not able to resist those luscious lips.

"This isn't going to be a thing," she said, freezing up a bit.

Was she trying to convince herself or me? I didn't need the warning. I couldn't afford a *thing* right now either, but I wasn't going to walk away from the most enjoyment I'd had in years, maybe ever. I'd make sure that she wouldn't get any fallout from Pavro's death, take her to Merlin, who'd do whatever he had to, and then walk away, letting her live out the rest of her life in peace without me. I might hang around for another month or two, but that would be it.

"Didn't we cover this last night?" I asked.

"Last night I thought it was going to be a one-off," she said, looking genuinely concerned about where things were headed.

One thing about Sassy: she didn't like any weak spots in the wall she'd erected around herself. Part of me wanted to take a wrecking ball to the thing, but the sane part of me would let it stand.

"This can be whatever you want to call it, as long as you don't call it finished. We both know it's a ways from that. Let it have a little life. We take what we need from each other, and that's all."

She stared up at me as if weighing my sincerity. I'd had women searching my every action, word, and gesture for hints of a commitment. I'd never been put on the spot to confirm my lack of one.

I should've been happy, but something about it didn't sit quite right. My ego wasn't used to being cast aside, but she was right: it was for the best.

"And when it's done, it's done. We don't make a thing over it," she said.

I couldn't help but laugh as I buried the blows to my ego. "I'll manage to keep my feelings intact."

I cupped her breast as I fit myself against her, remembering right where she liked to be touched, what had gotten her the hottest last night. A moan escaped her lips. We'd see who was so eager to walk away in a few days.

"I guess there's not too much harm if we have a little fun, right?" she asked, before she lost her words again.

Sassy

. . .

Cole walked across the bedroom, finding his discarded jeans, the muscles in his abdomen and back rippling with every movement. I wanted to lure him back to bed, and he'd just gotten up. Sleeping with him might've been the most dangerous thing I'd done—and I'd been in some real pickles.

He was zipping his jeans when his gaze jerked to the window. He grabbed his shirt next, picking up his pace as he threw it over his head.

"What's wrong?" I followed his lead and grabbed my jeans.

"Lonzo's here," he said before he headed downstairs.

I got dressed fast and followed.

Lonzo was already in the kitchen. "I've been calling you."

"What's wrong?" Cole said.

Lonzo's gaze shot to me before returning to Cole.

A stone dropped into my gut. I guessed what the problem was before he spoke.

"We knew they'd suspect you had something to do with Pavro's death, but they don't have enough proof to hang it on you. But they ID'd Sassy as your guest last night, and they're coming for her because they can."

Ever since Louis recognized me I'd known I was becoming somewhat higher profile, but I hadn't believed it would be this quick. And yet the vampires had the best surveillance equipment going. Of course they'd figured out who I was. I'd gotten sloppy.

Cole spun toward me. "Get dressed. We're leaving now."

"Can't you claim me? I thought they couldn't touch a human claimed by a shifter without going to the council? Aren't there rules for that?" Seemed there werc rules for everything with the vampires and werewolves. It was what Donovan did with my sister when they wanted her.

"Pavro's crew won't care. The pact is starting to fall apart and everyone knows it. They'll take you and clean up the mess afterward."

The reality that life as I knew it might be coming to an end, and not the way I'd thought, was throwing me into a bit of a tailspin. For someone who'd prided herself on the ability to pivot, I wasn't shifting gears or turning very well.

"What about my crew?" Did they know who they were too?

"Our sources say they're just coming for you," Lonzo said.

"Get your shoes or you're going barefoot." Cole turned back to Lonzo. "Get guys over here until we leave."

"They're on their way, but I don't know how much lead time we have. I got word they're on their way here now. I wasn't sure I'd even beat them here."

I wasn't typically slow to react. If I was, I wouldn't be alive. But something about the events of the last couple days made me nearly numb.

I looked once more at Lonzo. The way he kept looking out the window and the way Cole positioned himself near the entrance suddenly kicked my reactions into gear, like when I was on a mission.

Taking the stairs two at a time, I threw on the first pair of boots I found and my jacket.

Now what? Was everything I had gone? Was that what this meant? They didn't have proof I killed Pavro, but it didn't matter, did it? They'd come for me because a human life meant nothing anymore.

I'd always known that my story might end with a bang. You didn't kill vampires and blow things up and expect a quiet death. Whenever I had those thoughts in the past though, I'd known I was dying. As of now, I was still dying, but what if I wasn't going to be tomorrow? Then I'd be on the run for the rest of my very long life.

Fuck.

I could follow Pen and Donovan to Europe. My sister would be ecstatic. But to do what? Read the paper about how many humans had gotten killed? No. I wasn't walking away from this fight as long as I could stand.

Lonzo was answering his phone and Cole was waiting when I came back down.

"They're going to be here in two minutes," Lonzo said.

"We have to go." Cole grabbed my hand, pulling me after him.

"I have one last thing to—"

"Out of time. Whatever it is, we'll get it later."

"It's a passport," I said as he pulled me out the door.

"I can handle that, but I have to get you out of here, now."

Lonzo followed us, a hand on the gun at his waist. It wouldn't kill a vampire, but it would slow them down. He headed toward Cole's truck.

Cole shoved me in the driver's side of a silver Mercedes before getting in the passenger side.

"Drive north and avoid the highways. Drive fast, but not enough to be obvious." He started pulling guns out of the glove box, then from underneath the seat.

There were lots of clicking and locking sounds as I pulled away, too focused on what might be coming for us to look. I got down one block and could see another car speeding up, chasing Lonzo in Cole's truck heading in the opposite direction.

"Where're we going?" I asked after I got a few miles away and no one seemed to be following us.

"First to get you fixed and then out of the territory for a little while until I get *this* fixed." He had a line of guns arranged on the floor by his feet as he used his phone.

I continued driving with my vague instructions.

"We need to do it tonight and somewhere different. Things are heating up."

I couldn't hear the person on the other side of the call, but it could only be Merlin. There was a pause.

"Yes. Tonight. No, not there. The attic."

He stopped talking and switched to sending messages —to whom, I didn't know.

"Why are we going to see Merlin now? Wouldn't it be better if things quieted down first?" I asked. No one wanted a cure more than me, but could we afford a pit stop?

"It can't wait. They've been watching him. If they suspect a connection of any type to me, they'll kill him. It has to happen tonight."

"Why are they watching him?" The idea Merlin would be important enough to be on the vampires' radar made me want to both avoid the guy and seek him out, so I could pry some information out of him. What was he doing that they wanted to know about?

"They think he's a person of interest because of his research," Cole said.

"Which is?"

"I don't know all of it. Turn here."

I turned right onto a county road, having no idea where we were going, what would happen, where I'd end up.

He was back to messaging people on his phone, not

telling me a word about what was going to happen or what was being planned.

"Where are we heading after Merlin?"

"We're going to pack territory out of the area until I get things worked out," he said, most of his attention going to whatever he was messaging.

"Worked out how? If they think I killed Pavro, how does that happen?" I asked, feeling more shaken by the second.

He stopped typing and looked at me. "I don't know yet."

There was a long pause before his phone beeped and he went back to messaging.

I wasn't used to being out of the loop of planning, pulling strings, calling in favors, and negotiating. But this wasn't my world. The only person I could call was Donovan, who was an ocean away and would tell my sister, who'd be worried sick. That wasn't an option. The only thing I could do right now was drive and hope Cole could pull something off, or the life he might be saving wouldn't be worth the effort it took to save.

33

C *ole*

"Pull the car over here and park," I said. "Don't say anything until we get inside. There's lots of ears around this place."

The building was in the middle of the city, hiding in plain sight. Not the best neighborhood, but far from the abandoned outskirts where I liked to handle my business.

We walked into the foyer and then waited, knowing the occupants would already be watching for us the second we stepped over the threshold because of the silent alarm system. I knew because my pack had helped design it as part of payment for treatment.

The door opened and a young male human looked behind us before waving us in and shutting the door. He redid the bolt that locked the place up tighter than a bank vault before turning to us.

"He's waiting for you."

The place was a maze of hallways that all appeared the same, meant to confuse an intruder. After the third left turn, Merlin emerged from a doorway.

He appeared understandably less congenial than last time, which might be better. His friendly behavior was more unsettling than his distance.

"I need a word with you alone for a moment," he said, only giving Sassy the briefest of nods. He took a step toward the other end of the hallway.

"If this is about what you're planning on doing, it's being done to me. I should hear it," she said.

"This is about other business," Merlin said.

I didn't have any other business with Merlin.

"What's wrong?" I asked once we'd moved away. "You said you could fix her." I kept my voice soft enough that her human hearing would never pick it up down the other end of the hall. Merlin didn't know how lucky he was that we were in eyeshot of her, or he'd be slammed against the wall right now and I'd find out exactly what he was.

"I can, but there are a couple of issues that I haven't been able to work through. The more I investigated, the more it became clear she's right on the cusp. Her genetics are so close to shifter genetics that tweaking one or two things to make her immune to the Sucking Sickness might change her more than intended. When I do this, it might throw her completely over."

I kept my face neutral as Sassy continued to keep visual tabs on us. "How is that possible? And why didn't you mention that before?" I'd known Merlin was involved in some strange chemistry, but I had no idea how far it went.

"There's some shifter lineage in her past. I can't say

how far back, but it's there. If there is a line where the human ends and shifter begins, her toes are already hanging over it. I can't say for sure how close you have to get before it happens. She might be a shifter or something in between. If she changes, you were warned."

He spoke the way a person absolving themselves of all wrongdoing would. Nothing about the conversation was inspiring confidence. The only bright side was that Sassy couldn't hear all of this.

She was pacing down the other end of the hall, watching all the doors, the windows, every method of entry. Her hair was tugged up into a messy ponytail, her jeans clinging to every curve. She didn't have an iota of makeup on, and I'd never wanted someone more. She was absolute perfection, and if I told her the possible outcomes, she *might* say yes.

But I didn't know how deep the hate for the ones who'd subjugated her people was. Shifters were among them. Was it enough to say no? Thinking she could keep going for a while longer? This might be the only chance, and I wasn't going to let anyone take it away, not even her.

"Will she live?" In the end, that was all I wanted to know. I didn't care if she was human, shifter or some strange combination. I needed her to be breathing.

"Yes. She might be uncomfortable tonight, but she'll be okay. Whatever happens will happen fast, and then she should stabilize. Either way, it's your call."

It should be Sassy's.

"Give it to her," I said.

"I've got everything set up in here," Merlin said, walking into a nearby room.

"Sassy, he's ready." I tilted my head toward the room Merlin had disappeared into.

There was a slight hesitation in her step, as if she sensed that what was about to happen might be more than she'd bargained for. But true to form, she took a deep breath and walked over anyway.

She stopped outside the door, glancing in at where Merlin was setting up.

Her big eyes were staring up at me. I should tell her, give her a choice. But what if she chose wrong?

"Do we know what this is going to do to me?" she asked.

"Keep you alive."

The doubts were starting to build. She was looking past me to Merlin, wondering what she'd become. Having doubts whether death was really the worst outcome.

I blocked her view of Merlin. The more she concentrated on him, the more hesitant anyone would become. "Do you want to live? Because the woman I know would take any shot she had at doing exactly that."

"You know I do." She looked up at me as if demanding how I could ask such a question.

"Then this needs to happen, because right now you're teetering on the edge of death." I leaned close, face inches from hers, trying to make her understand how little time she had. "I can smell the amount of death on you. Your cells are dying quicker than they're being replaced. You don't have much time."

"And you're—"

"Positive."

She shuddered slightly and this one had nothing to do with being sick. This was it. If we didn't do this now, she'd die. It wasn't coming in the next few months—it was here. The next attack would take her life. Curtain closed. Pack it up. Game over.

She took another precious few seconds she couldn't afford, staring into the room.

"Sassy, we don't have time."

"Okay."

This was it. A mad scientist that was only talked about in the darkest corners was going to stick her with who knew what. And if I didn't let him, she'd die.

She walked in as if she still wasn't sure what she was doing, and I wondered how far I was willing to take things in order to save her.

"Roll up your sleeve." Merlin picked up a large needle.

Thankfully, he wasn't using the needlelike things that sprouted out of his hands.

"What's this going to do to me?" she asked.

Needle in hand in between us, he said, "Keep you alive."

Her last shred of resistance burned to the ground. He shot the needle into her.

"Now what?" I asked.

"Get me a blood sample in a few days so I can test her levels."

I didn't waste a minute getting her out of there and back into the car. As we pulled away, I spied a few vampires heading in the building's direction.

34

S *assy*

I leaned back, not paying attention to where we were going for the first time in my life. My head felt cloudy, like I wasn't anywhere. Even so, I could sense Cole's attention on me, as if he were waiting for something monumental to happen. As if I'd suddenly jump up and down, scream-ing, *I'm alive, I'm alive.*

I let my eyes drift closed, not caring where he was taking me. This might not be curing me, but it was doing *something* to me.

"Sassy?" Fingers grazed my cheek.

"I'm okay." I turned toward him, opening my eyes slightly.

"We'll be there soon."

Ten minutes later, the car turned into an opening in a chain-link fence. If I'd been scoping this place out for a hit, I would've kept on going. The place looked like nothing but abandoned, overgrown property, but there were telltale signs of life if you knew where to look. Like the downed power line that wasn't really downed but buried and probably was feeding electricity to something. The gaping hole in the broken fence that I'd bet anything was wired to light up anyone who touched it.

Cole flashed the high beams in a dot/dash pattern. A loud howl sounded from somewhere in the forest, and he began driving again.

A lone cabin appeared in the distance.

"Is it safe here?" I wanted nothing more than to crawl into a bed and fall asleep without thinking of vampires for a few minutes. My body felt like it was being ravaged by fever.

"There isn't a vampire alive that'll come anywhere close to here. It's shifter territory for miles. This is where some members from different packs go when they need a safe haven or to unwind. They know we're here, and they'll be watching for intruders."

I pushed the car door open and stood, resting a minute against the hood.

Cole walked over, hoisting me up into his arms.

"I can walk."

"You don't have to."

It was a log cabin, but the kitchen had stainless-steel appliances and stone counters. It was all open except for a bathroom off the back and stairs that led to a loft that he carried me up to, laying me on the bed.

"Wait, I need to get my phone. I have to let my people know. They'll be afraid I'm dead." I tried to get up.

"This won't get tracked," he said, handing me a burner phone. "Even so, keep it short and vague."

I hesitated, deciding to text Vicki, who would get the message out but not be inclined to ask questions.

It's Ghost. I'm okay. I'll be in touch soon. Have everyone lie low until we talk. There might be more eyes than normal.

I hit send, hoping she'd take that last piece of advice to heart.

There was more howling outside, close to the cabin. Cole turned his head slightly, listening.

"I'll be back soon. Rest," he said.

Cole

Sassy's breathing changed, the wheezing smoothing out at some point in the night. Merlin said it would be fast. A soft moan escaped as she tried to get comfortable but couldn't.

There'd been no other way. It had to happen if she was going to live. Sometimes a little pain was worth the payoff.

She opened her eyes, looking wild.

"It's all right. This will pass. The doctor said you might have a reaction, but it won't last long." I settled down on the bed, pulling her shaking form to me.

If there'd been any other way...

I held her close, trying to use my warmth to comfort her. At some point before dawn, she calmed, falling asleep against me. I should've gotten up and left at that point, but I didn't.

By the time the morning came, she didn't smell like a human anymore. She smelled like one of my kind, a shifter. How thorough the changes were remained to be seen, but if I ran into her on the street, *human* wouldn't enter my mind.

She stirred as she opened her eyes. It was clear she was trying to get her bearings and could feel the difference in her limbs as she moved.

"Do you want some coffee?" I asked, getting up and supplying an easy excuse to give her a minute to herself.

"Yeah, that would be good. Thanks."

It took her a half an hour to make it downstairs, her expression intent even as all she did was walk across the room.

She came forward, taking a coffee from me.

After a few sips, she squinted, looking at the cup. It probably tasted different. She was noticing layers of flavors she hadn't been aware of before.

Whatever Merlin had done, the smell of sickness was long gone, that was a certainty. How much she'd changed wasn't anywhere near as predictable, but she needed to be told something.

"Is it safe to walk here?" she asked, heading toward the door.

"Sure. Just stay within a few miles of the house. No one will bother you." Or I might not have to tell her anything. She might be figuring it out on her own.

35

S *assy*

I stepped out onto the front porch of the cabin and breathed deeply. My lungs filled until they couldn't fit a smidge more air, and it didn't trigger a coughing fit. The heaviness in my chest was gone. The tiredness that had dogged my steps for years had lifted. Even the allergies that usually plagued me seemed to be gone. With my sinuses cleared, I could smell everything. It felt as if I'd slept for a year, but in a good way, as if while I was asleep, my body had healed.

This wasn't like the last "cure" or after the doctor's treatments. Whenever I'd gotten "better" before, there was still a lingering feeling inside, like something wasn't quite right. It was like having a splinter you couldn't see but knew was there. When you're sick, you know it, no matter what anyone tells you. I could've had fifty doctors tell me I was healed and I wouldn't have believed them. Today I could have a thousand doctors tell me I *was* sick and it wouldn't matter. I *felt* it. This time was different.

I skipped down the front steps and then walked. When walking seemed too slow, I broke into a jog, which became a run—a very fast run that didn't seem to bother my lungs or muscles. I ran laps for a good half an hour before I stopped, but I could've gone all day. I hadn't even broken a sweat.

What had Merlin done to me? Would this last? Did I want it to last? I stretched out my arms and legs. I wouldn't mind if it stuck around for a while. Dodging bombs would be a lot easier in this new version of myself.

It'd wear off, whatever it was, just like the depression had after the first time I met Merlin. I'd probably be normal, or normal-ish, tomorrow. As long as I didn't slide all the way backward to sick, I didn't care.

I walked back into the cabin, and a newspaper caught my eye. How was I reading the fine print on a paper that was twenty feet away? No, this was officially beyond having a good night's sleep.

"Are you hungry? They stocked the kitchen for us."

They being the shifters in the area? I'd smelled them while I was running. I'd told myself I was crazy, but as I looked at the paper again... Maybe not so crazy after all.

Cole had the fridge open. "There are eggs, bacon..."

"No, I'm fine." I couldn't focus on food when the entire paradigm of my world was shifting.

Cole moved closer. "Sassy, what's wrong?"

"I'm wrong. I think there's something more than healing going on. I can smell the eggs that are in the refrigerator. I can read the paper over there on the table. I think Merlin did a little more than fix me."

I watched, waiting to see if he'd panic.

"Do you feel anything else? Like an itch all over that you want to scratch?"

"No. Why? I don't think this is an allergy. I think I'm physically different."

He nodded, not saying anything else about itching or allergies, but there was something about the way he looked at me that made me want to either fall down onto the couch or run for it.

"I'm going to get your doctor up here to run a few tests to check you out."

"Up here?" I asked.

"It's safer than going to him."

He was already messaging on his phone. He'd probably make one of the guys drag Doc up here, whether he wanted to come or not. If there was any chance of stopping Cole, I would try, but he was every bit as stubborn as I was, and I didn't have the fight to stop him.

"He'll be here soon," Cole said, putting his phone down.

"Do you think this is something to worry about?"

"No, but I think we'll get you checked and see what's going on."

Other than a more intent perusal, he seemed to be taking these weird side effects I was experiencing in stride.

Did he know something? When he'd talked to Merlin, my gut screamed it was about me.

"Is there something you're not telling me?" I asked, trying to focus on Cole even as my senses were overwhelmed with smells and sounds.

"Merlin wasn't sure the extent of the changes his cure might cause. This might be normal."

No one was going to convince me this was normal. Not for a human being, anyway.

"Normal how? Nothing about this feels normal."

"Doc will be here soon. He'll be able to tell us more."

He knew something he didn't want to say.

"I'm going to go hop in the shower," I said, looking for anything that might decompress me a bit.

Doc was at the door. He must've left the city as soon as Cole got a hold of him, or someone had forced him out. Either way, I sighed in relief at seeing him. I'd never imagined feeling good would be as worrisome as being sick.

"Everything all right? I got the notice from Lonzo and came right away."

"Sorry to drag you all the way up here. It probably could've waited until we got back."

Doc was staring at me, not remarking at all, but his eyes narrowed as if he were mentally cataloging a change. "You look better." He took a deep breath. "And you smell different."

"Yeah, that's part of why I wanted to see you. I've had a couple experimental treatments, and I think they might've changed something." That was the best description I had for what had happened.

Cole had walked over but remained quiet for a change.

"Is there somewhere comfortable I can examine you?" Doc asked, looking around the cabin.

"I'll give you a few minutes," Cole said, walking out the front door instead of taking charge.

I watched him through the window while Doc felt for my pulse.

"Your heart rate is faster than normal. How do you feel?" he asked.

"Good. Almost too good, if that could be a thing. How much faster?"

"Enough to be different." Doc dug into his bag, pulled out his stethoscope, and listened to several different places on my chest. He whipped out a blood pressure cuff and measured my pulse, looking more confused as he went. "Do you mind if I take a blood sample?"

I held out my arm. "You've done much worse."

He filled one vial, and then dug out another, and then three more.

"What was this experimental treatment you tried?" he asked, shooting for nonchalant and failing miserably.

"It was just something someone passed along. Figured I didn't have much to lose, so I gave it a go. Everything looks okay?"

He packed away my blood and then stood there for a few minutes, looking as stumped as I was feeling. But he didn't have the *get your things in order* face on.

"You seem perfect, for a human—I might even say better than perfect." He crossed his arms, looking at me like I was a mouse in a cage. "Where did you get this treatment?"

"Just a friend of a friend." No one had to warn me not to say anything about Merlin. Some knowledge was instinctual.

He nodded, knowing a bullshit story when he heard one. "Well, if you ever remember this friend's name, pass it along. I'd be interested in getting a sample. I think quite a few people might be interested." He looked at me like I was pulling some scam job on him, as if I knew what was going on but didn't want to share.

"And why is that?" I asked.

"Your heart rate is faster but extremely strong and constant. Your lungs sound better than they ever have. Your blood pressure is eighty over forty. If I didn't know any better, I'd think I was examining a shifter." He rubbed his chin. "And you have no idea what you took?"

"I don't. That I can swear to you."

He nodded slowly. At least he believed that part of the story.

"Do you think I'll be okay?"

He reached out, feeling for my pulse again. "I think you're going to be fine. Does your skin feel itchy at all?"

"No, not at all."

"Do you have any more of this treatment anywhere? Even the container it came in?"

"No. Sorry."

He lifted my arm, smelled my wrist, and dropped it, shaking his head. "You know I've been studying Sucking Sickness for a while, right?"

"Yes, that's why you were helping me."

He grew silent again, each pause making me antsier.

"What aren't you telling me, Doc? Just say it. Is there a problem?" I took my arm back, not liking the way he was looking at me one bit.

"Not a problem at all. I'm simply trying to figure out how you got from Point A to Point B when there are no known ways to do such a thing." He took a few steps to the left and then back toward me again, as if that would help him get his words in order. "You know that vampires are growing their numbers, right?"

It was the first time he'd ever started a conversation about the real world with me, and it wasn't helping matters.

"Yes. Even people who don't know what's going on have their suspicions with the amount of converts lately. You can't walk down the street without tripping over a new vampire." I'd even seen a flier recently for humans looking to convert—and a pair of idiots who were avidly reading it.

"That's obviously a threat to shifters and the balance of things. In the world we live in, with vampires trying to build their numbers, if we want to secure our future, we need to expand as well. Our process takes a lot longer, though, more in line with the human race, not overnight like vampires."

He was speaking to me almost as if I were one of his kind. I backed up a couple of steps until I was partially sitting on the table behind me.

If he noticed my shakiness, it didn't slow him down. "It's been known for a long time that shifter blood is lethal to vampires, so I had a hypothesis that there might be a connection between humans who get the Sucking Sickness, which makes your blood lethal to vampires, and shifters, whose blood is also lethal to vampires. It's not a huge leap to wonder if there's a genetic link between certain humans and shifters."

"You're saying I've got a link somehow to shifters? How is that possible?" I was the leader of the resistance. I targeted other races that suppressed humans. Yes, maybe I was soft on shifters, but I couldn't *be* one. That wasn't the way this could shake out. That would upend my life nearly as much as dying. And yet I was fairly certain that was exactly where he was going with this.

"I'm not sure when or how, but your DNA has always had some shifter genetic mutations in it, and from what I'm seeing..." He waved a hand at me.

And there it was. Somehow I was a shifter now? What the hell had Merlin done?

Doc kept right on talking, saying more in this half-hour than he'd given away in a year, probably because he considered me Team Shifter now.

"I don't know how this happened," Doc said. "There might've been some crossbreeding a few hundred years ago. We know shifters can breed with humans and have human children, but the reverse wasn't a possibility until recently. Probably because it took a while for enough shifters to interbreed that there were enough humans with the amount of DNA in their systems for them to have shifter children, the way your sister did."

And it kept getting better. "So you were trying to figure out who would make good broodmares to pluck from the otherwise useless human population?"

"It's not as if we'd be forcing anyone. There's plenty of women who would gladly have our children. It's only that vampires can reproduce rapidly, and we can't afford an imbalance."

We. He did think I was on his team.

"I'm still human."

Doc shook his head. "I highly doubt that."

Oh God, my sister. "Did Donovan know this?"

"No. He had no idea when he got involved with your sister. I, on the other hand was very curious when I heard about her, and did inquire into any siblings."

If I thought my knees would work, I'd stand up and punch him.

"And now here you are, presenting more like a shifter than a human," he said, shaking his head in amazement. "I'd love to know how you managed to make that last genetic leap."

When I didn't offer anything other than stunned silence, he grabbed his bag.

"I've got to get to the lab and run your blood. Let me know if anything else changes."

He was halfway to the door when I said, "Doc, you didn't tell me why you asked about itchy skin."

"Oh, yes—when shifters change, our skin usually gets itchy. I was trying to gauge if you would shift or not. Doesn't look like it, but you never know. I'll be in touch soon."

Cole had asked me about my skin. He knew. Had he known all along what was going to happen? Had Merlin told him?

Cole walked back in the cabin a few minutes later. "I talked to Doc on his way out. Said you're looking pretty healthy." He didn't look like a man delivering good news but one waiting to see what the fallout might be.

"He said as much."

"He also told me he took a sample to test."

Oh, he knew. When had he planned on telling me?

"You figured it out pretty fast, or did Merlin tell you?" I asked.

"Merlin wasn't sure, but he thought it was a possibility."

"Why didn't you tell me?"

"You knew there were risks. You didn't go in blind. You also knew there was no other alternative."

I took a step back from him, trying to sort out my thoughts. He was right. I did know there might be unforeseen complications or side effects, and so far there was nothing I could even complain about. I was healthier than ever, stronger, could run like I'd never been able to, no matter how hard I trained. So why was I so mad? It came down to one problem.

"Did you do this, help me like this, because of the deal or because you didn't like wanting the sick girl?"

"When are you going to get past that? I did it because I wanted to fix you."

Fix me? I guess to him I'd been broken. I'd be considered broken to a lot of people.

The feelings, sensations, and information bombarded me until I wasn't capable of having a logical reaction. I needed to treat this day like it was a mission, detach emotionally until I could get my head around it. Then react.

We stared at each other, and for once he seemed at a loss for words.

I backed away toward the bedroom. "I'm going to go lie down, maybe call it an early night."

He backed away toward the door. "I'm going to go touch base with a couple of the pack."

36

S *assy*

Cole hadn't come into the bedroom last night, giving me space. I didn't know if that was a good thing or not, but considering I couldn't figure out who I was at the moment, it probably wasn't bad.

I wandered out of the bedroom, and he looked like he'd been up for hours already. He watched me as I made my way to the coffee.

"I got off the phone with Doc. He already ran your blood work. Your genetics are coming back as shifter."

It had already seemed like a foregone conclusion to Doc, but still, knowing that genetically I wasn't human anymore, that I was now a race I'd once declared my enemy, it was a bit to take in. I was alive. I'd have years, maybe more than I'd ever imagined, to live the rest of my life. But what would that life be? Where did I fit?

I sipped my coffee for a few minutes, digesting it all but not knowing what any of it meant.

"Where does this leave me?" I asked.

"I don't think the vampires can touch you without violating the pact. That doesn't mean it'll go smoothly. They might put up a fight, but they'll either have to back off or war with every pack on the East Coast. It's not a line they'll be ready to cross—not yet, anyway."

But I wasn't a real shifter. I was a fraud. "Even if I'm newly converted? Not born?"

"It'll hold. If they tried to argue that, they wouldn't be safe, as *every* vampire is born human. You've got some options."

Options? That was something I wasn't used to hearing. I typically thought in "next week," maybe "next month," timelines. With those kinds of limits, it was slim pickings. Even the far-off attack plans I typically made sure could be carried out without me.

I groaned. What did this mean for the resistance? Would they follow a shifter?

"What were those options you were talking about?" I asked. For someone who wasn't dying, I seemed to have fewer choices than I'd had before.

"I can get you to wherever your sister is, or somewhere else out of this area if you want to cut ties and make a fresh start. Like I said, the vampire situation can be resolved as well, if you want to go back home." He paused. "Or you can stay with me. Maybe we give this thing between us a try, see where it goes."

Stay with him? Give it a try? He'd never acted as if a relationship was an option, not even before I'd quashed it, but *now* he wanted one. Apparently being a healthy shifter, even a fraud of one, made things much different.

I hadn't been good enough for him, but I still wanted him. It would be so easy to leave here, try to fit into his world and pretend that we were meant to be, but we were only meant to be now that I was "okay." I was good enough because I was like him. Inside, where it counted, I was still the sick girl. What if one day this genetic mutation wore off? Would I be unwanted again?

Still, I could push that all aside, ignore that I hadn't been enough, and embrace what we had right now. It might last a week, or a month, but sooner or later that resentment would boil up and my pride would demand payment.

I wasn't the only one with a lot of pride. Once I turned down his offer, one I was sure was rarely made, we'd be done. He'd walk away and move on. Nothing about Cole made you think he'd sit around and pine over a lost love. As much as it hurt, it wouldn't be as painful as the constant reminder that I hadn't been good enough for him.

"I think I should go home."

His jaw shifted and then he nodded. I hadn't expected a fight from him. No, he was above fighting for anyone, especially a second-rate human and a fraud shifter.

"Huddy has some business nearby tomorrow. I'll see if he can grab you and drive you back with him if you'd like, unless tomorrow isn't soon enough."

"Tomorrow is fine."

His eyes were as cold as ever. I'd expected the cut from him, but not this fast and easy. He gave me a nod and walked out of the cabin. I was fairly certain I wouldn't be seeing him again tonight.

· · ·

Cole

Huddy walked into the cabin, and my entire body tensed. She was leaving. I shouldn't care, shouldn't feel this impending doom, but I did.

"Hey," he said, clearly trying to gauge the situation.

"Thanks for coming."

Sassy poked her head out of the bedroom, and the awkwardness only grew.

"Heard someone needed a ride?" he said, clearly uncomfortable and definitely wondering what the hell was going on.

"Yeah, thanks for getting me. I just need a few minutes." She smiled, but it was clearly an act. The atmosphere in the cabin felt like a funeral. She walked to the couch and grabbed the sweater off it before disappearing into the bedroom again.

Huddy's brow furrowed as she walked past him, his nostrils flaring.

He turned to me, waiting for the door to close before he spoke. "You said she was going to officially be part of the pact, but I didn't believe it."

His sigh sent a blast of judgment through the room. Unfortunately, he wasn't going to leave it at that.

"I've been trying to stay out of this situation, but first you get her involved in your vendetta, then you fuck her and now she's changed into... I don't even know what you changed her into, but she sure smells like one of us. And now? Things don't look too good. What the fuck are you doing? What am I going to do if Donovan calls and asks how everything is going?"

"Huddy, you know I like you, but you need to stay in your lane."

"I *am* in my lane. I'm dead center in my lane. I care about the girl. She's good people, and her brother-in-law is my best friend. That makes this not only my lane, but my entire street."

I gave him my back, walking into the kitchen. I needed to put some space between us before I punched him in the face and then threw him out. The situation was too fresh and raw to poke at. When I turned back around, trying to make the final decision, I didn't do anything. His shoulders were slumped and he looked truly beaten up about the situation.

That was the problem with Huddy. He was too damned soft. No killer instinct inside this alpha. The girl he was protecting was more of a killer than he was.

"As far as fucking her goes, that's none of your business. I fuck who I want, and as long as they're willing, which all parties have been, it's no one else's concern. You of all people should keep your mouth shut on that one."

He opened his mouth anyway to argue but then shut it, shrugging and shaking his head. That man got more pussy than the local animal shelter.

"As to saving her, she's better off alive—or do you disagree?" I asked. There wasn't a person in my place that would've made a different choice. If they would, they weren't someone I'd bother with.

Huddy walked closer, keeping his voice low. "I'm not worried about her being like us but the ramifications of what was done. How? The doctor Donovan hooked her up with couldn't do anything but get rid of the symptoms."

That was one area I wasn't going to talk about. I

couldn't because I didn't know how it had been done. I wasn't sure I *wanted* to know.

"Doc said her DNA looks stable. Genetically she's more shifter than human, and that's how she's going to stay. She's going to live, and Pavro's people can't touch her without going to the council. They won't do that because they don't have proof. It fixed several issues, and that's all that matters."

"You're not going to tell me?" Huddy leaned on the counter behind him and crossed his arms, a deep scowl forming.

"No, and it's better that way."

Huddy's Adam's apple bobbed like it was the main event at a Halloween party. "There's only one possibility I can think of, and that's just a rumor. I'm not sure I'd trust *that* way with a pet hamster."

"Sometimes all options have to be on the table." That was the difference between Huddy and me—to accomplish what had to be done, I very rarely had a line I wouldn't cross.

"Did you go to... Is it what I'm thinking?"

I shrugged. This conversation was becoming a game of hangman, but I wasn't going to fill in the blanks. I didn't know how well she'd be received by the pack as it was. There was no room to risk prejudicing them more when she'd need their full support to pull off what came next.

His cheeks puffed as he blew out a stream of air that might've emptied him of a year's worth of breath. "So you actually care for her? And I mean more than liking her enough to fuck her."

"You're so out of your lane you're about to crash into the guardrail. I'm done filling you in for the day."

I didn't know what was going on with Sassy other than

she was ready to walk away from our situation. We'd had our fun and now it would end. There was no future for the leader of the rebellion and an alpha werewolf. She'd made it clear she didn't want anything else, and if Huddy thought we'd sit down with a cup of tea and hash out all the details, he didn't know me well.

Sassy walked back out with her jacket on.

I stared hard in her direction, still not quite believing that this was where it ended.

Her eyes met mine, her emotions shut down. Her walls were right back in place, like when I first met her.

"You ready?" Huddy asked, glancing between the two of us.

"Yes," she said, breaking our stare.

He headed out.

She followed, pausing with her hand on the door as I waited for her to say something. She didn't. After another few seconds, she walked out.

37

S *assy*

It was two days since I'd seen Cole, and as much of a mess as my life was, I couldn't think of anything else. Forty-eight hours of thinking of every touch, kiss, gesture, from the way he'd grazed his teeth over my sensitive skin to the way his palm felt as it squeezed my ass. The way he'd tasted, smelled, practically burned the place down when he fucked, to the stupidest detail, like the way he always handed me coffee in my favorite mug.

"So what does this mean? Are you part of the pack now?" Mattie asked, jarring me back to a meeting that should've had my full attention.

This was the first time I'd seen them in days, my group, my crew. They'd felt like family, and now Mattie was staring at me as if he didn't know me.

"You're saying you're a shifter?" he asked, jerking his

head back as if this was the worst thing that had ever happened to me. "How did this happen?"

"Experimental treatment. It had a weird side effect." I was standing at the table in headquarters as Mattie tried to visually dissect me.

Vicki and Harlow were staring at me with the same level of interest, minus the fear of contagion.

"Look, I don't care if you're one of them. You were one of us first," Vicki said. "I know where your loyalties are."

That was the problem. *I* didn't know exactly where my loyalties lay anymore. I'd never had a problem killing vampires, but shifters had always been a grey area. That grey was getting murkier by the minute.

"I'm not saying she isn't one of us," Mattie said, backtracking on what he'd implied seconds ago. "I'm only pointing out that the resistance as a whole might have a problem knowing their leader is a shifter. We have a lot of members who have beef with shifters, members who can't understand why we aren't taking out more of those targets already. Her taking a leave of absence might be the best move."

Harlow was the only one who hadn't weighed in yet. He finally shrugged. "There's already been a few rumors spiraling in the last day about a new member of the pack. I put out a couple of feelers this morning, afraid of what kind of reaction this rumor might bring. I didn't get great feedback."

I let Harlow's words sink in. There'd always been some pushback about not hitting shifters, and I'd always been ready with excuses about how I was getting food supplies from some of the members. But sooner or later, it was always going to be an issue. Now that I was a shifter, it was going to be an uphill battle. I knew this.

"She's Ghost. She's a legend. This resistance is what it is because of her," Vicki said, getting to her feet.

"And she's still Ghost," Harlow said. "I'm not trying to take anything away from her, but we might need some time for them to adjust."

I didn't know how to argue. I wouldn't trust me either.

"Nothing has changed. She'll still go as hard as ever," Vicki said, fighting back even as she was clearly wondering why I wasn't.

Mattie leaned forward. "Let's face it. She wouldn't go after the shifters before she was one of them. You think *now* she's going to?"

Vicki turned to me, her eyes pleading that I deny it.

"Maybe I do need to take a break for a while, until we see how people feel," I said.

Vicki's mouth gaped open.

"A short break. It doesn't have to be permanent," Mattie said, nodding coolly, even as we all knew that he didn't mean it.

"You only want her out because she wouldn't fuck you, you bastard," Vicki said.

"She's a fucking *shifter*, Vic." Mattie was turned toward Vicki but pointing in my direction. "How is she supposed to lead the resistance? You've got to be realistic here."

"*Stop*," I said, already seeing what this was going to do up and down the ranks. "It's still my call, and I think a break isn't the worst idea."

Harlow turned to me, looking grateful. Mattie didn't look at me at all. Vicki shook her head.

At some point I might be able to come back, but for now I'd have to hand the reins over or risk creating a chasm so large that the whole group might break apart. I grabbed my bag, seeing the writing on the wall.

Harlow gave me a hug. "As soon as things calm down, I'll let you know."

Mattie and I exchanged a chilly nod. He'd been my right-hand man, but now he couldn't stand to look at me. I wasn't feeling particularly fuzzy for him either.

Vicki followed me out to my bike. "He's going to ruin the group."

She was a tough chick. I'd seen her break an arm and not shed a tear, but she looked close to cracking right now.

"If I try to force myself on everyone, it might be worse. We have to let it play out. If they want me back, I'm here. I'll always be here for the people I care about."

Vicki never hugged, but she squeezed the hell out of me before waving toward my bike. "Get the fuck out of here before I give you a flat tire so you can't," she said, using laughter to keep herself glued together.

"Call me," I said, about to lose the last of the makeshift family I had here.

"You ain't getting rid of me that easy," she said.

I tried to smile, forcing myself to keep it together as I rode off. Refusing to look back at the legacy I was leaving behind. The people I'd seen nearly every day, who would slowly become less and less a part of my life.

For the first time in forever, I felt truly alone. I made it back to my house in record time and stood inside my kitchen, realizing that I didn't have anywhere to be. Nothing that I had to do. No plans I had to get done.

I'd survived countless missions, close calls, attacks, and even a disease no one had ever beaten. But as I saw a pair of vampires heading up the road to my house, there was no doubt this was going down as one of the worst days of my life.

Cole had said it might be bumpy as things were

worked out. I was going to find out how bumpy it was soon. Was this going to be some bumps and bruises, a concussion that would lay me out flat, or a lethal blow?

I grabbed a scrap of paper and jotted down a note.

Cole, please tell my sister I love her.

My hand froze. There were too many things to write and not enough time. Those ticking seconds seemed to strip away everything to the core of what I needed to get out.

Two vampires were approaching slowly, as if waiting to get intercepted. Except no one was stopping them. I hadn't seen a shifter in days. The bottom line was that Cole had saved me and I'd walked away.

If I was going to die, he needed to know one thing. I had to get it out, one way or another. It was something I'd fought admitting to myself, but as I stood here, thinking I might never see him again, it was so brutally clear that I couldn't deny it.

If you get this note, for whatever it's worth, I did love you.

That was it. It was all I had time to jot down. They didn't bother knocking and kicked in the back door. It hadn't even been locked.

"You'll need to come with us," one of them said. He looked familiar, a face I'd seen around the neighborhood that registered as out of place.

"Fine," I said, knowing I didn't have a choice.

A hand was hooked on either arm anyway. They marched me out the back door as I wondered if I had a shot at taking one of them out. I didn't think I had the strength of a full-blooded shifter, but I was a lot stronger than before. Plus I wouldn't go down without a fight.

They were walking me toward a dark sedan where they might split apart and I'd get an opportunity to test my new strength.

The sound of Cole's truck announced him first, and my brain seemed to short-circuit as my limbs grew weak. Vampires trying to kill me I could handle. Seeing Cole was something entirely different.

I closed my eyes, willing myself to get it together. This was not the time to fall apart.

"Stop." Cole's voice carried easily, deep and commanding. He was every inch the alpha.

I jerked my head up to see him walking toward us, and my heart bled from the sight.

The vampires stopped walking as Cole stood between them and their car. The one who seemed to be calling the shots said, "Get out of our way. We have orders to take this human to—"

"She's not human. She's part of my pact, and you have no authority over her. You can't touch a shifter unless you're bringing them to the council and have enough proof for a possible conviction."

The lead vampire froze, as if his common sense was conflicting with his orders.

Cole took another step forward, his gaze shooting from their hands on my arms to the vampire's face. "You better think about what you're doing or it'll be you in front of the council next. Unless you're saying you can't smell a shifter when she's standing right beside you?" Cole held out a piece of paper.

"She doesn't smell human," the lower-ranking vampire said, his grip loosening.

The lead vampire dropped his grip on me to take the paper from Cole and look at it while I read over his shoulder.

Right on the top of the sheet in bold, it read, *Species: Shifter. Lycan. Werewolf.* At the top corner was a picture of me.

I'd never seen official pact papers, but it looked legitimate as far as I could tell. There it was. I was officially a shifter.

"I'd let her go," Cole said, staring down at the other guard, who seemed to have forgotten he was holding me.

His hand dropped from my arm. The two vampires looked at each other for a few loaded seconds.

"I'll need to make a call," the lead vampire said.

"Be my guest, and you can take that with you. I have more copies, plus another one that's been registered with the pack headquarters and forwarded to your people."

The lead vampire walked ten feet away, his phone to his ear, as his companion stood next to him, waiting to hear the outcome.

Cole stayed where he was, as did I. The words I'd jotted down in my note burned in my chest even as I remained silent.

His attention was on the vampires. I didn't care. All my attention was centered on Cole.

"They want a meeting," the lead vampire said. "Now, at Franklin Park."

"Fine," Cole said. "We'll meet you there in twenty."

The second they departed, Cole made a call. "I need the pack at Franklin park now. And I mean everyone."

He hit end, and just when I thought I'd have a moment alone with him, Lonzo and Derek walked out of the backdoor.

"House is clear," Lonzo said to Cole before they both gave me a smile and a nod as they came over.

Lonzo took a deep breath as he came to stand beside us. "Oh yeah, you're a full shifter now."

Derek laughed.

As happy as I was to see the guys, my heart was craving a few minutes alone with Cole.

"We should head over there," Cole said, taking a step toward his truck. "Do you want to ride with us?"

"I'll take my bike," I said, choosing to ride solo over not being able to talk to him the way I really wanted to.

"Sure," Cole said, not fighting me.

I rode alone, but Cole's truck was behind me the whole time until I turned the corner toward the park, and he swerved to go in front of me.

There were shifters piling into the park on one side, and vampires filling the other, an invisible line keeping them to their respective sides.

I got off my bike, realizing shifters were still flooding into the place. I was getting nods as they passed me—and more than a few deep breaths as they checked my credentials, shifter style.

Lonzo and Derek walked toward the front of the line to a female vampire who was getting the most attention.

There were fairies buzzing about in the trees, looking for a little gossip, but other than that, no other species wanted to get anywhere near this.

Cole stopped beside me and, with a slight tilt of his head, silently asked if I was ready.

I nodded, not even sure what was throwing me off my game more: the vampires, the shifters all showing, or that I was close to Cole again and it was shredding me to feel this cool distance looming between us.

We walked down the invisible line until we stood in front of the female vampire. She looked young, even for her species, but I could smell her age, which was beyond gnarly.

"Sassy, this is Blanca. She's taken over Pavro's position."

She was slender and taller than me, giving me a regal stare as she sized me up.

"What is the purpose of this meeting?" Cole asked.

"Don't play stupid," Blanca replied.

"I know what you think, and it's all a rumor. There's no proof she had anything to do with killing Pavro—not that I'd imagine you're that upset about it anyway."

Her plump lips flattened together until they were a mere line. "You know nothing. I'm devastated over his loss."

Cole let out a laugh. "Yes, I know. I've heard. We could get into those details if you'd like, or we can get to the main point of this meeting. Sassy is part of my pack. Either produce evidence or back off."

Blanca turned her attention to me. She stepped closer, and Cole did the same.

"I'm confirming her scent," Blanca said. "It's hard to know where the stench is coming from with so many of you."

I took the liberty of moving closer to her and tilting my head back, practically daring her to have a taste.

"There is no way her scent would ever pass for human," a male vampire close to her said.

"How did she come to be a shifter when she was supposedly human only a week ago?"

"Spontaneous mutation," Cole said, smiling. "We can try to get into more details about that and many other things if you have the time."

I didn't know what dirt he had on her, but it had to be something bad the way she shifted her attention off me, the venom in her eyes solely directed at him now.

"We'll leave her be, but this is a one-time offer. She steps out of line, the deal is off," Blanca said.

"And if someone comes for her, even a rogue vampire, you can throw away the pact."

"This meeting is over." She was gone in a blink. Then, one by one, the vampires disappeared like dots on the landscape.

Cole nodded, and the shifters began to disperse. I got a few smiles as some of them left, but I didn't take the overall lack of a warm welcome to heart. No one seemed to want to hang around the area now.

Except for the flying busybodies.

"You're not part of the pact. There's no reason I can't break your little necks," Cole said.

The fairies flew off.

It was almost worse after they did. We stood, looking at each other, four feet apart, like casual acquaintances might.

He spoke first. "For a little while, I'm going to need you to be seen at the club. The vampires need to view you as part of the pack. It'll shore up the deal, but I don't think they'll bother you anymore."

"Okay." There wasn't a moment of hesitation. As far as

keeping me alive, he was right up there with Pen. It was my heart that took the beating when I got involved with him.

Fuck it. Tell him how you feel. Just get it out and let the chips fall where they may. Being with him can't hurt as much as being away from him, can it?

He looked over at his truck and then back to me. Was he trying to leave? Was I keeping him here?

"If any of them do bother you, just call the guys. They'll get me the message," he said.

Call the guys. It felt like a noose was tied around the main artery to my heart and life was being strangled out of it.

"Sure." That was the one word I could manage to get out without my voice shaking.

"How have you been?" he asked, as if he were going through the motions with someone he hadn't seen in a while.

"Good. You?" I asked, falling into the same tone and pattern, even as what I really wanted to do was wrap myself around him.

"I've been good," he said.

The conversation trailed off. This was it. I might see him in passing from time to time, but we were done.

This wasn't the ending I wanted, even though I'd been preparing for it since the first time we'd met I didn't have a crew any longer, and I also didn't have him. Turned out losing the crew wasn't nearly as devastating as losing Cole.

He glanced over at his truck again.

"Okay, well, I'm sure I'll see you around," I said, giving him his out. I gave him a wave as I made my way to my bike.

He got in his truck, following me long enough to make me think he was going to make it all the way to my house, walk in the kitchen uninvited, and tell me he couldn't live without me.

One block before we got there, he turned and drove off.

38

S *assy*

The club loomed ahead. I'd said I would come. I'd promised. It wasn't my reception by the shifters that worried me. It was Cole. Lonzo had said he was going to be gone tonight. This was the perfect opportunity to start upholding my end of the deal, even if part of me ached to see him.

But it was *his* place. Being this close to anything connected to him was...*something*.

Get in. Get out. Don't let your emotions tie you up in knots. Treat this like a mission. Shut down your nerves and feelings and get it done.

The door to the club opened before I reached it. Derek was smiling and waiting.

"Glad you came. A lot of people are anxious to meet you."

Lonzo stood right beside him, tilting his head and motioning for me to follow.

"Why do they want to meet me?" I asked.

"They know you're Ghost. Even if you weren't a shifter, anyone that's killed as many mosquitoes as you have is welcome."

"I can't shift. They know that, right?" I ran a hand over my sweater, wondering if it was too white, or too short, or just wrong. I definitely should've worn different pants.

"Not all of them can shift either. I mean, I can, and I'm pretty fucking spectacular, but I won't hold it against you," he said, busting my chops like I was already part of the pack.

"Lonzo, I'm not a real shifter. I know what Doc says, but I'm not, and I know that."

He stopped at the door that led into the main club room, just close enough that people were already peeking at us. "Sassy, you're a shifter now. The only person that doesn't know that is you. Now come on. A lot of people are excited to hang out with you."

This was going to be the worst night of my life. I would be in a room full of people who were all more than I was. It was going to be like living with Pen again, except times fifty.

I walked in anyway because I'd agreed to be here. These people had backed me up when I needed it. Even if they snubbed me now, I still owed them the respect of showing up.

I stepped into a room packed with shifters, the place where I'd always gotten cool but polite gazes, and was overwhelmed by the amount of smiles directed my way. There were three drinks lined up for me before I got to the bar, and I was greeted with more names and faces than I'd remember in one night. I'd barely start one conversation before another person interrupted.

There were a few holdouts lingering on the other side of the bar, but that was to be expected with any group. There were probably more people against me in my own crew. Or what used to be my crew.

I was introduced to most of the room, all of whom knew exactly who I was. They didn't ask how I'd become a shifter, or how much of a shifter I was, or if I could turn. What they did ask about was how many vampires I'd killed and how I'd done it. Apparently Ghost was a bit of a legend, all the more so because, as they had their hands tied because of the pact, they'd vicariously reveled in my adventures.

By the end of the night, I was starting to feel like I'd been accepted. Even though I'd lost one crew, I might've found another. It was turning out to be one of the best nights I'd had in weeks...until it wasn't.

Cole walked in, and the tension spiked through the roof. He gave me a nod from across the room and then walked into the back.

That was all I got now.

A nod.

That was where we were, and I'd have to be fine with it. After all, I was the one who'd turned down the potential for more, even if it had come a little late and with a lot of holes.

Cole

. . .

Derek followed me into the office.

"Sassy looks pretty good," Derek said, as if I hadn't noticed.

"She's nothing if not a survivor." I continued to my desk, waiting to hear what he wanted. When he kept staring my way but wasn't forthcoming, I nailed him with a look. "Did you want something?

He ran his palms over the front of his pants. "Well, it's actually about Sassy—"

"I told you, unless she's dying, I don't want to hear it. Considering she's in the club right now, and she's not dying, the subject is closed."

"But—"

"Whatever it is, I don't care. I don't want to hear her name again."

He opened his mouth.

"No. Now, if that's all you wanted, I have business to finish up."

He left the office, and I poured myself a drink. I flipped on the monitor, watching the club floor. I'd wanted to fuck her the minute I met her, and nothing had changed. If anything, the feelings had only grown stronger, and the distance hadn't done a damned thing to help.

How her and Pen were sisters was a perfect example of a diverse gene pool. Other than a resemblance in the bone structure, they couldn't be more different. The way I saw it, there were three kinds of people in this world. The first was the forgive-and-forget type. The second kept it cool but plotted your death as they went to sleep at night. The third didn't forgive *or* plot. They grabbed the nearest weapon and stabbed you to death the second you wronged them or cut you out of their life cold and hard.

Pen was the second type. Sassy was number three all day long. You always knew where you stood, and it was clear at the moment that I was standing in the freezing cold.

Now I needed to move on, the way she appeared to be. There was nothing left for me there.

39

S *assy*

My sister's name lit up my phone. If I knew she wouldn't keep calling, I might've let it ring. As much as I loved my sister, this was not going to be a pleasant call.

I accepted it anyway.

"Hey, what are—"

"Why haven't you come yet?" she asked. "You said you were going to come, but Huddy is telling me you keep giving him the runaround on dates. It's bad enough I had to find out you were sick *after* you got better, but now you're lying about coming to visit?"

"Pen, I'm going—"

"What's there for you? I bought into your excuses last

time, but you need to come here, and now. Sassy, you don't understand. It's normal here. It's like the war hasn't happened."

I couldn't remember which country she was in at the moment, so I was afraid to ask which "here" she was referring to. It was too risky. I'd surely get yelled at for that too.

"I will. I'm just not ready to leave quite yet. I've been kind of busy."

That wasn't a lie. I might not have a crew anymore, but I'd decided that didn't mean I couldn't be useful. There were plenty of ways I could still take nips out of the vampire regime. It just took more planning when you were a resistance with only one person. Luckily, planning was my strong suit.

There was a long pause as Pen probably skimmed notes on the next point of her argument.

"It's him, isn't it?" she finally asked. "You can say it was nothing but a quick hookup, but that's not what I'm hearing."

Huddy was the best and the worst, all at once. I didn't know when my sister and him had become gossip buddies, but it was really becoming an issue.

"What's he saying now?" I didn't need to specify who "he" was. It definitely wouldn't be Donovan. You had to like small talk in order to want to gossip. He didn't like to talk, period.

"You know he worries about you. He thinks you're *his* little sister." She laughed, as if the two of them powwowing over me and what I should be doing was the funniest thing.

"I'm not staying for Cole. We're done. We're so done we're burned charcoal."

"I don't think so," she said, as if she had a clue from across the ocean.

"Trust me. He's moved on." She didn't see the way he'd barely glanced my way when I walked in the club, as if I weren't even there.

"Huddy says he hasn't slept with anyone since you."

I scoffed, and loudly so she didn't miss the point. "That's such bullshit. Huddy has no idea what Cole does." I loved my sister. I really did. But the *I know better* side of her wasn't my favorite. Being right so often had gone to her head, and now she was under the misconception she could never be wrong. Donovan giving in to her constantly did not help matters either.

"Fine. Don't believe it, but Huddy has good sources. *He* even said he thinks the reason Cole hasn't left the pack yet is because of you."

"He hasn't left the pack because there's no one to step in." Cole was probably still trying to find a replacement. The D.C. pack wasn't an easy one to handle.

"Look, I need to just say it. If you won't leave because of him, and he won't leave because of you, you might as well be with the guy."

I swallowed, trying to get past the pile of stones in my throat. "He didn't want me when I was sick. How can I be with him now?"

"You *were* sleeping with him when you were sick, right? So how is that true?"

"Yes, I know that, but he didn't want anything more until I was a shifter." I shouldn't have answered the phone. I could've muted it and then pretended to be in the shower. If she'd panicked, she would've sent Huddy over.

"Maybe it had nothing to do with you getting healthier but the timing," she said.

"He was *repulsed* by my sickness." The only thing good about this conversation was it was like taking a knife to an old scar, cutting it back open and then packing it with salt. When I went to the club tonight, if I did see Cole, I'd be likelier to punch him in the face than hide in the bathroom crying, like I may or may not have on a previous occasion.

"I don't know. This sounds so different from the version of what Huddy is saying that it's hard for me to make heads or tails of it."

It was my opening to close out this conversation before she made me want to blow up the entirety of D.C., just to get to Cole.

"I gotta go. I have to get ready and make my weekly appearance at the club."

"Okay," she said, finally accepting defeat.

"Why is it you only come once a week? You need to hang out more. Everyone here loves you," Debra said.

When I first came, it had been all obligation. The second time, a small part of me had looked forward to it. The third time, I'd had a tinge of excitement. This time, I'd looked forward to having a drink and unwinding with everyone, or mostly everyone.

The doorman had greeted me as if we'd been friends for years. I'd walked into the main club room, and the bartender started pouring me a bourbon neat. I was now sitting with Debra and her boyfriend Al. The tables I passed had all smiled and waved.

Yeah, there were a couple of people who glared, but even their hostility had turned lukewarm at this point.

"I'll try. Sometimes my schedule gets in the way." Or

Cole's. Whenever he was definitely going to be around, which was often, I tried to not be.

"Oh, yeah. I'm sure," she said. There wasn't a shifter in the place that hadn't picked up on the weird vibe when Cole and I were here at the same time.

As if I'd dreamed Cole into reality, Debra and Al looked over my shoulder. The room's noise level dropped a hair as the tension seemed to increase by a thousand. No one had to tell me that Cole had walked into the club.

I grabbed my glass, finishing it while I feigned ignorance of the new arrival. Lonzo had said Cole had a meeting until late tonight. Apparently his information was wrong yet again. I was starting to think he was either clueless or lying.

"I'll be back in a few," Al said, as if he'd gotten waved over by someone.

Debra filled the gap, moving closer. "You know, I didn't want to ask, but there's been a lot of talk about what went down between you and Cole. The way he stares at you makes me think at least some of it's true."

I didn't know anything about his stares. The most I'd ever seen was a cold nod. He might've been staring at my back like he wanted to drag me out of the club by my hair, for all I knew.

"There's usually a grain of truth in most rumors, but it was really just a fling." I leaned on the bar, keeping my gaze fixed ahead, even as I could feel his presence. I could even smell him. I'd missed his scent.

Debra looked over my shoulder again, her eyes narrowing before she turned back to me, taking a sip of her drink as if she needed it as well.

"What's wrong?" I asked.

"Nothing. Just someone I don't care for."

Debra was one of the friendliest shifters I'd met. I hadn't realized she had people she didn't like.

Curiosity drove me to look over my shoulder. Cole was standing across the room talking to Lonzo. Sarah, one of the few shifters that had given me a cold shoulder, was running her hand up his back.

He'd definitely moved on. Or backtracked. I'd heard rumors as well.

I turned around, waving for a refill, when I should've left. But then Cole would think he'd chased me out of this place, that I was scared of him or something. Nope. We wouldn't let that particular rumor spread. In a few minutes he'd probably go off to his office and I'd pretend I never saw him.

Actually, I was glad I saw her hanging on him. I'd been dreading it every time I came. It was due. There was nothing left between us, and this made it final. He could hang out and drink at the next table, have his whore climb all over him. He could do whatever he wanted, as could I.

"You all right?" Debra asked.

"Fine. Great." I tilted my glass back.

Debra smiled and nodded like someone who didn't believe me for a second.

"What's the guy's name again?" I said, signaling a few chairs over.

"Oh, that's Eli. Nice guy."

Every time I came here, he smiled a little bit wider, as if the obvious break from Cole was giving him hope a relationship might be up for grabs. I hadn't been interested in getting involved with another shifter, especially not one from this territory, but why not? Cole had moved on, so why shouldn't I?

I shot Eli my best smile before glancing away. When I looked back, he was still staring.

"Oh no, I'm not sure that's the best idea," Debra said.

"Why? I'm single. Everyone is single. We can all do what we want."

I glanced at Eli again. He took the bait this time, heading over.

Debra stood. "He can have my seat, as I don't want to be too close when the fallout hits."

"There won't be any," I said.

Eli slid into her chair. "Hey, how've you been?"

I leaned on the bar in a way that accentuated my figure. "Good. How are you?"

"Feeling pretty good right now." He pointed to my drink. "Need another?"

"Would love one."

Cole

Sassy was sitting on the other side of the club, laughing like she was having the time of her life, and I couldn't stop staring at her, as if she were the only other person in the place. Her hair, her lips, the sound of her voice.

Instead of thinking sane thoughts, like how I was going to leave this place, all I could think of was the conversation I'd had earlier with Donovan. Sassy was leaving here, and she hadn't even bothered to give me a heads-up.

Even when her walls were fully erected, as they were now, she had this *fuck off* undercurrent that turned me on.

She could have everything going against her and she'd still be tough as nails.

I kept thinking back to her curling into me, her guard dropping. When she was around me, something different clicked into place. I used to go through life thinking the best we could do was settle all our scores before we died. She'd stared at me as if I were her savior, and instead of wanting to run, I wanted to be whatever she needed. Everything else took a back seat.

After everything we'd been through together, I had found out she was leaving from her brother-in-law. She hadn't even bothered to swing by and say goodbye, or "fuck off," or something. She came to *my* place and thought she was going to drink and flirt and have a last round with one of my pack members before she disappeared?

I was the one who walked away. She'd saved me some headaches going forward by breaking it off first. I should be relieved.

So why wasn't I?

Well, fuck her. She wanted nothing else to do with me? I'd show her how well I was moving on.

Sarah sidled up to me, and instead of urging her away, I gave her a smile. Normally when Sassy was here, I went into the back. I was tired of avoiding people in my club. I made my way to a table, and Sarah followed me. She climbed onto my lap a second later, wrapping an arm around my neck. Her other hand landed on my stomach, just high enough to not be indecent, but we were talking hairs, not inches.

Sassy was leaning closer to Eli. Even before she was a shifter, she'd been desirable to any male who had a pulse. The guys also knew her sister had given birth to an alpha.

Now that she was a shifter, they couldn't stop sniffing around her. Lonzo said she had a thing about not being able to shift. There wasn't a single guy in here who gave a shit about that.

Sarah leaned over to tell me something. It turned out to be her tongue in my ear. I should take her into the office, fuck her until I erased Sassy from of my mind. Sassy wasn't mine. Didn't want to be, and even if she did, it wouldn't matter. She'd walked away from me once. I didn't give second chances.

Sarah squirmed on my lap, making her intentions clearer, if that were possible.

So much for my big thoughts. I still couldn't stop looking at Sassy across the room.

She wasn't looking my way, but I knew her. I knew when she leaned in, arching her back, it was for me. When she lowered her lashes and glanced over, running her tongue over her lips, that was for me too, not him. She was showing me exactly what I couldn't have anymore.

I should let her keep going. She'd walked away from me. It was her choice. But she had to make a spectacle here? In my club?

Eli reached out, touching her waist, his fingers sitting low enough to graze her hip, and my skin began to tingle.

I stood, and Sarah fell off my lap.

"Cole, you got a minute?" Derek said, stepping in front of me.

"Not really," I said.

"It can't wait anymore."

The kid looked like he was going to make me beat him if I wanted to get him out of the way. He'd been haunting me for weeks about Sassy. Might as well let him get it out of his system while I was already pissed off anyway.

"Fine."

He nodded to the side.

I left, and he followed me into the office. If I was going to hear him out, I needed a break from the spectacle Sassy was making.

"You know how you don't like to talk about *her*?" he asked.

"I have no problem talking about *her*. There's just nothing I care to hear. She's a fringe member of this pack. But say whatever is bothering you so much. Let's be done with this."

I'd shut him down so many times that I'd lost count, and I was getting tired of the constant reminder.

He dug into his jacket and held out a slip of paper. "This. I saw it in Sassy's house the day the vampires showed up. I grabbed it in case there were problems, and I think you should read it."

I grabbed the paper from him, immediately recognizing Sassy's messy writing.

If you get this note, for whatever it's worth, I did love you.

"I've been trying to give it to you for weeks. It's not mine, and I felt awkward keeping it." He shrugged. "Plus, to be honest, it's getting *really* weird out there with you two."

"You did the right thing." I pocketed the note and left him, marching back into the main room. Someone was giving me some answers.

40

S *assy*

"If you toss those back any faster, I'm going to have to get you a bottle soon," Eli said, laughing even as I sensed he was a little alarmed over me being drunk or something.

He didn't get it. He wasn't the one who'd watched the person they loved get climbed like a jungle gym.

"A bottle might be a good idea," I said.

Eli's attention shifted to behind me.

"No. It's not," Cole said.

I didn't know what happened, what silent power Cole wielded, but Eli took his drink and stepped away from the bar, and me.

"I'm sorry. I thought you two were finished," Eli said.

Cole stepped into the gap between us. "Keep moving," he said to Eli.

I went back to staring behind the bar, sipping my

drink, having no desire to find out why Cole was standing beside me.

It was strange how I'd felt more civilly inclined toward him a month ago. Then the days had passed and the anger kept boiling up, obsessively almost, until there were nights I could barely sleep. Top that off with tonight's little show and all bets were off. He'd walked away from us without a hiccup, and it made the pain that much more real.

"In my office. We need to talk," Cole said, as if I'd acknowledged him.

I turned toward him. "I'm fine here." Every single person was listening. The situation wasn't ideal, but it was better than being alone with him.

Cole wasn't going to back down. Whatever his problem was, he was as angry as I was.

"You don't get to come into my club and fuck my pack members," he said, his voice low and lethal.

"You mean like you were about to do over at the table? Like that? Is that what you're referring to? Something along those lines?" I asked, beating the hell out of the question the way I wanted to beat him.

"If you give a shit, why didn't you give us a chance?" He leaned an arm on the bar as he angled over me. "I think I liked you better when you were dying. You had a bigger set of balls. Now you're a scared little girl running every chance you get."

"Fuck. You. I'm not scared of anything," I said, shoving at his chest.

"Then why'd you walk away?" he asked, his eyes intent as if he really cared.

I knew he didn't.

"Maybe I got bored."

My words were sharp but my body was all soft curves, lips parted. It happened every time I was near him, whether I wanted it to or not.

He pulled the letter out, the one I'd jotted down before the vampires grabbed me. I'd told myself so many times the wind had blown it away or that I'd thrown it out without thinking. And here it was.

"What's this?" he asked, holding it up in front of me.

A whisper spread through the bar. Damned shifter eyesight. Now the whole place would know I loved him and was rejected week after week.

"That means nothing. I wrote it when I was feeling good. Now that I'm sick again, it means nothing, I'm sure, so you should run for the hills."

"You're sick again?" His voice was thick, like his insides were grinding against themselves. He dipped his head, looking as if I'd rocked his world so hard that he couldn't speak.

He deserved it, and yet I immediately wished I hadn't said the lie.

I might've told the brute that if I didn't find myself slung over his shoulder in the next second. He had a knack for getting me pissed off like no one else, and it seemed that hadn't changed.

I pushed off Cole's back so I could punch him in the kidneys.

"Punch me all you want. We're fucking talking," he said as he continued to walk into the office, the last place I wanted to be with him.

My last look at the club was Huddy covering his face and shaking his head. Derek was talking to him, shrugging and looking guilty. No one else seemed to be fazed. If anything, there were more than a few *about time* expressions.

Cole opened the door, kicked it shut with his heel, and then dropped me to the ground. At least no one else would hear this fight, because it was going to be a doozy.

The second my feet hit the ground, I came out swinging. I landed a solid punch to his gut. It didn't matter if he was bigger and stronger. I had rage on my side.

My knuckles felt like they'd collided with granite, and he didn't budge. I landed another punch. I looked up, gauging his pain level.

He looked the same. Furious, but with concern still crowding it out.

"Are you sick?" he asked, his voice gritty.

"What if I am?" So much for coming clean.

"Don't push me on this. Are you sick or not?" he asked, gripping my shoulders.

There was too much hurt in his eyes to keep the lie going.

"I'm fine. I'm a shifter, remember? One of the chosen few who are good enough to be with you." I shook my head, frustrated with myself for not being able to hurt him. I brushed off his grip, though. It wasn't much, but it was something. "Why do you even care? Go back to your business," I said, putting even more space between us.

"Why? So you can get back to yours?" he asked, following me.

"Why not? I'm single, and you're clearly fucking people."

"I haven't fucked her since us."

He said it like I was the reason, but it couldn't be. Pen and Huddy had to be wrong.

"Well, I'm sure there were others." I waited, caring too

much for my sanity. Had he moved on or not? Right this second, it didn't feel like either of us had. "There's others, *right*?"

"There's been no one," he said, seeming almost annoyed with himself. "I can't seem to fuck anyone else because you're the only one I want."

That was the best and worst answer I'd ever heard. As much as it was right, it didn't fix the real problem.

"You don't love me, if that's what you're implying."

"I don't?" he asked, raising a brow.

"No." People in love didn't act this way. Did they?

I was half the equation, and I'd been about to hump Eli on the bar out of principle.

"Please elaborate on that. I'd like to know why, because it sure feels like it to me."

"If you love me now, it's only because I'm a shifter. You certainly didn't want me when I was some sick human."

"Because I couldn't. I knew the second I met you that you were something special. And no, I didn't want to watch a light that burned as bright as yours get snuffed out right in front of me. Some part of me always knew that I wouldn't be able to handle you dying, and it only got worse the more I was around you. So yes, I didn't fuck you, and that's why."

"Then what's changed? What if I do get sick? We don't know what will happen."

"If you do, then it's the option of last resort. I call in a vampire and we change you."

He said it so flatly, so matter-of-factly, that this wasn't something he'd thought up on a lark. He'd planned this.

"You'd have a vampire change me? You hate vampires." The anger was drained. Everything but shock was gone.

"It wouldn't matter because I fucking love you, and I don't care what shape or form you're in as long as you're you."

Clearly he wasn't thinking straight. "You're a shifter. Vampires are your enemy."

"I don't care if you're a shifter, a half-dead human, or a vampire. It doesn't matter."

"No way. You wouldn't." I was still staring at him, but nothing about him read as bluffing.

He picked his phone up off the desk as I stared, dumbfounded.

He made a call and then put the phone on speaker. "Huddy, you know that favor we were working on a month back with Emanuel? Can you please tell me the fine points of what was involved?"

There was a pause. "On the phone?"

"Yes. Just do it."

"Is she really sick? Are we going to have to go that route?" Huddy asked.

"She's fine. She doesn't believe what the plan was, though."

Huddy broke out into a deep laugh. "I don't blame her. Turning the old alpha's sister-in-law into a vampire is pretty unorthodox."

"Thanks."

Cole hit end, tossed his phone on the desk, and moved closer.

I was so focused on what he would've done to save me that I seemed to miss the bigger picture. I didn't realize why he was moving into my space until his hands were on my hips, pulling me into him.

It was like some sort of internal mechanism when he

touched me. I completely melted down. Thoughts short-circuited and I became all *grab me, touch me, want me.*

"Why did you write that note?" he asked.

"Same reason you were going to turn me into a vampire," I said, curling my arms around his neck.

I kissed him, because if he said one more word I might crumble and start weeping.

41

S *assy*

"You know you weren't supposed to shack up with him. He was only supposed to watch out for you," Donovan said.

"He did watch out for me, and he still is. He's very good at it, by the way."

Donovan groaned. "So the rumors are true, aren't they? Instead of him keeping you on the straight and narrow, you've taken him down. Why did I imagine it would be different? Your sister warned me you had a knack for corrupting people."

Anyone who thought Cole was *ever* on the straight and narrow didn't know the man that well.

"I wouldn't exactly say *I* corrupted *him*." What we were about to do was his idea. Yes, I was a willing participant, but I didn't have the clout to pull it off.

"I know what the two of you are up to. I still hear things. Your sister is going to lose her mind if she finds out about any of this." His tone was that of an older brother trying to scare me. Luckily, I was immune to those kinds of shenanigans.

"Then I think we shouldn't be talking about this," I said. "You can't tell her what you don't know. It's worked for us in the past. I think we should try it again."

Cole was leaning against the truck, tapping an imaginary watch as he waited for me outside my—*our*—house. He'd moved right back in after the night at the club and never left. We'd both never cared for the mausoleum Donovan and Pen had lived in.

"I gotta go. Tell Pen I love her. I'll get another throwaway phone and call in a few days, but we're heading up to the cabin for a little R and R right now." That wasn't a lie. R and R could stand for recognizance and resistance. There was no law that it had to mean rest and relaxation.

"Try not to start an all-out war if you can show some restraint?"

I only hesitated for a split second. "I'll try *really* hard."

"Are you ready for this?" Cole asked, grabbing my hips and tugging me against him.

"I'm always ready," I said, smiling at my dual meaning.

"Oh no, we cannot be late for this meeting," he said, laughing even as he dipped his head to capture my lips for a kiss.

As much as I wanted to disappear back into the house,

I pulled back after a few moments. This meeting really was too important.

"Whatever we agree to, that's it," he said. "Shifters are loyal and fierce. We make a deal with them, there is no getting out of it."

"I've been ready for this for years."

"Then let's go."

We drove back to the cabin, and it seemed fitting to have this meeting at the place I'd become a shifter myself.

When I got out of the truck, Cole walked beside me, but he didn't take my hand. It was there if I wanted it, but in this male-dominated society, he didn't want to lend the impression I needed him or that I wasn't a full partner in this meeting.

There were supposed to be three other alphas meeting us. When we walked into the cabin, there was only one shifter there.

He rose from the couch and strode over to us. "Dante," he said to me.

The name rang a bell.

"There were supposed to be a couple more people," I said, looking about as if they'd pop up out of the woodwork.

"Yes, but I told them I'd handle it," he said, every inch of his tall frame exuding alpha energy. He smiled, as if that was all the explanation needed, his dark stare making me imagine he could handle anything that was thrown at him.

Cole moved his arm to my hip, making it clear that even if I didn't need him, I was duly claimed.

"I'm glad you decided to join us," I said.

"I'm thrilled to have you on board, *Ghost*," Dante said, making it known he was aware of my past. "You too, Cole."

"On board?" I asked, getting a hunch that the situation might be not quite what it had seemed. I'd been under the impression I was going to lure their shifters to our side once the pact fell apart, which everyone was aware might already be happening. Seemed something else might've already been in the works.

"I've been waiting for you folks for a while," Dante said. "We've got a lot of work ahead of us."

Torn Worlds will continue with Dante's story!

You can get my newsletter two easy ways: Either text **Augustine** *to 22828 or click here to sign up online.*

Or, follow me on one of these platforms:
https://www.facebook.com/groups/223180598486878/
http://www.donnaaugustine.com
Twitter handle: @DonnAugustine

ALSO BY DONNA AUGUSTINE

Savage One

Wyrd Blood
Wyrd Blood
Full Blood
Blood Binds

Torn Worlds
Gut Deep

ACKNOWLEDGMENTS

As I branched out into romance, I was afraid I might lose some of my people. If they wanted to dump me, they hid it well!

If they did dump me, I wouldn't blame them. Let me tell you, being a beta for me is not usually a fun job. I'm typically running behind and dump the book on them with nearly no notice, and very limited time to read it and turn it around. Lisa A., Donna Z., Camilla J., Lori H., Tammy K. and Ashleigh M., love you gals!

Made in the USA
Las Vegas, NV
27 September 2021

31231753R00173